READY TO LOVE

BOOKS *on the* UNDERGROUND

READY TO LOVE

JON APPLETON

Roffo Court Press

First published in Great Britain in 2016 by Roffo Court Press
Text copyright © 2016 Jon Appleton

1 3 5 7 9 10 8 6 4 2

ISBN 978-0-9935473-1-7

Typeset by Hewer Text UK Ltd, Edinburgh
Printed by Clays Ltd, St Ives plc

jonappletonbooks.com

Remembering Belinda

PART ONE
THE LAST TO KNOW

In a decade of adulthood, Minna Jepson had had three proper boyfriends, which was neither feeble nor excessive. She went with the tide, but there were gaps when nobody floated her boat, and moments when 'any port in a storm' applied. But she wanted to be in love. It wasn't just because everyone else seemed to have a partner. She was self-sufficient but, well, there were times when she felt not lonely, not needy, but that life would be so much sweeter if there was someone with whom to share it. Knowing she could love (because she had done so before), she wanted someone else who would, in turn, love her.

Minna was a staunch believer in commitment. She considered herself lucky to have parents who were still happy together. Grandparents, too, whose like-minded friends were also in for the long haul. They had rhyming names like Jill and Phil and Ray and Kay – the exception being Paul and Pauline. Her younger sister was partnered constantly, if not consistently. Lisa discarded boyfriends like pairs of tights. She must have worn them in layers, because there was always some new, unladdered lad at the ready. In short, if there was a gene for romantic longevity, Minna hoped she'd inherited it.

Minna really thought she'd hit the jackpot with boyfriend number four: Leo, who was her junior by eighteen months. When she listed the qualities she was seeking in a partner – a list she regularly revised, changing fonts and indentations – by and large, they were attributes of Leo's. But after fourteen months together, Leo told Minna that he was gay.

Callie, her best-friend-since-school, had been comforting but curt. By the time Leo dumped Minna, Callie was deep into her idyllic marriage to Todd, whom she'd met on a blind date arranged by a magazine. All Minna got was a lip gloss.

Callie said, 'Don't give yourself such a hard time. It won't be long before you'll look back on all this, and shrug it off.'

Minna dabbed the tears from the corners of her eyes. 'What makes you think that?'

'It might have gone wrong for worse reasons, Min,' said Callie. 'Relationships fail all the time.' It was clear she was referring to a world beyond her own blissful realm. 'But the way it's happened, you get to walk away blame free.' Callie spread her hands. 'So move on, Min. Count yourself lucky and move on. Leo's a nice guy – it's not as if he's suddenly turned into a demon – but he's not for you. Just go out and find someone who is.'

It might have been intended as encouragement, but suggested only that the woman who had taken five weeks to decide between two near identical shades of apricot for the tablecloths at her wedding could, if required, be decisive.

*   *   *

In the year just gone, Minna had turned thirty, and two months after that, began dating Julian Callender. (There had been nobody special since Leo. Until she met someone fabulous, Minna was, by and large, cool with being a solo unit.) Julian had come to work at Macsamphire Strutt burnished with a reputation for troubleshooting, just a few weeks before Minna joined as an analyst. The recruitment freeze that had swiftly followed was unconnected to either appointment. Julian proved his worth so fast that his one day a week soon became two. His contract was extended from three months to six. The day the memo circulated announcing he had agreed to stay on as permanent part-time was one of unmitigated joy. Minna herself had received an e-mail confirming that her probation was over, and she was now a fully paid-up member of staff. She felt relieved: Julian was so impressive that she'd feared he'd be a shoo-in while she'd be surplus to requirements.

Julian was a likeable guy. Minna got the sense that Adam, the only other man on the team, wanted to enlist him as a regular drinking buddy or partner in some blue-sky business scheme. The other women, Kerry and Stephanie, were flirtatious, but no more so than those on this floor, the ones above and below, and in the sandwich shop over the road. If Minna were honest, she remained a little jealous that Julian's was the more creative role. Her cultural life was by no means barren: she could happily spend a Sunday with a bonnet drama box set, and she never missed the new Cathy Kelly. But the way her colleagues enthused about some technical or creative problem Julian had solved, or how he'd won over a truculent client – each comment liberally laced with awe and devotion – made her feel out of step, which she did not much like. And then, one Friday evening, early in June, during Adam's birthday celebration she found herself regarding Julian afresh.

Minna's team were in their favourite haunt, a pub called Monroe's, just off the Euston end of Tottenham Court Road. They ordered tapas and the wine flowed.

Luckily, the tapas plates had been emptied and cleared away when Kerry checked her phone and let out a bark of alarm. Enquiries were made and the source was revealed as a tenant SOS. She and her partner didn't have children or pets: 'We rear maisonettes,' she joked. 'They're just as demanding, though a lot more profitable.' The situation wasn't urgent but Kerry was nothing if not diligent.

Minna wasn't intentionally prying, but she happened to glance at Kerry's phone and was confronted by a close-up of a pair of hairy male feet submerged in water.

Julian voiced mutual puzzlement. 'I can't quite see what this has got to with repairs to one of your properties . . .'

'It's actually really helpful,' Kerry informed them. 'We encourage tenants to send photos of damage. It helps us diagnose the problem and plan the solution.'

'Oh *now* I see it,' said Adam, taking the phone from Kerry and enlarging the image. 'The tap's come off. You would have thought he'd have got out of the bath before taking the picture, wouldn't you?'

The evening never really recovered after that. But they'd done well. Minna surveyed the discarded bottles and considered the conversations that had poured forth from them. She mused on the marvel of wine: it has no knowledge, and yet it harbours many views and the skills to disseminate them.

Minna didn't feel drunk, just mellow and end-of-weekish, but even so, she found herself engulfed by melancholy. She recalled that Julian had set the mood plummeting with a story about disadvantaged countries. Travel was his thing, which Minna did not find very relatable. Apart from university, parental trips across the channel to purchase alcohol for Christmas, a spot of inter-railing, a skiing trip to Switzerland, and summer hols with her sister, she'd been London-based. Travel seemed so *effortful*, but Julian was a dab hand who could negotiate the trickiest situations. He'd winkle out the most co-operative camel in a pack; he'd know which noodles in a market stall were cooked fresh and not reheated. He knew the precise local price of a beer and its correct temperature for serving.

By now, aside from the staff, Minna's team were Monroe's sole occupants.

'Just off to the gents,' said Adam, as Kerry snapped shut her phone.

'I'd better ring Dave,' said Kerry, 'and see how we're off for gland nuts.'

'I need a fag,' said Stephanie.

Julian and Minna found themselves alone. He smiled. 'Something I said?'

It wasn't an especially comical remark. She should have still been irked that Julian had droned on about poverty at a birthday celebration – it was as appropriate as planning a picnic in Ramadan. Actually, you could question his motives. There he was, stomping on carbon feet, but not as an aid-worker or a peace-promoter or anything beneficial to the greater good, but as a tourist—

But all that mattered, was that he seemed to be flattering Minna now. So she smiled back. Her spirits lifted immediately. She regarded her wine glass and saw that it was empty. But whatever agency had promoted this delicious new contentment, it was not working under the auspices of alcohol.

Minna smiled again. Julian had a nice smile, she thought, as if noticing it for the first time. She felt as if she was catching up with everyone else at last.

But silence loomed. One of them had to *say* something, but all Minna could summon were the results of an office-wide poll in which the majority had chosen to reinstate Fair Trade Coffee over supplying the bathrooms with anti-bacterial handwash.

'Personally,' she told Julian, 'I'd like both but there must be cost implications, and I'm not sure the handwash is eco-friendly.' Mercifully, she stopped there, although privately, the sentence trilled on: 'Actually, you *are* quite sexy, aren't you?'

Mercifully, again, Minna realised that she was not toiling alone. Julian rewarded her attention lavishly. He made jokes that she found so hilarious that she was convinced he'd scripted them for her. He delivered revelations perfectly tailored to enhance her own points of view or to introduce new and instantly life-enriching perceptions.

All this took place within a time frame of roughly three minutes and when the others resumed their positions, Julian and Minna were mid-snog.

'Don't let us interrupt . . .'

'And there I was feeling bad about abandoning you.'

'Only said the other day you don't see Minna and Julian chatting very often . . .'

'So how long has *this* been going on?'

Julian drew back from Minna slowly, so that she did not feel an abrupt detachment. He said, 'Anyone fancy another drink?'

Adam hesitated, as if tempted. 'No, I've got to be up early to take the girls swimming, so I'd best not stay.' He was referring to his twin daughters, who were three.

'I've got a quiet day planned,' said Stephanie. 'But in the evening I'm going to the theatre with Janine.' Interchangeable to the uninitiated, the members of Stephanie's social circle fulfilled specific functions and operated on a rota. Along with prescribed activities, they had designated meeting points. Days of the week varied but a tennis friend never angled for an invitation to cake decoration, or vice versa. She added, 'There's a new play on at the National and we got ten-quid tickets.'

'What's the play?' asked Julian.

'I've no idea. Janine read about it in the *Metro*.' The request for specifics overstretched the brief. 'I'm going to the theatre with Janine.'

'Dave's making noises about an early trip to B&Q.' This was Kerry, of course. 'Think that means I should make a move.'

9

Minna suddenly had an incredible thirst. 'I'll stay,' she gushed. And so they did.

Wasn't dating a colleague *asking* for trouble? Didn't everyone know that? Then again, when you thought about it, colleagues should date all the time. We see more of the people we work with than family and friends. It's *friends* you shouldn't go out with – that's the line that can't be crossed – and Julian wasn't a friend. None of the team was. And aside from having little in common other than sharing an office, Minna had never dated someone with such curly hair – it could do with a cut – and despite the fact that none of her other relationships had lasted, she saw no reason to switch policies now.

Minna found she very much enjoyed the business of getting acquainted with Julian. He was the only person she knew who didn't own a television. But who needs TV when you've got a million real-life stories running through your head? Julian showed her photo albums and played home-made videos on his iPhone. Minna quickly found herself in thrall to his every word. Soon they were a couple.

Sometimes, Julian and Minna spent the whole weekend in Julian's flat in W2. Julian would cook an authentic African or Indian meal, with Minna's assistance. It was summer, but she was more than happy to forgo picnics in Greenwich or swimming in the ponds at Hampstead Heath. She didn't go clothes shopping because there were no parties to attend. It appeared that she dropped out of several social loops, which she was slow to realise, because she spent less time on Facebook and on the phone to girlfriends. She told Lisa to find someone else to take her place on the Ibiza holiday, even though she had begged to be included back in the depths of winter.

Sunny days sailed over Praed Street and swallowed Minna and Julian with them. When they ventured out, things invariably went wrong, but that only added to the fun. It was hilarious to think that Julian had made it through Amazonian rain forests with just a scratch on his left ankle and a thirst, and yet the car he borrowed from a mate – someone never seen by Minna – died just before Hillingdon en route to their Oxfordshire B&B. Trains were cancelled, bus timetables expired, and taxis sailed past, despite having their lights on.

As the weeks went by, Minna came to notice the way Julian's stories tailed off, as if their retrieval had unearthed disappointment, not fulfilment. She wondered if Julian had pursued travel as an act of evasion. She didn't want to spoil their days together so she didn't ask for reasons. Besides, as his girlfriend, wasn't it her privilege as much as her burden to see what was hidden to others?

'This is nice, isn't it?' said Julian, squeezing her frozen hand on the way back from somewhere cold and muddy.

She squeezed back. 'Yes, it is.'

She kept telling herself it *was*, and would be even nicer when she told the team on Monday morning. How they relished tales of Julian and Minna's weekends. She always managed to satisfy their curiosity, which made it so much easier to conclude that she too was satisfied. Even so, it seemed as if the rest of the world was wearing rose-tinted spectacles, and Minna felt excluded all over again.

After four months, Minna realised that she had made a big mistake and she ended the relationship. It happened in Australia, which was an expensive way of doing things, but effective. The occasion was the wedding of an old friend of Julian's. The team at work was, naturally, thrilled. Callie was impressed, because her own honeymoon had taken her no further than Torremolinos.

Minna embraced the opportunity and the end of the summer sales. It was a privilege to be invited when she and Julian hadn't been together all that long – and you couldn't ask for a better public induction than a wedding. It chimed with the extremes of Julian's life as described, if not experienced. And how romantic! Sex between them was great, but Julian wasn't a great one for public displays of affection. Maybe his hands were so used to carrying maps and compasses or those walking sticks – the ones for the outdoorsy, not the elderly – that it felt unnatural to entwine his fingers with smooth, human flesh. All that could change.

They would stay with Julian's older brother, Adrian, who lived practically on the water. So far, Julian's family had been as scarce as his friends. Not even Minna's mother had succeeded in extracting more than his parents' names. Julian had promised to take Minna to meet his folks but the logistics were difficult, because they had retired remotely to a hamlet in Dorset. So she was fascinated to meet Adrian. Cut from the same cloth, how alike were the Callender brothers? She and Lisa were evidence of just how wide and deep a gene pool could be, but since there was only a two-year age gap between the boys, perhaps they had been close. Then again, Adrian had lived in Sydney for nearly a decade.

'He married an Aussie girl when he was twenty-one,' Julian explained.

'Wow. And they've been there ever since? Have they got kids?' Julian hadn't mentioned any nephews or nieces.

He shook his head. 'The marriage only lasted a year. She went back to Perth and Ady stayed in Sydney. He must like it, I guess.'

'That's so sad,' said Minna. 'What went wrong?'

'They got bored of each other, apparently,' said Julian.

'After only a year?'

Julian shrugged. 'You wouldn't think it possible, would you?'

Minna decided to leave the subject there.

But she was not cast down! Spring in Australia as a London autumn closed in promised so much. At last, she'd see Julian's spirit of adventure. It would rub off on her, and she'd learn new skills.

Minna read a charity-shop-purchased *Lonely Planet* guide on the plane. Every now and then, she nudged Julian, who was watching back-to-back movies, and shortlisted possible excursions. Without looking away from his screen – and without exception – he said things such as, 'Oh, I went there. No need to go again.' 'It's really not up to much – just desert really.' 'But I swam with dolphins in the Galapagos.'

They arrived in Sydney at six a.m. on the Friday, body clocks out of sync – wasn't Julian used to crossing time zones? – but wired with excitement. As their taxi pulled in, Adrian greeted them briefly, handed over a set of house keys, and cycled off to work. They'd see little of him after that.

The tourists showered and changed and had coffee. Then Minna said, 'Right. Our first day in Australia. What should we do?'

Julian was scanning a listings supplement from the weekend paper. How thoughtful of Adrian to provide it. Unfortunately, as the morning wore on, it became clear that reading was all Julian was intent on doing.

'I feel a bit knackered, Min,' he said at noon. 'Think I'll have a kip.'

'I thought the best way to fight jetlag is to stay up all day and go to bed at your normal time.'

'Maybe it's not jetlag,' he said, 'it could be something I ate on the plane. I'm feeling pretty rough, actually.'

'OK,' she said, kissing him on the forehead. 'Have a sleep, but I might go for a wander. After all, it's my first day in Sydney. Don't want to waste a minute.'

He squeezed her hand. 'Good idea. Ady's bought plenty of food, but if you come across a chemist, something for a dodgy tum wouldn't go amiss.'

Minna savoured opening the front door to a view of the boats on the harbour, and the scent of eucalyptus. Then, all of a sudden, the air was filled with a screech and Minna was surrounded by an angry cloud of black and white. No one had warned her about magpie nesting season. The notion of a week-long house arrest was only marginally less attractive than being dive-bombed whenever she stepped into the street. She respected the birds' protective instincts, but regretted the fact that her summer sale purchases wouldn't look quite as gorgeous as intended when teamed with a patchwork of surgical gauze.

Julian recovered in time for Saturday's wedding, so it was a genuine shame to arrive at the gardenia-garlanded venue to be informed by the groom's parents that it had been cancelled at short notice. The bride had announced the night before that she was pregnant. By someone other than her husband-to-be.

'Well,' said Minna, 'that's a shame for them, but it got *us* here, and we've still got three weeks to fill.'

But six days later, in Melbourne, during an episode of *Australia's Got Talent*, Minna found she could go on no longer. She turned to Julian, who had not stirred from the television for twenty minutes, and said, 'I'm sorry, Julian. But I'm not happy and I can't do this. I'm going to use the internet downstairs and change my ticket and book a flight back to London.'

Julian looked perplexed. 'I don't under— I mean, I didn't realise – Min, does that mean we're splitting up?'

Minna's heart began to thud. 'Yes, Julian,' she said. 'We're splitting up.'

His expression looked as though she'd pulled the world apart and stranded him – the intrepid traveller – without a passport, or money, or any local lingo. As if Minna was the bold adventurer, when she'd never felt less courageous in her life.

Leo was still a vital person in Minna's life. After he'd dumped her, there'd been a period of cool silence, but Minna hadn't wanted to fall out permanently. She had sent the first, tentative text but it was Leo who suggested hooking up. Now they were the closest of friends.

Since the start of the year, Minna had listened to Leo speak enthusiastically about his new boyfriend, Darren, whom she'd seen in pictures, but was yet to meet. Minna decided to fix this with an invitation to her shared flat in Balham, the Saturday of the second week of March. Apparently, Darren disliked the gay scene, where Minna and Leo usually met. Her flatmates, Niamh and Sharmila, pledged their absence. In solidarity, Sharmila went round with the Hoover, and Niamh cleaned the bathroom.

By late afternoon, the flat looked good. Minna found an old throw rammed at the back of a cupboard and splashed it across the sofa to vibrant effect. Minna prepared smoked salmon blinis with a dill garnish. She removed all the plastic from the pre-prepared trays and put them out with the recycling and opened red wine to breathe. She put her iPod on, the playlist carefully constructed. Then she had a long bath and carefully selected an outfit for the evening, settling on a polka-dot patterned skirt and a black T-shirt. By six o'clock, her flatmates had departed, leaving Minna alone with a calming dash of wine as she awaited her guests.

When the buzzer went just after half past, Minna felt chilled and fabulous. She opened the door to be confronted by a giant bunch of brightly coloured flowers, from behind which out stepped Darren. Introductions were made and pleasantries exchanged. The loving couple promptly parked themselves on the two-seater sofa, a pinkie from one hand interlocking with that of his lover's. Minna felt a little twinge of envy, but she shrugged it off.

'I haven't met a florist before,' she remarked, by way of a conversation opener. 'Not socially, I mean. But that's how you two coincided, right?'

Leo and Darren exchanged a conspiratorial look. 'Kind of,' Leo began. 'I took the day off work to go and see my aunt, who was in hospital. I thought I'd better get her some flowers, and since I had time to kill before the train, I rocked on up to Darren's stall.'

'It must have been fate,' Darren said. 'I believe M&S do a decent range of chrysanths at their Colchester store.'

'Please,' objected Leo. 'I would never buy *anyone* chrysanthemums. They smell *rancid*. Anyway, I bought the flowers and I remember thinking, *He's quite nice looking*, as you do. I thought he gave me a signal—'

'No, you gave me a signal. Definitely.'

'Only in response to yours.'

'You *definitely* made the first move.'

'Did not.'

'Did so!'

A good host is both indulgent and goal-oriented, so Minna interrupted, 'So you noticed each other. Then what happened?'

Darren laughed. 'Nothing. He buggered off to Colchester for the day.'

Minna asked, 'Did you slip your card inside the flowers? It would have had your phone number on it. Maybe your name ...'

'Please!' Darren scoffed. 'I wasn't desperate. Besides, he knew where I was. Not likely to be going far, was I?'

Leo reprised the story Minna had heard before. 'I did think about him, Min, on the train and throughout the day. It was late when I got back to London – cancellation after cancellation – and the station was pretty much deserted. I went down to the tube, to the Hammersmith and City platform and guess who was there, waiting for the train?'

Darren nodded. 'I'd just had a drink with a friend on Shoreditch High Street and was heading off to a gig. So we didn't have long to talk. But we exchanged numbers, arranged to meet up at the weekend, and the rest, as they say, is history.'

'Three whole months,' said Leo with a gleam of pride, as if he were speaking of millennia.

Minna felt the need to keep it real. 'What do you like best about your job, Darren?'

'Everything,' he said. 'I had no idea what I wanted to do when I left school, though I liked gardening. I thought about doing agricultural science but I'm a city boy at heart so the idea of life on a farm held no attraction, basically. After a few twists and turns, here I am.'

'He's built up the business single-handed,' Leo said proudly. 'If Darren doesn't do it it won't get done. So, three mornings a week he's up at six and off to the flower market at Vauxhall. I went with him once. It's an amazing place.'

'It sounds like heaven!' she said.

'You could come along one day,' Darren offered. 'If you don't mind an early start and squeezing into the van.'

'That would be great!' she said. Hay fever was an issue, but it hadn't been bad this year, and she was totally beguiled by Darren. 'You must be frantic during rush hour! I bet time flies. Much more interesting than my job. In an office.'

'I thought you liked your job,' Leo said.

'I do,' Minna confirmed. 'But when you hear about something like Darren's, well, there's no contest, really.'

Darren shook his head. 'I disagree, Minna. Working in an office *can* be really exciting.' He glanced at Leo, who coloured as if trying and failing to issue a warning, but carried on regardless. 'OK, I'll come clean. Leo told me you'd dated one of your workmates. I'm dying to hear more about that. It sounds outrageous.'

Minna shot a look at Leo and witnessed his twist of distress. He must have thought that she thought he'd betrayed a confidence. But Minna had no appetite for reproach. Darren's look held no judgement, and Minna found herself relaxing. Why not tell Darren? Why not give it a go?

The words flowed without rancour: it was bliss to hear Julian's name sound like a whistle on the breeze instead of a brick against a window. But Minna's voice cracked when she spoke of her sudden flight from Australia. At first essential, her decision had quickly become an improbable extravagance.

It was only as the plane soared, then achieved its altitude, that her nerves began to calm. And then it struck her that her accomplishment really held no ambition: she was simply going home.

But to what? Oh, there was washing and ironing and catching up. She'd deal with it all in good time. What mattered was work – specifically, there was the team to face. She'd e-mailed an explanation, and to say she'd be in on Wednesday. Mid-week was surely less disruptive. But she was in no doubt that the news would not be welcomed. She imagined dismay hanging like an ash cloud over every work station. She had maintained the very lowest of profiles.

A couple of weeks back in the job, Julian e-mailed her, appealing for the private word she had so far avoided. He said, 'It's time to seek pastures new. Fresh challenges beckon, Min.'

Minna had been filled with panic. 'You don't have to do that,' she'd cried.

Julian had shaken his head. 'I think it's for the best. There's plenty of work out there. I had a few conversations back in Sydney, you see. After you'd – well, after you'd—'

She halted him. 'But you can't leave—!'

A look of hope lit Julian's face, making him irresistibly sexy. 'Me,' she thought. Or did she mean 'them'? Adam, Stephanie and Kerry. Minna didn't know, so she said nothing.

At Christmas, Julian had dropped by the office with a monolithic Stollen from a grateful client. He was careful to speak to everyone, moving clockwise, leaving Minna until last. Julian was as funny and charming as he'd been on their first date – on so many dates. She didn't want him to go so when he suggested they have a drink, she agreed. Why not? The week was chock-full of parties and dinners and another wouldn't hurt. It had led to nothing more than the agreement to regular catch ups from New Year on.

After two months, these reunions had become the stuff of folklore, and the novelty eroded. They talked about work – Julian's *other* work – and their families. Then they systematically went through every weekend they'd shared, not necessarily in order, but fairly comprehensively, as if each were an old-fashioned slide being popped into a carousel projector.

'Have you been back to Lewes?'

'I wonder if that funny old tea shop ever got the oven fixed?'

'Do you think someone's finally noticed that the town's name is spelled wrong on every window in the high street?'

The farewell, after coffee, was as low-key as the beginning and middle.

'Well, brilliant to see you.'

'And *you*.'

'Must arrange the next one – the weeks go so fast.'

At work the next day, Minna had said to the team, 'It was good to catch up.'

'*Wonderful* Julian!'

'So glad the old boy's doing well.'

'Oh, Julian.'

On it went. Minna was currently awaiting Julian's e-mail – it was his turn to make arrangements – so the April date could be slotted into the diary. It was an obligation, only it wasn't terrible, by any means. None of it had been, really.

Returning to the present, to her eager guests, she wrapped it up. 'There really isn't much more say.'

Darren's eyes gleamed. '*Au contraire*, there's quite a lot to say!'

'Darren . . .' whispered Leo, frowning.

'Go on,' Minna offered. She liked Darren. 'Was there something else you wanted to know?'

Darren needed no encouragement. 'I want to know how you coped at the end. You had a range of unsustainable emotions.'

Minna enquired, 'What do you mean?'

Leo whispered, 'Darren, babes, is this really such a—'

Darren said, 'You were angry that Julian had ensnared you in the relationship when he clearly had no intention of putting any effort into it.'

Minna was startled. 'I was never angry.' But the theory wasn't so outlandish that it could be rejected out of hand. 'Well, I suppose that maybe . . . I suppose that's possible . . .'

'You were angry that he didn't do more to try to get you to stay.'

'He didn't,' she admitted. He'd let her walk out of the hotel. Out of the country.

'And you were angry at yourself for going.'

'Darren . . . *babes* . . .'

Minna said, 'But I had to leave. I told you. I couldn't stand it any longer.'

'Yes, but that's when the guilt really caught fire. Until then, there was still time for you to be more patient with him – more pro-active in booking trips away, instead of just praising suggestions that rarely amounted to anything.'

'I just sort of went along with him . . .'

'You could have switched off the slide projector, taken down the maps and got out a fresh, unmarked atlas and planned your own journeys,' said Darren.

'Julian knew so much more. He'd done everything before he met me,' Minna pointed out. Shouldn't that have been a warning?

'You could even have had a row,' said Darren, 'instead of all the silences which Julian may not have interpreted as you wishing you were somewhere else.'

'He isn't a confrontational person,' said Minna.

Leo saw an opportunity to add value to the exchange. 'Half the time they were at work. They had to be professional. They couldn't have had blazing rows, even if they'd wanted to. So it all just bubbled up under the surface.'

'Yes,' Minna agreed, more in support of Leo than the truth.

Darren nodded. 'I think you've hit on something. I don't think Julian is the problem here,' said Darren.

Having beamed at Darren's approval, Minna and Leo exchanged puzzled glances. 'He's not?' she said.

'He's not?' Leo echoed.

'No,' said Darren, confidently. 'I think the people who are really to blame are Minna's colleagues.'

'My colleagues?' Minna whispered.

'Yes!' said Darren. 'Why should they even have cared? Presumably, none of them need to harvest their own happiness from yours?' He continued, 'Why didn't they warn you that dating Julian might actually lead to complications? All romantic scenarios are beset by obstacles and setbacks, but an office romance is more challenged than most.'

'I knew that,' said Minna. 'I just put it out of my mind, because—'

Darren interrupted, 'They had become stakeholders in whatever happened between you and Julian. They were entitled to a view, perhaps even a say. And yet, they were not equipped with all the facts.'

Leo made a noise that sounded like a dead bird dropping from the sky.

What if Darren were right? Minna let him continue. 'Go on.'

'When it was over, and Julian left, you, Minna, had to deal with the fallout from the team on your own. You had to be polite when you could have pointed out to them that they were free to see whomever, whenever they liked.'

'Well, of course they were . . .'

'Darren . . .' Leo cautioned, flashing Minna an emergency request or apology.

'They didn't need your permission to see Julian, as if he *belonged* to you.'

She brayed, 'As if!' But Minna sensed a stab of loyalty towards her colleagues.

Darren's focus did not waver. 'But you said none of this, Minna, did you?'

'Well, I . . .'

Leo appealed to her. '*Min*, you really don't have to . . .'

Darren patted Leo's head. 'I don't mean it unkindly, babes. I think Minna understands that.'

Leo was practically wheezing with anxiety. 'Darren, hon, I think you've said enough. Perhaps we'd better go . . .'

'But I don't want to go,' said Darren. 'Minna, do you want us to go?'

'No!' The shrillness of her voice made Leo jump. But Minna didn't feel crushed by Darren's assault. She said, 'The oven's on so I think I'll pop the food in. I don't know about you, but I'm starving. Leo, would you mind opening another bottle?'

Leo murmured in tones of surrender, 'Sure, Min. Happy to.'

'Just relax, Darren,' she said, as he presented his glass to Leo, who was grimacing as he refilled it.

'Awesome,' Darren beamed. 'We can chat some more over dinner.'

A new week unfurled and consumed her, the way they do. On Wednesday, Minna bumped into a colleague in the kitchen on the floor below. As the only member of IT who could conduct a coherent conversation, Astrid was the initial port of call for many on the payroll. Most importantly, she'd been the first person to show an interest in Minna when she joined the firm. They worked on separate floors but always stopped to chat in passing.

Minna hadn't seen Astrid in ages, and did a double take. In lieu of hello, she said, 'What's happened to you?'

Astrid paused in her efforts to boot up the state-of-the-art coffee maker. 'What do you mean?'

'Last time I saw you—' facts cleared inside Minna's head '—you had a broken arm.'

Astrid laughed warmly, disentangled her fingers from the most expensive piece of technology the office boasted, and wiggled them. 'I've been out of plaster since December. Has it really been that long?'

Was it really *three months*? Longer, even? 'Crazy,' Minna confessed.

Astrid explained. 'Well, we had a mini-break before Christmas so I missed the office party. Then we went skiing in January.' Again, Astrid shook the repaired appendage. 'That was a real test of the healing process, I can tell you.' She pressed the ostentatious on-switch and the machine began to purr. 'Let's have lunch, Minna. Catch up properly.' Minna eagerly assented. Astrid checked her watch. 'Why not Friday? Shall we meet downstairs about one? I fancy the Italian down the road. What do you say?'

'Brilliant,' Minna replied, trying to cap her excitement which seemed excessive. 'There are a few work questions I've been meaning to ask you ...'

Astrid smiled, as coffee flowed into the glass receptacle. 'Jot them down in an e-mail. I'll get to them just as soon as I can. No point in letting them spoil our lunch, is there?'

Minna agreed, and cheerfully went on her way. But several questions assailed her as she headed downstairs, then back up again to accomplish the task she'd undertaken when she encountered Astrid (the fetching of padded envelopes), and then down again.

Why doesn't our floor have a swanky coffee-machine like that? Why haven't *I* broken any limbs? And why haven't I seen Astrid for so long – and not noticed?

As for the second question: nothing Minna did ever introduced the necessary element of risk. The first was satisfied by the fact that nobody had bothered to challenge the status quo. As for the third? Well, it was because of Julian. She'd neglected many people during the relationship. But it was over with Julian by December. That was *weeks* after Australia. So Minna had had no excuse for not seeking out her injured friend. She wouldn't waste any more time. Luckily, there wasn't long to wait, because the end of the week came gratifyingly fast.

The lunch was a treat from the start. Regarding wine, they threw caution to the wind and ordered a carafe. ('Well, it's Friday!' reasoned Astrid.) The conversation roamed with the freedom and agility of a Time Lord, not only around Minna's floor but the entire building.

'You must know as much as HR,' said Minna. 'After all, you have to set up new user accounts and security passes and inductions.'

'I know more than HR,' said Astrid. 'Let's face it. The window cleaners know more than HR. The guys in the post room know everything. But you're right, Minna. I get to dip in and out, like management, but without the bad press.' She sipped her coffee, for the wine was gone and the hour was up but Astrid seemed in no hurry to return to duty. 'Funny though – I've never managed to penetrate your lot's inner sanctum.'

'We usually go to the pub for birthdays,' Minna said. 'You'd be very welcome to join us.' Surely she would?

'Thanks. I know everyone of course, but I wouldn't say I knew them well. Who was the tall guy who worked on your team? He didn't last very long, as I recall.'

'That was Julian,' said Minna. A sudden lump had formed in her throat.

Astrid beamed, as everyone did at the mention of his name. 'Oh, yes! Yes. Julian.'

'We're still friends,' Minna said. 'We meet up now and then. I'll probably see him in a couple of weeks' time.'

'Shame he left, but that's life, I suppose. Mind you, he was quite a catch, wasn't he? I pity any woman who thought she had a chance.'

Minna's jaw dropped. Her throat was dry. 'That was me,' she croaked. 'I mean, we were more than friends, Astrid.'

Astrid's face creased into a puzzled frown. '*You* were? That's not what Kerry said.'

'What did Kerry say?'

'Yes. At least, I think it was Kerry. Or it might have been Steph. Or even Adam . . .'

'*Adam?*' Minna shrieked.

Astrid shook her head. 'Actually, no it wouldn't have been him. It was Kerry or Steph. Which one of them is the smoker?'

'That's Steph.'

'Ah – but I gave up when I broke my arm. Lighting up was a hassle and I knew it would do me good.' She tapped her chest. 'I had a nasty cough that's completely gone so it must have done. Now I smoke maybe three or four cigarettes week.'

'That's great, Astrid.' But the tremor in Minna's voice belied the assurance. Her speech was a hapless stutter. 'But – so – *who* told you? About me and Julian?'

Astrid spread her hands. 'To be honest, I'm not entirely sure.' Perhaps the incident that had precipitated the broken arm had also induced a delayed version of concussion. 'But someone you work with told me that you and Julian once had a snog in a pub but there was no more to it than that. She thought it was sweet, for what it's worth.'

Sweet? Minna fell upon Astrid's word, as if it were her own sword. (It was true, she supposed, that even though she had blamed Julian for their failure, she had absorbed practically all of the guilt herself.) But swiftly she rose again: *sweet* was so wide of the mark. The team had thought it was more than sweet. It had been the highlight of their year. You could almost say the relationship had belonged to them more than to Minna. Without them, she would never have taken things as far as she had—

Well, no. Not at all. Nobody embarks on a relationship just to please other people. (Minna floundered: Had she really thought that was the case?) Minna had *wanted* to make it work with Julian. She had been fond of him, and Julian – for all that he spent so much time in the past – kept wanting to be with her right up till the end, perhaps even afterwards. She'd grown fond of the curly hair, even his dodgy stomach. So *why* had they failed?

All Minna knew for certain was that the story was not Astrid's property. Was it too late to set the record straight?

'We *were* a couple. Julian and me. We really liked each other. Maybe we were even—' But her voice gave way.

Thankfully, Astrid's face was a twist of remorse. 'I'm sorry, Minna. I didn't mean—'

'No, I know … It's fine …' Minna broke off before she plunged into self-pity.

Ah, too late. Astrid pressed a clean napkin into Minna's hand which was when she became aware of the tears making tracks down her cheeks.

Minna apologised for making a scene, and Astrid gently cajoled her, and said not to be ridiculous. By the time Minna had calmed down, they'd been gone from their desks for an hour and forty minutes, and Minna was dry-eyed and composed. Nothing was said about her long absence. Not to her, at least, which threatened to start her weeping again.

At key points throughout the working day, Stephanie asked questions to stimulate discussion. On the stroke of nine: 'So what did everyone watch on TV last night?' As one o'clock approached: 'Who's got interesting plans for lunch?' Shortly after four came: 'Anyone up for a coffee?' And rising six: 'What are we all doing this evening?'

Everyone answered each question in turn, in alphabetical order of first name. Adam began and Stephanie went last, which was doubly appropriate as she was MC. Minna looked forward to these markers of time. So she was stunned on Monday when, in a bold departure, Adam left the office at lunchtime before everyone had discussed their plans. He returned about fifteen minutes later, and slammed a package on his desk.

'Is that your lunch?' Minna asked, fearing for the welfare of the contents of the white paper bag.

'Yes. It is my *fucking* lunch.'

Minna recoiled, but Kerry was not deterred. 'Your *fucking* lunch?'

'I'm sorry,' said Adam, mollified. The team seldom had recourse to swearing. 'It's just that ...' He glanced up at the three faces now assessing him. 'Never mind.'

'Just what?' said Stephanie.

Minna watched as Adam weighed up his options. This opportunity might never arise again. Intrigued, she prompted, 'Didn't they have what you wanted?'

It must have cut close to the bone, for Adam was wild. 'They had *exactly* what I wanted. That's the problem.'

Kerry shook her head, unfulfilled, and prepared to withdraw. Already she'd pulled a bag of dried banana chips from under her desk. She opened the packet. 'You've lost me.'

Minna felt duty-bound to investigate. 'So how is it a problem?'

Adam sat, so everyone was at eye level. 'OK. Get this. Every Monday, I go into the sandwich shop on Drummond Street.'

'The one with the hanging baskets?' asked Stephanie.

'I don't know. There might be hanging baskets. I hadn't noticed.'

'Anyway,' said Minna, over Kerry's crunching. 'Every Monday you go there to buy your lunch. Today's Monday. So that's where you've been.'

'Or was it closed?' Stephanie asked. 'You had to go somewhere else?' With feeling, she added, 'I hate it when people let you down.'

Adam shook his head. 'It was open. It always is. Even between Christmas and New Year, apparently. They're very reliable. So every Monday, I order exactly the same sandwich.'

'Really? Always the same?' said Minna, whose own repertoire was limited but not unfailingly consistent. 'What is it?'

'It's a curried chicken mix. I happen to like it.'

It wasn't to Minna's taste, but you embrace diversity. 'Sounds great.'

'Like I said, I always have it. Always with a little bit of butter. On a white bap. No salt, but pepper to season. Cut into halves, not quarters. No salad. No drink. No crisps. No chocolate. Never eat in. Always take away.'

'Every Monday the same?'

Adam nodded more vigorously than before. 'Every Monday. At the same time, too. *Served by the same guy.*'

By the tone of this statement it was clear that insult was being added to injury. Awe was impossible to muster, so Minna tried admiration. 'Wow. That's pretty regular.'

'*Exactly*, Minna. *Exactly.*'

Adam's focus was squarely and exclusively upon her. It was the strangest feeling, but not unpleasant. Why *me*? Had Steph withdrawn or been eliminated? Was Kerry too intent on her snack? Any pleasure was compromised by the fierce look on Adam's face. His teeth were clenched. His hands lay flat on the desk, restrained. He continued:

'*So why does he always ask me what I want?* Why does he always sound surprised when I tell him? And why does he always ask if I want halves or quarters. And salad. And a drink. And crisps. And chocolate. And if I want to eat in.'

Minna rallied, albeit with careful steps. 'Perhaps he forgets? I'm sure you're a favourite, but you can't be his only customer.'

'He *knows* it's me. *I* know he knows. I've been going there for months.'

Minna tried again. 'Maybe he thinks it's rude to assume you'll order the same thing. He could be trained not to second guess what people want.'

Adam frowned. Clearly, it was a new suggestion. 'I don't think that's part of a chef's training. If he is a chef. He probably isn't. They do lasagne but I doubt it's made on the premises.'

Stephanie stood up, about to leave the room, but not before issuing a parting shot. 'Maybe he doesn't *care* what you have. I mean, why would he?'

'But he sounds so eager,' said Adam. 'Like he's enticing me.'

'You're reading too much into it,' said Stephanie. 'We're talking *sandwiches*.'

With that Steph left, and Minna found her heart beginning to race. She said, 'Maybe he secretly wants you to try something else. To be spontaneous.'

Adam's hands flew up in the air in a flare of defeat. 'I can't *be* spontaneous. He won't let me. The moment I walk in, it's like stepping onto the set of a play. He has the opening line so I can't say anything until he speaks. After that, I'm locked in.'

Kerry tipped the packet to her lips to swallow crumbs. But not a second was lost as her remark was not just timely but the most pertinent of all. 'Perhaps you don't *want* to be spontaneous, Adam. Do you think that might be the problem?' And with that, she also left.

The man looked injured. He appealed to Minna: 'That's not a very nice thing to say.'

Confronting Adam's naked despair, it was Minna who felt helpless, and hopeless. 'You have to admit, it's a possibility.'

Adam wailed plaintively on. 'It isn't *true*, Minna. It isn't *true*. I *am* a spontaneous person. I am. At least, I *would* be, if I ever got the chance. It's difficult you know – with the twins – and Laura's *brilliant* – don't get me *wrong* – I love her, I *worship* her – and god knows *she* never gets a second to do *anything* out of the ordinary, except when her mum comes round – but *that's* only once a week – Laura and I are lucky – but sometimes – *just sometimes* – we feel we'd like to get off the roundabout – or the rollercoaster – or whatever it is – and do something *different*. Do you know what I mean?'

Minna had met Laura and the twins only briefly. Adam had swept them in and off the premises, as if fearing they would

34

embarrass him, or perhaps be exposed to some hideous infection.

Minna said, 'Yes! I know exactly how you feel,' but how could she, despite all the time they spent together? Her world beyond work was nothing like Adam's. It was as bad as thinking that they'd cared about her relationship with Julian! But if she took her words back it might offend Adam. So Minna privately amended them. We don't know how each other really feels. Was that something that could ever be fixed?

The day wore on, and then the week, with little promise of rewards for application. So Minna looked to her birthday in three weeks' time, in mid-April. Callie had suggested drinks and would let Minna know when she was free. Julian still hadn't e-mailed to make a new arrangement, which was out of character. Was he waiting to send a birthday greeting? Leo's call, therefore, was a welcome short-term distraction. It had been a fortnight since the dinner party, and she'd received only a brief text next evening, thanking her for a 'fab nite'. He asked if she were free on Saturday night and she readily agreed.

Minna had a lot to get through on Friday. So when she logged on she was taken aback by a string of e-mails from disgruntled clients which revealed a flaw in the software. Her first thought was to call Astrid, but she hesitated, as if their every encounter now risked being soured by debilitating disclosures. Kerry had referenced a similar problem only days ago. It would take all of a moment to ask, and just minutes more to resolve. But again, Minna stalled. Kerry's indomitable competence made her wary. So Minna resorted to the Help Desk, and was put immediately on divert.

It was ten to ten before Minna clocked that the first of the day's routines had been missed. No good would come of getting agitated, so she elected to be calm. No one else had said anything. It was liberating to be spared the ritual, like being reprieved of an onerous chore at the eleventh hour, but unsettling, too.

By five past, however, she perceived a twitch being volleyed between Adam and Kerry, and so took the initiative to ask, 'Did Steph say she was going to be late?'

Adam shook his head. 'Not to me.'

'Nor me,' Kerry concurred. She summoned a website. 'No problems with public transport that I can see. Besides, everyone else is here.'

'Maybe she's got the day off?' Adam asked. 'Carol might know.' Adam put his phone on speaker and dialled their manager's extension. Carol sat next door, and was not known for being a uniting influence. If not resentful of her responsibility to those on her report, Carol shelved their welfare low down on her list of priorities, as she got on with her studies in advance business management.

'*I'm currently out of the office. Please leave a message or press zero to get back to the switchboard.*'

'Does that really work?' Minna asked. 'Pressing zero, I mean. My phone always goes through to accounts payable.'

Kerry shrugged. 'Depends who's on the front desk whether messages get relayed back. So, what's happened to Steph?'

'Medical appointment?' hazarded Minna. 'Maybe she reckoned she'd be finished before work began so she didn't think to mention it.'

'Let's try her mobile,' said Kerry. But the number wasn't in use. 'Maybe she's changed it?' She addressed Adam and Minna frankly. 'Come to think of it, how I do know I've got *your* up-to-date details?'

Phones were produced and contact lists scanned. Then Minna said, 'What about Steph's home number. I'm sure I've got that somewhere.'

But again, nothing.

'She lives alone, doesn't she?' Adam said.

Both women nodded, sharing Adam's bleak thought. 'She *could* be there, couldn't she?' said Minna. 'What if she can't pick up the phone? She could have lain there all night.'

She imagined the *Evening Standard*: WOMAN'S CORPSE LEFT TO ROT IN LEWISHAM FLAT. CALLOUS COLLEAGUES CLAIM, 'WE THOUGHT SHE'D MISSED HER TRAIN.'

'The longer she's been there,' Kerry pointed out, 'assuming she *is* at home—'

'Which we can't,' Adam warned.

'—the greater chance there is of someone who expected to be in touch with her, failing, and being concerned. And acting on it.'

'Someone could be taking care of her already,' Adam suggested. 'They wouldn't necessarily think to call work. Work isn't a priority in a case like that.'

We're not a priority, corrected a voice in Minna's head.

'Assuming she has had an accident,' said Kerry.

'Which we can't,' said Minna. 'I know.' She tried to look on the bright side. 'No one's come looking for her *here*. That's a good sign. No one's expecting her. She hasn't failed to attend any meetings.'

'But she could have sent a text,' said Kerry. 'Has she tweeted?'

Minna checked her phone. 'Not this morning.'

'Who else can we ask?' Adam said. 'In the company. Who is she friendly with?'

'Maybe that's not such a great idea,' said Kerry. 'We don't want to get Steph into trouble.'

Minna had a rare brainwave. 'What about her real friends? She's got *millions*.'

If the phrase 'real friends' caused offence, it was suppressed. Adam and Kerry seemed only relieved to pursue Minna's suggestion. 'Where do we start?'

Minna thought on. 'We need to find out where she was last night. And with whom. She might have got food poisoning, and had to stay at a friend's. Out of London.'

'Good point, Minna,' said Kerry. 'Let's look in her diary.'

But Stephanie's desk was locked, and no one knew the password to her computer.

'We should be able to sort this out ourselves,' said Minna. 'What *was* Steph doing last night? She did tell us.'

Adam pondered. 'She might have said she was going to the theatre. With Jessica.'

'Not Jessica,' said Kerry. 'Isn't it Julie she goes to the theatre with?'

Minna thought. 'I think it is a J name. It might be Joanne.'

'Joann*a*?'

'Joanna sounds right,' said Kerry. 'But I don't think she was going to the theatre last night. That was two Mondays ago. Remember?'

Adam and Minna shook their heads. 'So what was last *night*?' Minna asked. 'She was definitely doing something.'

'She was always doing something,' said Adam. He corrected himself. 'She *is*, I mean. She's always doing something after work.'

'I think it was cookery school. Leith's or something. With Lorraine?'

'They don't always alliterate,' said Adam. 'It'd be easier to keep track that way, I admit. Movies with Meredith. Shopping with Sinéid.'

'So how do we find this cookery friend, whoever she was?' said Minna.

'Or *he* was,' said Kerry. 'Is. This is hopeless.'

Minna sighed, because she had begun to feel united with her colleagues, instead of threatened by them. 'Let's try and eliminate some candidates by going through the people she's mentioned.'

By eleven o'clock, a whiteboard had been wheeled in. Names and occupations criss-crossed its surface as if all were suspects in an enquiry, and the office soon resembled a police incident room. There were lines from Sarah to tennis, from Tracey to clubbing. The theatre friend had been identified as Janine.

'Inga's the cyclist,' Minna said. 'We can rule her out. Cycling's a weekend activity.'

Kerry brandished a marker pen, deftly slashing at names and pursuits.

'So that means,' said Adam, 'last night Steph was bowling with Rachel.'

Minna said, 'So now all we need to do is find Rachel, and ask if she knows where Steph is. Shouldn't be too difficult. How do we go about it?'

'Easy. Try Facebook. We could look at the "interests" of people with that name.'

'But that might be private information,' said Minna. 'We might not even get that far, if Steph's profile is available only to friends.'

'Not a problem,' said Kerry. 'She's one of my Facebook friends.'

'She isn't one of mine,' said Minna, hoping it sounded more like an observation than a complaint. She whispered to Adam, 'Are you Steph's friend on Facebook?'

'I think so. I mean, I think I accepted. Ages ago. But I never look, to be honest.'

'Here we go,' said Kerry, commanding her colleagues' attention. 'Right. Stephanie has two thousand and seventeen friends. And, with any luck, amongst them will be someone who knows where and how she is.'

Suddenly, the door swiftly opened and Stephanie walked in. She sat down at her desk. 'Morning,' she chirped, without peering up from her screen. The others swivelled simultaneously towards the centre of the room. After several minutes, Stephanie looked round and, with unnecessary aggression said, 'Yes?'

They all spoke at once: 'We thought something had happened to you . . .'

'Did *anyone* know where you were?'

'Steph, we were worried sick!'

Stephanie ruthlessly extinguished their distress. 'What's the big deal?' She turned back to her monitor, as if it were more agreeable company than her co-workers. 'Frankly, I'm surprised any of you noticed I wasn't here.'

The others converged on a look of shared bewilderment, then dispersed in their disparate inadequacy. Minna was cast adrift, excluded again – the feelings that had topped and tailed her months with Julian. What if this breech were permanent? Could she plug the gaps that might furnish an unbroken path back to her team mates?

Gaps were everywhere, when you looked. Minna felt the urgent need to close them, and stop others from rending open.

She wondered what had brought this little team together in the first place, because they all performed such very different tasks. Was it determined by the availability of seating? The four of them were wedged into an office that was smaller than most others, having once been halved in size to create a sound booth.

Minna supposed they'd arrived last, and had been squeezed into an overspill zone. But it was such a comfortable social fit that Minna embraced the idea that it was all to do with personality. Just what might that mean? She knew only that they were somehow unlike the black-and-charcoal knitwear-sporting crowd in her previous job (for which she was glad). Nor like any of the other teams who worked throughout the building – one of whom was rumoured to never put pen to paper unless it was Moleskine, while another was virtually paperless. So what was the link that united Minna's lot?

Perhaps they shared parallel career paths. On her Film Studies course, Minna had dreamed of a career in which words and pictures were spliced and paired in thrilling combinations, not sold to the highest bidder. But then, her Exeter experience seemed to belong to someone else. On a visit to her parents' at Christmas, she retrieved her old prospectus and examined its temptations. A myriad career opportunities presented themselves: journalism, publishing, film and television, arts administration. Minna had fondly imagined that you floated from one industry to another, via a private screening or gallery opening – a glass in hand as relevant as a CV – sustaining your status as a networker.

Minna's family was light on role models. Lisa's vocation as a dancer had been a one-off act of divine intervention. Both senior Jepsons seemed to have perfected the skill of shuffling, ever so slightly, back and forth, within their respective professions.

Minna had spent three years working in a vintage clothes shop off Portobello Road, before bagging a job as the office manager for a production company in Brewer Street. Latterly, that role had moved her along an unexpected trajectory, and she unearthed a talent for which she had never experienced any passion – as an analyst. And, not long afterwards, spurred on by friends and flatmates, she got through two interviews and was offered the job at Macsamphire Strutt. It had been almost too good to be true.

So what had been Adam's journey, and Stephanie's and Kerry's? For all Minna knew, the little team, like Minna herself, had drifted into their jobs and stuck, like limpets, as the tides of commerce and creativity ebbed. Which offered no clues to their compatibility or not. *Dare* she ask? She would hate for them to think she was stirring. Because she felt she had said enough, and done enough, already.

Friday's final throes were a race to tie up loose ends, and Minna was happy to let work absorb her. As they shut down their computers and tidied their desks, the team disclosed their weekend ambitions, after which Steph left promptly. Kerry lingered, waiting for a phone call, apparently. There was nothing pre-meditated about the fact that Minna got to the lift at the same time as Adam, but she was pleased she had.

'Do you think Steph will be all right?' Minna asked, as the doors closed behind them. 'Maybe we should have asked her out for a drink.'

Adam shrugged. 'Come on, Minna. What else can we *do*? When it's all said and done, it's not our problem.'

If the attitude sounded harsh, the tone wasn't. She said, 'You're right. I just don't feel as if we've made a difference.'

He regarded her kindly. 'We did our best.'

Minna smiled, but wished the day had ended with a more upbeat resolution.

A thoroughfare throughout shopping hours, by seven o'clock on Saturday night Old Compton Street was reclaiming its milling, village atmosphere. Tourists deserted venues and regulars flooded in. A few aged parents, being inducted to the scene by idealistic sons, kept one eye on their Selfridge's shopping and another on the exits.

Minna expected to see Leo and Darren, arm in arm, but was not overly disappointed to see Leo by himself. Impressively, he was only one Kylie-chorus late. When he and Minna had dated, he'd always been punctual, if not early. His standards hadn't slipped; it was just more time-consuming being homosexual. Minna had made an effort, because their evenings were special. She was pleased to see that Leo had too.

They shared a bottle of wine, then went for a pizza at nine which they wolfed down in hunger. Afterwards, they had more wine and shots at the Friendly Society, where they'd even had a little dance, before moving on to G-A-Y to spot celebrities, take pictures of each other, and dance some more. Crossing the road, they nearly got run down by a reckless Rickshaw, requisitioned for a party in Clerkenwell to which they were invited by way of compensation. Delighted to be asked, they declined in favour of more local drinking and dancing. Minna was having a brilliant time but agreed with Leo that they'd have just one more and then catch the last tube home.

Much of their conversation had extolled Darren's virtues, though tactfully Leo had steered it away at several points to make Minna the focus, which was a bit of a downer, if she were perfectly honest. She apologised, 'I wish I had some news of my own.' The mood in her office had shifted, but it seemed too soon to comment on the result. 'Now, back to Darren,' said Minna. 'I really like it that—'

Leo interrupted. 'We probably said enough about him the other night.' He sounded tetchy.

'Oh, I didn't mind the questions,' said Minna. 'Darren's very confident in his opinions. You have to admire that.'

'Well, thanks, Min. Means a lot to hear that from you.' He sounded sincere.

'So let's keep talking. Tell me something he didn't pass on himself.'

'Well . . .' Leo havered. 'There *is* one other thing about Darren . . .'

'Go on. I'm ready for it.'

'It isn't a *big* thing, not really. It's not *physical.*' She was pleased to hear it. 'No, no.' He twisted his fingers around the stem of his wine glass. 'It's just that . . . The thing is . . . you see . . . he's not out. You know . . . O.U.T.'

'Oh,' said Minna. 'What's the reason? Religious, cultural, a family inheritance?'

Leo shook his head. 'None of those, no.'

Carefully, she probed. 'Does Darren have a problem with being gay?'

'Doesn't seem to. He's very comfortable inside his own skin. And mine.'

Minna ignored the smug remark. 'And he's definitely gay?'

'Oh yes,' Leo confirmed. They'd had this discussion: people weren't bisexual in his book, just greedy. 'We have a great time. We just don't do the scene. It's not everyone's bag.'

'But *you* crave it,' she reminded him. 'You're like a kid in a toyshop.'

'Sure . . . I just suppose I always thought I would enjoy it with my boyfriend – I mean, it's brilliant being here with you – but it's, well . . . I'd like to hold hands in the street with a guy, kiss in a taxi.' He paused. 'So part of me thinks it'd be kind of stupid to be with someone who wasn't up for that too. Don't you think?'

Suddenly, Minna shivered. *What* did she think? Only that she didn't want to think about it. Only that she *couldn't*.

She said, 'But you really like Darren. You're such a fabulous couple.'

'Thanks, Min. I absolutely do like him. I'm making too big a deal of this, actually. Really, it is OK, because everyone knows.'

'Everyone knows what?'

'That Darren's gay.'

'But you said he wasn't out.'

'He isn't. He doesn't *need* to be. I mean, hello – thirty, single, living alone in a Eurovision-themed flat in the East End, works as a florist. It's obvious.'

'But if he hasn't told anyone he is gay, then how can you say everyone knows?'

'They just *do*, Min,' Leo said wearily. 'So it's not a problem.'

'Then why did you mention it?'

Leo nodded vigorously. 'No, it's *fine*. I don't mind that he doesn't want to come into Soho or meet my mates. I don't mind that he went to Romford for the weekend to see his folks and I couldn't even text him. Relationships are all about compromise, aren't they?'

'This one sounds like it's based on secrecy.' She'd meant to offer reassurance, something like, 'The main thing is, you really fancy Darren. And he fancies you.' But then she said, 'Hon, if it's even a tiny problem now, just think how much worse it could get.'

Now he flared. 'You're just saying all this because you're jealous because *you're* single.' Where had *that* come from? Leo had never been so neurotic when they'd dated.

'That's rubbish.' Minna snapped. 'I'm just trying to be helpful.'

She and Leo never argued. At worst, there were tipsy tiffs which descended into random slanging matches once the gist of the original argument had fled for safer ground, but nothing more than that. In spite of the fact that Leo had dumped Minna, they strictly adhered to a conduct which ensured each never let the other down.

But this was about Darren – the kind of person who is happy to assassinate the characters of others while spurning introspection. And how did it reflect on Leo – no stranger to deception himself?

Worried now, Minna said, 'We're not going to fall out over a guy, are we?'

A flicker of a grin spread across Leo's face. 'We broke up over one. All of them, actually.'

Minna laughed. She couldn't help herself. So with hugs and kisses, and assertions of enduring love, they parted company.

But in the morning a sullied Sunday awaited Minna – another hangover, and worst of all, her memory of her little dinner party a fortnight ago was irrevocably dimmed.

Minna had considered it a success. The food had been well-received and a lot of wine consumed. The conversation flowed just as freely, with no further reference to partners past or present. Or colleagues. At the end of the meal, Darren and Leo washed up, leaving the plates disarrayed but drying, to join Minna in the living room. She'd turned up the music and they pushed back the coffee table and danced. She couldn't quite remember getting to bed, but had slept soundly till late morning.

Minna had confined herself to her room until such a time that she could be sociable. But she soon got bored, and forced herself down to the gym. When she got home, she found Sharmila alone at the kitchen table, leafing through a Sunday supplement, as serene as a receptionist in a private skin clinic. (In fact, she worked in banking.) Often, Niamh and Sharmila operated as a double act, which tended towards conspiracy. Their eerily similar appearance was coincidental – both were pale-skinned with raven hair – but perhaps they had a pact to conserve energy by taking it in turns to speak. When Sharmila did not acknowledge Minna's arrival, Minna assumed she was on standby rather than shutdown.

Eventually, Sharmila had looked up. 'So how did it go?' she asked.

Minna replied, 'Leo said they had a great time.'

'Did you believe him?' said Niamh, who had suddenly entered the room, perhaps prompted by Minna's return.

'What kind of question is that?' Sharmila asked.

'A perfectly reasonable one,' her best friend said.

'Explain what you mean.'

'Well, if it all goes wrong and Minna happens to let slip at the end that she'd had her doubts about Darren from the start, then Leo is going to feel disappointed that she said nothing to warn him.'

'He'd be furious.' Sharmila was entirely in agreement now.

Why were they speaking as if Minna wasn't there?

She dismissed the scenario. 'But I liked Darren,' she said. 'He was interesting to talk to. And Leo adores him, which is terrific.' Then she reflected, 'Not that Leo got to say much. Darren has quite a dominant personality.' But she admired his certainty. It was refreshing to meet someone who was so sure of himself.

'Well, maybe that's no big deal,' Niamh assured her. 'After all, the night was all about Darren.'

'No it wasn't,' Sharmila protested. 'It was about Leo. The dinner was for him.'

Niamh said, 'What about you, Min? Did you enjoy yourself?'

Minna dealt with the facts. 'It was pretty stress-free on the organisation side.' The kitchen was in chaos but bore no lasting damage. '*Yes*. Yes, I did.'

Her flatmates nodded in acknowledgement but they were not yet done. Sharmila challenged, 'You got what you wanted out of it?'

Niamh said, 'What *exactly* was your goal, Min?'

'She wanted to make sure Leo is happy with Darren.'

'And is he? You said he was sidelined a little.'

Sharmila explained, 'Leo might have been nervous being in your flat with his new boyfriend. I mean, back in the day, *he* slept here, didn't he? So it stands to reason that he might have felt awkward.'

Niamh nodded. 'But it was kind of you to organise the evening. Very selfless.'

Her friend took over. 'But was it the right thing to do?'

Minna frowned. 'Why wouldn't it be?'

'Perhaps it's better to leave well enough alone.'

'Assuming all is "well enough,"' said Niamh.

'Minna said they seemed very happy together.'

'I'm not talking about Darren and Leo,' said Niamh. 'I'm talking about Leo and Minna.' When Minna looked puzzled, Niamh explained. 'Well, it must look as if you're interfering in Leo's life . . .'

'In his happiness,' said Sharmila, catching on fast. 'As if . . .'

'As if you can't let go.'

'Or won't,' said Sharmila. 'It's a fine line between being friendly and suffocating.'

Again, a glance was shared. Niamh began, 'We wondered—'

'Although we didn't like to say so at the time—'

'Perhaps the reason things didn't work out with Julian was because you hadn't moved far enough away from Leo. Is that a possibility, Minna?'

'I'll bet it's much easier catching up when you're both single,' Sharmila offered. 'I'll bet you prefer it.'

Minna bridled. 'That's not true! It was Leo I phoned from Melbourne when it all went wrong with Julian.' Leo had urged her home so they could talk further – so Minna could rant again. Besides, wouldn't Darren have said if he felt Leo was the problem? But could Darren be wrong? After all, Minna had known Sharmila and Niamh far longer.

Harangued by hindsight, because none of this had bothered her at the time, Minna was in turmoil. But then a wild insight intruded, and elbowed out remorse. How could *any* of them have formed an opinion before she had settled on her own? Then she subsided into a gloom which, for all her habitual optimism, she had to concede was familiar. Hadn't it always been the case that other people had a clearer view of her world than Minna did herself? Wasn't she always the last to know?

Next morning – another Monday – Minna emerged from Euston Underground station and joined the reassuring jostle of friends and couples exchanging final words of reassurance. She allowed brusque commuters to pass, but found she was too slow to avoid that third type of person, who stands alone, equidistant from others of their ilk: the distributors of free samples and fliers. Within minutes, she had scooped up two fistfuls of documents and a packet of yoghurt-coated oat cakes, and carefully stored them inside her bag. She was wary of lingering, lest anyone thought she was begging.

At the office, Minna fetched coffee from the kitchen and switched on her e-mail. Soon enough, she was joined by her colleagues, and once everyone had logged on and been revived by drinks, they turned inwardly and formed a circle to facilitate the day's proceedings.

When asked about her weekend, Minna paused. She could talk about Leo, or about Leo and Darren but the latter could conjure Julian and that seemed too far removed from the agenda for a brand new week.

She said, 'It's this morning I want to tell you about. On the way in I just happened to pick up all these fabulous vouchers.'

'Vouchers?' said Kerry, as if she'd been offered ketamine instead of cashback.

Adam, the family man, continued. 'You can save a lot of money with vouchers.'

Kerry nodded, as if willing to be persuaded. 'No one expects to pay full price for anything. I'll happily change brands to make a saving. And if there's another bargain to be had a couple of weeks later, I'll change again. Who *needs* favourites, after all?'

'I like routine,' Steph cautioned them all.

Adam shrugged. 'We know we ought to shop around, but who's got time to actually do it? I guess that vouchers take the hassle of choice away, and still offer variety.'

Adam and Kerry's advocacy was all very well, but with her decisive remark Steph had frozen herself out of the conversation and immersed herself in work. Why she was being so evasive?

Minna waved her paper hoard as if it were a manifesto. 'Look! I've got about twenty pounds' worth of savings right here!'

'Go on,' Kerry challenged. 'Tempt us.'

Minna reeled off coffee and sandwich combinations, hair and nail procedures, gym memberships, magazine subscriptions, digital TV packages – speaking so quickly that interruptions were not permitted.

Steph still seemed aloof, and Minna dared to investigate. 'Hey, Steph, here's one for a private opening in a gallery in Shoreditch. Champagne and canapés. One night only. Tonight.'

Without looking up, Stephanie said, 'I can't tonight. I've got zumba with Leonie.'

'But there's champagne!'

Steph was unmoved. 'I said, I can't. I've got my zumba class with Leonie.'

'But you can do zumba any night of the week, can't you?' said Adam.

'No. Only every second Monday and only with Leonie.'

'Take Leonie with you,' Kerry suggested.

'Champagne gives her migraine. Anyway, we're going to zumba. Leonie and I.'

Minna said, 'You might find an even better class on a different night. Have you thought of that?'

'We haven't got time to look. I'm busy every night. Tomorrow I've—'

Minna's tolerance levels were humming but it seemed Kerry's had already snapped. But Steph was not her target. Eyes narrowed with suspicion, Kerry observed, 'You've got a lot of vouchers, Minna. Did you actively go out seeking them?'

Adam sniggered, boyishly. 'Soliciting!'

'They're everywhere,' Minna declared. 'Some mornings, you just can't move for them.'

'And today was one of those mornings?'

Minna eyeballed Kerry with unprecedented nerve. 'It was.'

'Why don't *you* go, Minna?' Adam suggested.

It felt like an attack. 'No! It has to be Steph! Because . . . she likes East European art.'

'Everyone likes art,' said Kerry. 'You wouldn't admit to not liking it, anyway.'

'Steph likes art, she's *told* us,' Minna persisted. Stephanie interrogated Minna with a penetrating look. Minna might have withered, but wondered if there was a point to be made, if only she persisted. She scoured her pale scraps of memory until she struck gold. 'Remember, last year, you went on that plate painting course in Greenwich?' Her sister had been there just a few weeks later.

Slowly, Steph nodded. 'Yes, I did. That was with Kate. We decided to get into crafts.'

You could see Adam was thinking: Crafts with Kate. They *do* alliterate. Leonie only got Zumba because Steph didn't know anyone called Zoe, presumably.

Minna was triumphant. 'See! I knew it.'

Stephanie frowned. 'But I don't see her any more. She found another friend to go with. So I switched to madrigals with Gaynor.'

Two hard *G*s, but Minna decided another facet of Steph's social policy was being fulfilled. The co-participant in any pursuit must not be replaced by another. If the protagonist removed herself from the activity, the endeavour itself needed to be abandoned, and both a new partner and entertainment sourced as its successor.

'You can go tonight, Steph,' said Minna. 'Meet new people. Or ring up a friend who's at a loose end.'

Steph dug her heels in. 'I don't want to go!'

Kerry said, 'Minna, why don't you leave the vouchers in the kitchen for people to help themselves?'

How virtuous she sounded. Minna could have slapped her. 'No!' she cried. 'No, we can't do that!'

'What's this *about*, Minna?' said Adam, treacherously.

'Yes, what's going on?' demanded Kerry.

All eyes were on Minna. She felt like a dissident or troublemaker, but realised – suddenly and brutally – that she wanted only to please them. She wanted to encourage them to take a moment in the spotlight, as she had done, during her time with Julian. (Maybe Adam had taken his already, on account of the sandwiches. Had Steph's disappearance been her own little statement? God help them all if Kerry took a stand.)

Or perhaps Minna simply wanted to make up for disappointing them in her failure to love Julian? Would it always come down to that in the end?

She held her head high. 'Steph, last Friday, you were really out of sorts. You came in late, which you never do. Was it because you're fed up? You want to change your life.'

Kerry and Adam seemed to have shrunk in their seats until they achieved the size of staplers. Minna felt horribly conspicuous, as if ensnared by a spotlight. An image of Darren's beguiling smile appeared in her head. She quashed it.

'I was late because my heel broke,' Steph said. 'I had to wait and get my shoe mended. I couldn't be arsed to go home and change them. That's all.'

'Oh,' said Minna. The light went out. Darkness seemed to leech in all around her. 'Well, I'm sorry to hear that.' The others adjusted, like layers of tissue paper subsiding into a gift box. Minna was the foiled rosette, frivolously plonked on top.

Over the next few days, Minna swapped her boots for pumps and renewed her gym membership. The weather was glorious throughout. Monday was 1 April and at the end of the week was Good Friday, which pitched Easter just one week prior to Minna's birthday.

Don and Maureen had pledged to visit old friends in the Lakes, and having considered the volume of traffic projected on the consecutive weekends, opted to travel on Minna's birthday, when there would be fewer people on the roads out celebrating. Minna didn't mind. (She'd been at school with a girl embittered by being born on December 25.) Minna's mother assured her of cake as well as chocolate eggs. She would be with family, because Lisa had promised to join them. That's what counted.

Still no word from Julian. Perhaps he really was planning a surprise! But Minna began to fret that she'd scared him off: that she had unwittingly revealed the dread she felt in anticipating their meetings. (A dread which never amounted to anything as damaging as her prediction.) Or had Julian bored of *her*, and finally decided to move on.

But what if there was something wrong? Did she have any right to be concerned? *Oh Julian*, she willed. *Get in touch. Please . . .* She sent a text: Hope you're well? Let me know if you want to catch up again. Mx. And then regretted its brief, unemotional composition. Where was the lure in that for Julian to respond?

In her MC capacity, Stephanie opened Thursday's e-mail before the others. The heading – IMPORTANT INFORMATION RE OFFICE MOVE – might have alerted a twitchier team but her colleagues ignored it, much in the way they ignored fire alarms until they stood at the window and watched the last person spill onto the pavement below.

'I think a team catch-up is in order,' said Steph.

'So what's new?' said Adam.

Kerry said, 'Yes – what's so important about an e-mail? You're sure it's not a delayed April fool?'

Steph shook her head. 'It's no joke. It appears we're moving offices.'

Kerry gave it due consideration. 'Somewhere with more regular heating, I hope,' she said. 'It's like a Siberian winter on the third floor and a baking desert on the sixth. The whole system needs an overhaul and that can't be done with a hundred per cent occupancy.'

'I'd quite like to be nearer a Waitrose,' said Minna, wanting to contribute. 'One of the Little stores would do. So long as there's a salad bar. It's got to be hygienic if it's Waitrose, doesn't it?'

Adam nodded and added, 'Being closer to the Jubilee line would make a difference to my morning drop-offs. I reckon I'd save eleven minutes.'

Minna was impressed. 'You can work it out to the nearest minute?'

He spread his hands. 'I have to be specific. You get charged if you're late picking up your kids where my girls go. What about you, Steph? I suppose being central is pretty important, because of all the stuff you do in the evening. I just hope we're not going to end up on some shiny new retail park on the outskirts.'

Kerry growled. 'All glass atriums and marble pillars. Style over substance.'

'It must be cheaper to run than somewhere in central London,' said Steph. 'You get more space for your pound.'

'More bang for your buck!' Adam cried. It must have amused him.

'I wouldn't want to work in Ealing,' said Minna, thinking of Leo who struggled with Rayner's Lane. 'You might as well be on the moon. Steph, tell me we're not going to move out to Ealing.'

Stephanie shook her head. She'd used those brief moments

to study the e-mail, so was reliably informed. 'No. We're not actually leaving the building.'

'Oh,' said Minna. 'Are we switching floors?'

'The carpet's new on level two,' said Adam. 'Because of HR. I wouldn't mind working there. Haven't they got that nice coffee machine, too? I've heard it's amazing.'

'Yes,' said Minna. 'It's impressive. Though if we move in there, won't IT have to relocate? I wonder what they'd think of that?' She could imagine Astrid up in arms.

Again, Steph referred to the e-mail. 'They're not moving anywhere. In fact, it looks like we're the only team being affected.'

'So where are they going to put us?' Adam asked.

'I wouldn't have thought there was any spare space for four people,' said Minna.

Steph wiped her eyes with the back of her hand. She sniffed, and said, 'They're not going to move us as a team.'

'Then what?' Adam asked.

'Yes?' queried Kerry, sharply. 'What?'

'They're splitting us up. They're re-deploying us to different teams with whom our—' she fairly spat the next word '—*specialisms* are most compatible.'

But the others refused to absorb the news so readily. 'Specialisms?' Minna said. 'I wonder what they mean by that?'

'In my case,' pondered Adam, 'I couldn't begin to guess.'

Steph, having absorbed the facts, considered them. 'I suppose I could sit with R and D, if I had to. Or maybe I could split my week. R and D on Mondays and Wednesdays, say, and then, on Tuesdays and Thursdays, I could—'

She got no further, interrupted by an impassioned wail from an unlikely source. Practical Kerry – the last bastion of robustness – rose to her feet in a single glide. She towered. She glowered. Then she tipped back her head and howled: 'But I don't want to work anywhere else. I only want to work with you.' Tears glittered in her eyes.

Silence followed: evidently, there was residual embarrassment at the risk of exposed emotions. But no one wanted to shun Kerry's efforts. To Steph's credit, she succeeded in cracking the silence. 'I never knew you felt like that . . .'

'Oh, Kerry,' Adam opined. 'I'd miss you too. We all would, wouldn't we, Minna?'

Kerry looked to Minna, as if Minna were the author of all that had happened and all that would come to pass. It wasn't an accusation but responsibility was implied, and it weighed on her, heavily. Minna longed to steal away: she'd thought of doing that, after the vouchers. After Julian. Found a new office to work in, avoiding all contact and opportunity for reproach. But she couldn't ignore the fact that a bigger part of her now wanted to stay and get it right. Perhaps she'd been misguided or naïve in the past, but Minna hadn't betrayed anyone, she hadn't let anyone down.

From this rose the brightest insights of the past few days. None of this was about the last of them having his or her turn, simply because it was owed. Nor was everything connected to the fact that Minna had dated Julian, and they had not. It simply wasn't an issue. (If ever it had been.) Only Minna would beat herself up about it if it became one, and it wouldn't help anyone if she did that.

Don Jepson collected his elder daughter from the station just after eleven on Saturday morning and drove her home. The familiar sight of the house was instantly heartening. Once inside, Minna was overwhelmed by the most deliciously welcoming scent of baking.

'In your honour,' Maureen revealed, as she leaned across the kitchen counter to kiss her daughter. Minna gratefully inhaled the smell of her favourite lemon cake, cooling on a rack. 'It's for tomorrow, when Lisa gets here. She'll scalp us if we don't. I'll open a packet of Hobnobs for now. Are you ready for a cuppa, or do you want to put your things away first?'

'Oh, they can wait. It's fine.'

'Well, you're in Lisa's room. We've had a clear out.'

The day Minna went to university, her mother had ordered new curtains and a sewing table from John Lewis. Minna had a couple of cartons stowed at the back of a cupboard, while Lisa had retained her hold by sculpting possessions into structures too elaborate to dismantle.

Over a pot of tea, mother and daughter began to chat about work and home – everyday conversation. Minna relaxed, and it was almost as if she were on holiday – which, she supposed, she was.

It was as they washed up the tea things that her mother's bombshell dropped. 'Did you want to do anything before the Gillespies arrive?'

Minna felt something other than crumbs lodge in her throat. 'The Gillespies?'

'Yes. They said they'd get here for six. They're staying overnight *en route* to Southampton. Now, I *think* we've got everything, but you wouldn't mind nipping to the mini Tesco if we're caught short?'

'You mean Barbara and Tony Gillespie?' Minna qualified.

'Of course. How many Gillespies do we know?'

'Abigail's parents?'

'*Yes*, Minna. *Those* Gillespies.'

'Abigail – who never said anything that wasn't designed to wind me up. For years.'

'Well, you can't always get on with everyone,' Maureen observed, plunging her hands into a sink full of hot, soapy water.

Minna nodded, but she still felt the wounds of the past open like the mouths of Venus flytraps. She hurriedly smothered them with the Elastoplast of maturity. But still she felt entitled to point out, 'You never told me they were coming.'

Maureen bridled. 'Didn't I? Well, they only phoned on Monday.'

'BT operates a 24/7 service, Mum.'

'Of course I know that,' her mother said.

Minna got up off her stool, and stood by the pantry doors, out of her mother's culinary equivalent of a flight-path. 'It's just that if I'd known they were coming, then . . .'

Then what? Would she have stayed away? How awful to feel alienated. She *belonged* here. At least, she had once.

Maureen smiled. 'Don't worry, dear. You won't be in the way.'

'I didn't mean—'Minna gave up. Then, 'Abigail isn't coming, is she?'

'No, don't be silly. She and Robert live in Paisley. Lovely wedding it was.'

'When did you go to Scotland?' Minna felt a twitch like a trapped nerve.

'The wedding was in Carshalton,' said her mother, rinsing plates. 'They wouldn't have had such a good turnout from your year group if it had been too far afield. It was terrific to see so many old faces.'

'When was this?'

'Last October. When you were in Australia, having a blast with Julian. How envious some of the single girls were, I can tell you. Not Callie, of course. She's landed on her feet, husband-wise.'

'Callie was there?'

'And Todd. Yes. So many of your old friends, all doing well for themselves.'

'Abigail didn't go to Callie's wedding. I didn't even know they were friends.'

'Didn't you, dear?'

'No.' She fought back, 'Callie never mentioned going to the wedding. *You* never mentioned it.'

'Oh. I suppose we assumed you were too caught up in your own happiness.'

'Well, I wasn't.'

'We weren't to know that, were we?' said Maureen, in perhaps only her third ever comment about Minna and Julian's relationship. 'We assumed you'd turned the invitation down because you had better things to do.'

'I didn't get an invitation,' said Minna. 'At least, I don't think I did.'

Could she, even at that late stage, have been so consumed with Julian that she had overlooked this opportunity? Minna had basically neglected her social calendar – but would she have even wanted to attend the nuptials of her nemesis? Maybe, thanks to Julian, she'd had a lucky escape.

After a sandwich lunch, Minna went to her room – Lisa's room – to unpack the few things she'd brought with her. There were clothes in the cupboard left from previous visits, and this prompted her to inspect the boxes of her youth. Everything was in order, but more than that, it was all exactly as she'd left it, years ago. Now and then, in nostalgic moments, Minna rifled through these effects, reflecting on earlier, more innocent and possibly happier times. But there was nothing to suggest she'd gone wrong at any point.

Later that afternoon, Minna took herself off for a walk into town, mobile at the ready in case her mother texted with shopping she required. Mentally, Minna was preparing for the evening ahead, trying to work out why she couldn't stand Abigail. Their enmity hadn't been seated in psychological combat. There was no rivalry for a coveted academic qualification, sporting trophies or tier of social standing.

Whatever had repelled each girl from the other brooked no influence over their parents. It may have been no accident that the senior Jepsons and Gillespies spoke as if they had never been gifted with progeny, despite evidence to the contrary. Minna just smiled at references she didn't understand or gave sympathetic nods to tales of people she'd never heard of.

After dinner, they sat in the living room with coffee and port. Minna was relaxed, though she seldom drank much in her parents' company. Then, all of a sudden, 'Rolling in the Deep' thundered from the handbag at Barbara's feet. Everyone jumped.

'Oh, it's Abbie!' she whispered, as if the esteemed caller had requested anonymity. 'Oh, hello, darling. You'll never guess who's sitting next to me right now. Not in a million years.'

I'm sure she doesn't need to, thought Minna. Everyone knew about the weekend except me.

'Yes! That's *right*! She *is*. She's right *here*! And of *course* she wants to say hello!' Barbara bleated, elbowing Minna. 'Minna,' she said, 'it's Abbie. Go on, say hi!'

The phone was thrust in Minna's ear. 'Hello, Abbie.'

'Minna!' squealed Abigail, as if she'd trodden on a spider. 'How hilarious you're spending Easter with your parents. Will you hunt for eggs in the garden in the morning?'

'I'm actually here for my birthday. So how *are* you? Sorry I missed your wedding.'

'Oh ... well ... you *were* missed, of course. It would have been fun to catch up – but I guess this is our chance so we'd best make the most of it! So how's life with Julian? He sounds great.'

'That's all in the past, I'm sorry to say.'

'Oh. *What* a shame. I'm sure you did your best to keep the spark alive, but sometimes it isn't enough.'

Minna knew what was coming and said, 'I ended it.'

Abigail soldiered on. 'Really? I wouldn't have thought someone like – I mean, *shame*. What a shame. Anyway. I've loved catching up, but I must fly. We've got people—'

Minna played to win. 'Your in-laws?'

'No, real friends,' trilled Abigail. 'So I'd better go. But it was nice to talk. Perhaps we'll get together one day. Meantime, happy birthday. Of course, I'm not thirty-one for *months*.'

It was years since Minna had gone to bed in a sulk in the house she'd grown up in and it was a lacklustre option tonight. She wasn't annoyed at being displaced by the Gillespies. She slept easily in her sister's bed. Well, why wouldn't she? She woke early to a silent house, pleased, because she wanted to be up before the guests. But she did not want to linger.

She assessed the immediate future. She knew that the point of coming home was to seek consolation and avoid the unforeseen, but she couldn't expect her parents to subvert their own plans to suit hers. She was OK with this. So what was a reasonable expectation for the rest of the weekend? It wasn't even half over, and while it had been pleasant, nothing had *happened*. As it stood, Minna would be glad to be back to work on Tuesday, which was a tragic way to think. Not that she was dreading it. But if she returned to London, she could try to salvage the rest of the break.

Minna enjoyed breakfast with her parents. There was no demeaning hunt for eggs in the weeds by the back step – the foiled chocolate glistened on the sideboard. It was ten before the guests surfaced, by which time Don and Maureen had embarked on their weekend routine, in which Minna was happy to play a pre-arranged part.

Soon after, Lisa phoned to declare her first delay. It wasn't a promise but her ETA might be noon. Shortly after, she called with the update that half past one was more likely. Everyone should get on and eat. Maureen provided a salad, which the Gillespies enjoyed, before announcing their departure – they wanted to be back in time for *Antiques Roadshow*.

Maureen had reserved Minna's birthday cake for family only, so Minna was happy to wait until guests had left before blowing out the lone candle, and tucking into her slice.

Then Lisa phoned to say that three might be viable, but only if she could make her connection at Reading. Safer to say four. Or possibly five.

'Tell you what,' Minna infomed her parents, stabbing the crumbs of the excellent cake with a fingertip. 'It's crazy for us all to sit here waiting. There must be stuff you want to do and there's a party in London I sort of promised I'd go along to . . .'

It was a lie, but it felt more like a sort of necessary sacrifice. Minna had no plan but the nub of a feeling that she was better off gone.

Her parents' smiles were flavoured with relief. 'We don't want to hold you up . . .' said her mother. Her father added, 'I suppose you could catch up with your sister in London. Well, with any of us, really.'

'I've had a wonderful early birthday,' said Minna, sincerely. There had been gifts outside her door that morning, piled onto the breakfast tray. She promised not to unwrap them until it was actually her birthday. 'And a fun Easter, as well.'

Her parents smiled again. 'Well, that's all we wanted, darling, of course it is . . .'

'So I might go back to London,' she said. 'Sorry to miss Lisa but – well, who knows what time she'll actually arrive?'

Don agreed that yes, this was a quantity unknown. 'If you're sure, dear. Let me check the timetable, and then I'll run you to the station in good time for the train.'

Minna accepted, and farewelled and thanked her parents again, carefully stowing a slab of foil-wrapped cake in her hold-all. When Don seemed keen to linger on the platform, she kissed him on the cheek and said, 'I'll be fine, Dad. You might as well head off home. Unless Lisa's texted to say she's on the next train . . .'

'Wouldn't that be lucky?' said Don, but as he checked his phone he shook her head. 'No news. I'll go back. I can easily head out again. It's no problem.'

She squeezed his hand. 'Give her my love, and enjoy the rest of the weekend. I'll call you in the week before you head up north.'

He told Minna to take care, and she promised them both she'd be fine.

It was no surprise that the London-bound platform was virtually deserted. Wouldn't there be more imports for big family dinners than city-bound escapees? Minna stood apart, near the station entrance, reading the ads on the boards across the tracks, in lieu of the eye test she ought to have attended in November.

From where the tall guy in the winter coat came Minna didn't know, but suddenly he had penetrated her personal space. She assessed the moment in which you decide whether or not to take offence, and chose against causing a scene. The man – Minna thought he was her own age, possibly a little older – seemed decent. But why wear a coat in such a mild April? She theorised psoriasis, which was something of a dampener, and entirely out of keeping with the tenor of the day. To Minna, today was one of possibilities.

Waiting for the train, she couldn't help but catch the man's eye and he nodded appreciatively in response. There was no turning back.

'I'm Seb,' he told her. It seemed a reason to be cheerful.

'I'm Minna,' said Minna, remembering she wasn't in London now, so pleasantries weren't likely to result in a knifing. 'Happy Easter, Seb!'

'Happy Easter, Minna. Are you off to see family?' He had a nice voice – it had a lilt, which suggested he might have been Welsh.

'I've just been,' she answered. 'I know we're only halfway through Easter Sunday, but my parents are busy. It's no problem. I had a nice time. What about you?'

'I'm heading off to work,' said Seb. 'I'm based down here most of the time, but I have to go to London for my job.'

Naturally, she asked, 'What do you do?'

'I'm a TV weatherman.' Seb spoke with caution, as if he could never predict how this news would be taken.

Something stirred in Minna. A memory. But the tug of the past was powerfully repelled by an impulse from the present. Already she'd acknowledged that rare fluttering which can only signal attraction. Seb was giving off a similar vibe.

(Minna had had sex, since Julian. Oh yes. Just as she'd had uncomplicated couplings after Leo. There had been an internet date in the dark days of January when they'd had trouble with the boiler and Niamh and Sharmila had been away. But not dates as in events which were the forerunner to a relationship.)

The train which had commenced its journey at Alton pulled into Farnham station, jolting Minna into the moment. Seb said, 'Shall we?' and Minna, startled at first by his presence, eagerly answered, 'Yes!'

Their carriage was nearly empty, and so they chose a bank of seats designed for six. They faced each other, but at an angle, so there was no awkward knocking of knees. Before he sat down, Seb had shrugged off his coat in a movement that was languid, despite its bulk. He had a T-shirt on underneath, which revealed a flat stomach and pleasantly but not overly-developed biceps. The skin on his arms was perfectly smooth. He looked very clean, which suggested to Minna he might be a stalwart of breakfast TV.

Both were settled, and the train began to move. Although the route announced on the tannoy was familiar to Minna, there was a distinct novelty to this journey, as if it were an inaugural voyage.

Enchanted, attracted, Minna resumed the conversation, 'So who do you work for?'

'Mostly it's Radio 4,' he said. 'It's much more forgiving than telly.'

Minna asked, 'How did you get to be a weatherman?'

'I've always been fascinated by weather,' Seb told her. 'I still like waking up in the middle of the night during a thunderstorm. But I don't like snow.'

'Me neither,' Minna admitted, pleased to establish common ground. 'Much. So did you talk into a hairbrush and pretend you were live on air?'

'I never wanted to be on *Top of the Pops*,' Seb pointed out. 'And I grew up with two older brothers and had to share a room till I was fourteen. There wouldn't have been much of an opportunity to rehearse.'

'You must have had special training,' Minna suggested, little tendrils of envy scampering all over her, but not unpleasantly.

'I studied Meteorology. Then I got a job with the Met Office, and I was deployed to the RAF for about eighteen months. They're big on weather.'

Minna was enthralled. She didn't suppose he'd worn a uniform, but still, what an amazing first work placement. 'What happened next?'

'I went back to Wales, and worked on radio there. That's where I met Becky.'

Minna coloured. 'Becky?'

'My ex-partner. She's from London, so after we had Katie—'

'Your daughter?' said Minna, hoping for a kitten.

'That's right. We moved over here, to be nearer Becky's parents. I got a job. Then we split up. About eight months ago.' He winced.

Minna twitched. 'Oh. I'm sorry to hear that. So are you single? You must be really busy. I bet you have to work nights. Quite hard to maintain a social life.' She thought of every possibility to squeeze random people out of Seb's life. She stopped when she realised she might be squeezing herself out, too.

'I used to do the breakfast slot' – Minna felt restored by a stab of triumph – 'and that meant working through the night. I'd finish at nine a.m. and be knackered. Becky didn't like it, so I pulled back from that whenever I could. Not that it did us any good.'

'And now?' Minna asked, hopefully. They were at Woking. The journey was half over but luckily there was a delay while the train was connected to another set of carriages, gaining an influx of passengers, before being conveyed further on.

'Now I do whatever they need me to, in London or down here. Sometimes it's twelve broadcasts a day. Sometimes it's back room office stuff. Or blogging. There's so much to prepare. It's not about guesswork.'

'I'm sure it's isn't,' said Minna, not sycophantically, she hoped.

'People think we get up and blag it but we don't. There are loads of reports and charts to compare and compile. And we spend ages looking at social media because viewers' photos and reports are really useful. That's what I like about the job. You talk about science and think about people locked away in lab coats. I do science, but it's for everyone.'

Tendrils writhed across her body again, but these weren't inspired by envy. Minna went hot and cold. The train moved on. Next stop, Surbiton. Then Wimbledon, Earlsfield, Clapham Junction . . . Almost the end—

'So, Minna, what do you do for work?'

'I'm an analyst.' She added, 'Facts and figures,' because she didn't want him to think about neuroses.

'Who for?'

'A firm called Macsamphire Strutt. You probably won't have heard of them . . .'

Seb reluctantly shook his head. But he wasn't put off. 'Tell me more. What sort of clients do you work for? What's your firm's USP? You know – how do you keep the edge?'

She answered the first part easily, and spoke of the colleges and schools they dealt with, the professional organisations, and web publishers. But she stalled at the second. It's not *just* me, she wanted to say. No one ever talks about goals or attainments. But how could she know that was true? It would be another two days before she could ask Adam, Kerry and Steph. They might be none the wiser. By then Seb would be long gone.

Vauxhall.

'It's difficult to define what makes us special ...' she hazarded. 'People keep coming back, though. It seems to work.'

The look on Seb's face conveyed disbelief more than disappointment.

The train pulled in to Waterloo. The final announcement was made, reminding people to collect their possessions. Wordlessly, Seb and Minna got to their feet and left the carriage, and followed the trail of passengers heading towards the ticket barriers and through to the station concourse.

Why isn't he saying anything? Minna panicked, herself bereft of comment or enquiry. Was he thinking ahead to what awaited him at work? Or forming a proposal to put to Minna – or awaiting one from her? Minna had given no clues as to how the rest of her day would unfold. She could easily be persuaded. Could she be persuasive?

They slowed, letting others stream past. Seb said, 'I don't have to be at work just yet. I need to put in a few hours but it's flexible – I'm not actually on air until tonight. Do you fancy going for a coffee or something to eat or ... Well, we could hang out, if you're not busy.'

I'd like nothing more than that. And yet Minna resisted. It

74

was a ridiculous, stubborn sort of feeling, totally unjustified. But entirely difficult to shift.

'I can't, I'm sorry,' she said, abruptly. There was some obstructive power inside her determined to make this difficult for them both. Or, rather, to make it difficult for Seb. As if it would, in turn, make it easier for her. But how?

'You can't?' He seemed to accept it, but then— 'Or won't?'

'Can't! Of course . . .' But the two words might as well have meant the same.

'Why "of course"?' Seb wanted to know. His defence swiftly crumbled. 'Oh, you've got a boyfriend . . .'

'No!' Minna screeched, but inside she was quaking.

'It's OK,' Seb told her. 'You don't fancy me?' He blanched. 'Sorry, Minna, I shouldn't have said that . . .'

'No, no. I do. I *do* fancy you, Seb. And the rest of my day is completely free. The rest of the weekend, in fact.' Try my life, if you want, she almost added.

'Then why don't we have a little time together? Just an hour or so.' Her silence was stony. He tried again. 'Please, then, tell me where I'm going wrong.' He looked away. 'I don't do this often, I swear. Tell me if I've offended you and I'll try to put it right.'

He had nothing to apologise for, but still she did not help him. Yet she knew it ought to be a landmark day. 'I can't explain it.'

'Is it because I've got a kid?' Seb asked.

Minna didn't hesitate, 'No!' How could having children be anything other than life-enhancing? Parenthood was a skill to admire, not be repelled by. Minna didn't know any children, not really, but she didn't have a problem with them. She could probably handle being sisterly to a child with experimental nail art while watching DVDs and eating Jaffa cakes. Naturally, at a practical level, Katie wouldn't be around all the time. Visits would be carefully planned. There would be boundaries to keep aware of and stay behind.

Seb tried again. 'Is it because I'm still on good terms with my ex? Would it be better if we'd fallen out?'

'Of course not!' If it was a case of daggers drawn, mightn't that suggest some awful characteristic of Seb's. Or if it existed in his ex-partner, an attraction in him to the wrong sort of woman?

Seb battled on. 'Is it because I'm only in London part of the week?'

'No, not that . . .' Minna knew from experience how unwise it was to spend all your time in the company of one person. You missed out on your own life.

'Is it the early starts? Honestly, I'm used to getting up really quietly without disturbing anyone. I don't put my shoes on until I'm practically out the door.'

'No,' Minna moaned, bored and resentful of her own refrain but unable to access any others. 'It's none of those things, Seb, I promise you.'

'Then why?' He looked needy. 'Is it because—' he paused, as if peering in to an abyss within him '—I'm a weatherman?'

Some professions are universally deplored. An incorrect weather report or a disappointing forecast irritates but is seldom the root of lasting grudges. How could Seb suggest that it was?

'No,' Minna rallied. But why couldn't she say yes to his other question? It was coffee not commitment.

There must be something. Some*one*. Inexplicably, Minna thought of Jeff, who worked for Go Aware on the ninth floor of her building. He was thirty-seven. Thick, dark hair, piled up a little too high, which made the rest of him appear somewhat short, but that wasn't offputting. Quite large feet, encased in shiny tan brogues, with a stippled pattern at the toe. There was a Russian connection, professionally speaking, which was potentially exciting, but Minna hadn't quite got the gist of it. They had exchanged lingering looks for some time, and around Valentine's Day – but not to mark it – she had agreed to go for a drink with him. It had been a bit strange because he'd talked a lot about his ex-wife's disastrous fortieth birthday. 'She crashed and burned,' he told her. Minna felt rather scorched herself. It was hardly conducive to fostering an intimacy of their own. They wound up the conversation soon after, and Minna put thoughts of Jeff aside. It felt a little ruthless but was the right approach. She could do without the complication of his company.

Did the same apply to Seb – or was he a *further* complication?

Minna knew what it felt like to two-time – imagined how it felt, that is; she'd never done it. As swiftly as she'd recalled meeting Jeff, she remembered an incident from last summer, before Australia, with Julian in the Marylebone High Street branch of the White Company. It had been a rare reconnaissance to the outside world, and who did she bump into but Leo? What was he *doing* on unfamiliar territory? (There was a Westfield virtually on his doorstep.) Minna had felt like a rabbit caught in headlights, the glare intensified by the stark brightness of her pale surroundings.

'Julian!' she'd spluttered. 'This is Leo! Leo! Julian!'

Julian and Leo had behaved impeccably. They'd been polite, exchanged a cordial hello, and then Leo disappeared to the cash desk, to pay for candles. Nothing more was said. In fact, *they* had come out of it well, but Minna remained haunted.

Worst of all, she felt that she'd undersold Leo to Julian. She'd spoken of him as a friend, because she couldn't bring herself to call him an ex. Leo had the advantage over Julian in knowing more about Julian than Julian knew of Leo, which was ironic, since there was so much more to be discovered about Leo, if only Julian had asked. If only Minna had said. But would Julian have *wanted* to hear all about her ex-boyfriend?

She'd favoured neither of them, ultimately. She might as well have condemned them both. Was she about to make the same mistake with Seb? After all, he'd offered a multiplicity of detractions. Or would it be an error to let him go?

From his bag Seb pulled a small notebook and a pen, and began scribbling. 'Minna,' he sighed. 'Here's my number. I really would like to see you again so, if you feel like getting in touch, Minna, here's where you'll find me.'

'Thank you,' she said, quietly, having to tug at the slip of paper for it was clenched tight between Seb's fingers. They tussled briefly, playfully. But it was not enough.

'Well, OK, Minna. See you around, maybe,' Seb said gently, and turned away.

Minna wouldn't – couldn't? – watch Seb go. She hurried across the concourse, head bowed against anyone who might read her expression, or any shiny surface that might confront her with her own ashamed reflection. But who was looking?

PART TWO

CUSTODY OF THE LE CREUSET

It was nearly a year since Jeff's wife informed him that their marriage was over, on a warm Saturday morning in May. They'd both had weeks busy with work commitments, so had spent little time together, which was fairly typical, unfortunately, but not unique to them. Perhaps it was easier to speak of partings when distance had crept into the relationship. Still, Jeff had been doing his best to kick the weekend off to a good start. All the windows in the flat were open and fresh air and light flooded in, cleansing everything. He had a load of washing on and had made real coffee as he always did. He was about to take it to Sarah in bed. She'd been dozing when he got up but suddenly there she stood before the kitchen door, unblinking and unflinching.

Clutching a cup, Sarah told him. Not impassively, but calmly, as if she had practised the words so she would not trip over them. It was a faultless delivery, which also meant that mercifully, it was short. Was this why she'd worked through last weekend – the first of the May bank holidays – claiming she had to completely rewrite a presentation? She'd refused his help, and he'd felt like a spare part. Jeff hadn't a role to play in her rehearsal.

They had been together for six years, married for five. They'd had a happy holiday earlier that year in the Canaries and a recent weekend in Sark. Just last autumn they'd painted the flat and were currently negotiating new carpet. Sarah's bombshell *was* out of the blue. (He adopted these platitudes when explaining to other people what had happened.)

Blundering over possible responses, he said, 'Have you been planning this for long?'

Sarah didn't attempt to lie, but she faltered, slightly. 'I've been wondering ... well, what else is out there ... as the big birthday got closer.'

Sarah had insisted on keeping her fortieth in February low key. Her parents, Vivien and Ken, had taken them both to Claridge's for afternoon tea. She'd done nothing at work – did they even know? – but her long-ago bridesmaids had taken her clubbing. Girls only, possibly scheming. (Don't torment yourself, but he did.) Jeff would have put on any celebration she'd wanted – he even made suggestions – but in the event, he cooked the simplest supper prepared with infinite care, and served with the best champagne. Sarah was still thinking about what she wanted as a gift, she'd told him: so don't rush out and waste money on any old thing. Fine, he'd wait. But perhaps she was waiting to leave him, and wouldn't care for another item to pack.

Jeff said, 'You've known you were heading for forty for years. Thirty-nine of them, to be precise.'

Sarah smiled at his feeble attempt at humour, which was generous, because she wasn't normally given to jokes. She said,

'It's been longer than that, actually, but I didn't want you to worry. I wasn't ready to tell you or to do anything. I suppose, I didn't want us both to end up being miserable. I still don't.'

'I'm not,' he said. 'At least, I wasn't.'

'Oh, Jeff, that's the brilliant thing about you. You're such a trouper. You're always optimistic. That's why you'll be OK without me. I know you will.'

The fact that she would flourish away from him evidently did not need saying.

He began to squirm against her judgement. 'I thought we were good together.'

She nodded, emphatically. 'We have been. We had some great years. And, don't forget, you rescued me in the first place.'

Jeff groaned. 'Just because your mother says that doesn't mean you have to.' He paused. 'Does she know?'

Sarah shook her head. 'Nobody knows. Well, except for—' She cited the bridesmaids. He rarely saw them, and wouldn't now. 'I had to talk to you first, of course.'

'To tell me, you mean,' he said, and could have kicked himself. Because perhaps Sarah had intended a debate in which they were both engaged. Maybe he could win her over—

'Oh, Jeff. I'm sorry. I really am. But I can't go on like this. I need to be free.'

Too late, he said, 'What about a trial separation?'

'Wouldn't that just be delaying the inevitable?'

He flung it back at her, but it wasn't a deft move, more like pancake batter smearing the ceiling instead of flipping neatly into the pan. 'You tell me. It's your decision.'

She groaned.

'Is there someone else?' he asked, aware that it was a line from TV or film, and therefore of little personal relevance to him.

'No!' She seemed indignant. 'Do you think I'm having an affair?'

'No.' They hadn't mentioned sex, but he'd detected no drop-off in enthusiasm of late. Had Sarah? 'I don't want to replace you,' said Sarah, with a faint smile. 'I just don't want to be attached.' She sighed, as if perhaps there was something she wanted more but couldn't yet identify. She seemed about to hazard a guess, but stopped.

The simplest thing would be to accept Sarah's assurance that he would move on as seamlessly as she would. Presumably, Jeff could resurrect his admirable skills, and transfer them elsewhere, to someone else, eventually.

Besides, Jeff and Sarah weren't practised at arguments or cold silences – and Jeff doubted he'd become proficient even with a crash course.

Once the initial sense of bombardment had eased, Jeff determined to try to reverse Sarah's decision. Neither ventured any talk of moving out. For a time, it was as if she'd put the decision on hold. He slept in the second bedroom, as if he had a cold and was snoring. Nothing was said for weeks and no one phoned or got in touch to say they were sorry to hear the news. To Jeff it was a golden opportunity to rewind the clock: he must display the traits that had made Sarah fall in love with him in the first place. He couldn't home in on any particular quality, so he tried to display every facet he could think of.

Then, one day, Sarah said she was moving into a friend's spare room, and Jeff understood that his plan had failed. And he realised his mistake: Sarah left because Jeff was just himself. He hadn't changed. In the time he had left, he started looking properly, and saw that she had. Sarah's movements seemed lighter, her smile seemed bigger. She began to make calls in a room away from him and laughed more than he'd ever heard her.

She asked, 'Do you hate me?'

Jeff looked at his soon-to-be-former-wife. To him she was still beautiful: with those big green eyes, her little, slightly snub nose, the freckles she tried to conceal with make-up. Already he had started to miss them. It took all his effort not to crumple. To ground himself, he looked through their back catalogue of hiccups: moments of frustration, confusion, irritation, disagreement, resentment – of which there had been plenty. Only, they weren't much use now. All of them had been overcome (at which he sourced a thrum of pride). But there was no recovery from *this*. So there could be no point of comparison, could there?

'I could never hate you, Sarah,' he said.

It confused him the way Sarah tried to make him feel better. It seemed like a taunt when she said, on the eve of her departure: 'I don't blame you, Jeff.'

Originally, Jeff had planned to be absent on moving day, but he was glad to have stayed to hear this. Anyway, she might have needed help carrying things – or with all the preparations, might have forgotten to get cash out and needed a twenty for the taxi. No amount of money could outvalue this reassurance. And it *was* true. She hadn't, so far.

He honestly hadn't meant to sound bitter when he said, 'Oh. Well. That's great, isn't it?' But perhaps there was no other way for that response to emerge.

Sarah's eyes lit up, but Jeff only detected a further drop in temperature. 'But I hope it will be,' she said brightly, once again looking to that future which Jeff could not foresee. 'I hope it will make things OK, eventually.'

'Really?' Hope quickened his heart.

'I am grateful to you, Jeff. For what we had. For what you gave me. You've been a fantastic husband in many ways.'

But not all, he thought. Not enough.

'Just not for me,' she confirmed, to brook no misunderstanding. Even if you counted her jokes, Sarah was a woman of few words. Now Jeff knew why. Keep it brief and you reduce the risk of what you say being misconstrued.

Jeff played down his mother-in-law's account of the way he 'saved' Sarah because he knew he had gained much more than he had offered. Admittedly, when they'd met, Sarah had been at a low ebb. They'd chanced upon each other in a bar, and he'd distracted her from people, and had taken her home to the flat he was sharing at the time. Nothing had happened between them – by the time Jeff returned from the bathroom, Sarah was fast asleep.

Next morning, she admitted she could not recall much of the night before. She was embarrassed even to be naked with him, but she wasn't frightened. She accepted his account. She thanked him – though it was clear she couldn't be sure why she was grateful. He gave her his number 'in case', and saw her out. She didn't need directions to the station, she didn't need money for a cab. He thought that was the end of it. He began to put her out of his mind.

But she hadn't forgotten him. She left it a day or two but then called him with an urgency. Later, she employed more words than she'd offered at the time: 'I wanted to see if you were real.' She joked she'd had her best night's sleep in ages in his bed. Seriously, she said she felt safe with him. Then she admitted it wasn't just safety. 'I can't explain it,' she said. 'But I want it, Jeff. I need it.' She needed him, she meant.

No master of words himself, Jeff soaked up everything Sarah offered. It was more than a good start. He took her out to dinner, and that night there was hardly any sleep at all. Few words – except the ones that had begun to form in his head, where they had to remain for it was too early to say them aloud. When he set out to find out all about her, missing her, not wanting to call too often, there were reams to discover. She was a highly successful lifestyle coach. Ambitious. A high achiever. But she'd also assured him that in other ways she was a complete disaster.

'He saved me,' Sarah told people. 'He made me realise that if I carried on the way I was I'd have burnt myself out. More than that, I would have missed out on all this.'

By which she meant Jeff. She smiled at him, and her audience – no matter who it was (and the story was told quite widely) – would signal approval and Jeff couldn't help but bask in their adoration. And Sarah's, too. Life only got better when they married. They couldn't have been closer but still they kept finding themselves drawn to each other.

Sarah's professional star kept rising higher and higher. She changed jobs, left them, freelanced, was lured back. She always took the cream of her clients with her wherever she went. Jeff built a life based on the reflected glory of their connection. It didn't matter that his own career wasn't a tenth as impressive as Sarah's. Probably, it helped that they weren't outstriving each other. In place of satisfaction in an upward career trajectory, Jeff enjoyed the blossoming of confidence from a successful home life. In fact, the only confidence he had was what he placed in his marriage. And then it ended. Sarah left. She didn't need him any more.

It might have been easier if Sarah *had* blamed him. Blame is a universal language, like semaphore. But you need flags to wave, like hostages. Otherwise people can easily forget that anything has happened. Was that why Jeff permitted the dinner service a key role in his divorce?

Admittedly, there hadn't been much else to play with. The couple had decided not to have children – Jeff had adopted Sarah's unreadiness, and then they stopped talking about it. He hadn't minded. Nor, so far as he knew, were his parents, Celia and Nigel, disappointed not to be rewarded with grandchildren. (Jeff's older brother Steve and his partner Alyx were childless too. They weren't married, either. 'If it aint broke ...' Steve explained and indeed, their union seemed the opposite of broken.) There had been no pets, no kit to divvy up or dispose of, no maverick works of art to rehome. Just ordinary furniture and a fairly extensive set of le Creuset kitchenware – in the original, timeless Volcanic, though two dozen other colours were available. The wedding list had comprised little else.

Sarah had always referred to them as the pots and pans. Calling a spade a spade is one thing, but did it help to strip everything back to its components? Did it make something easier to get rid of? Jeff appreciated the urge to dismantle. When he was ten, he'd gone through a phase of unscrewing any electrical appliance within reach. He levered off panels that hid batteries and wiring and removed casings so that all remained were circuit boards, naked and cold to the touch. But he'd been ten, not forty. It was a phase he'd passed through, not a hobby he'd picked up in later life. More importantly, his intention had always been to put everything back together again, not to conceal evidence of his meddling, but for the satisfaction of creating something.

(For a short but desperate window, he wondered if Sarah had been testing him. Did she pull their life apart so she could watch him put the pieces back together? Did it turn her on? Would she be proud of his triumph and fall in love with him all over again? Or did she predict that he would fail, which would justify her decision to leave?)

Jeff's childhood hobby hadn't always gone to plan; he'd often got a bollocking from his parents. *That* hadn't abated over the years. When Jeff phoned his parents last May, in a state of shock, Celia answered. Until then, he hadn't minded which parent picked up the phone. But he found that he was glad it was his mother. 'Mum, Sarah's leaving me.'

To which Celia replied, 'Why, what have you done?'

'Mum!' he'd moaned, and she'd backtracked at once. But her initial snub lingered, because it chimed with his own beliefs. Jeff *did* blame himself – it must all have been *his* fault. But Celia's dismay was her own: she liked Sarah, perhaps not as much as Alyx, but then Alyx had had a head start because she and Steve had met at university. Also, in a domestic unit dominated by men, Celia had lost one of her daughters-in-law, a valuable ally. Celia and Sarah would have girls' days out, now and then.

Jeff knew Sarah's own mother had been equally critical, because Vivien shared her views with Jeff. 'My daughter actually called them *pots and pans*?' Vivien screeched. Jeff hadn't meant to incriminate Sarah. As it turned out, his mother-in-law needed no assistance in criticising her only daughter. 'They're le Creuset, and they're high quality. She doesn't deserve them, Jeff. So keep them. Do.'

But, Viv, why are you siding with me? I couldn't look after your daughter. Why trust me with the stoneware? But of course he was too timid to say this out loud.

Jeff had only phoned Vivien because he couldn't seem to catch Sarah on any of her numbers. He feared she'd changed them, but she hadn't. There were many more people to inconvenience by doing that than merely Jeff.

The gift suggestion had been Jeff's parents' – he and Sarah had accumulated enough to start a home together in their former lives – but perhaps Viv's habit was to tend towards the proprietorial. She was within her rights because all four parents had reached across and befriended each other, with nothing in common but the pairing off of their children. What number of hopes and expectations had been dashed in the wrapping up of Jeff and Sarah's marriage? Could there be as much of a stigma in being parents of divorced children as there'd once been in the reverse?

In other families, blame might have snaked across the marriage lines. But here, they turned on their own. Still, Jeff felt it would be wise, going forward, to keep at arm's length from his in-laws.

Le Creuset wasn't a brand that Jeff's brother had heard of, even though for many years Steve Sullivan had driven a Citroën, and his collection of Asterix albums was complete. Steve was an architect who ran his own business. He was a natural at working with whatever scaffolding a scenario required. This he did on his mid-week catch-ups with Jeff, which had become a regular occurrence since Jeff had started living on his own.

A dozen years of site visits across London had equipped Steve with a vast knowledge of pubs. When he summoned his younger brother, it was usually to a venue that was unfamiliar to Jeff. The establishments were often hidden gems, frequented by long-standing locals who'd gone in for their tea by the time the brothers descended. Tonight's was all the rarer for being unspoilt by office workers, being half a mile off Camden High Street.

Steve was three inches taller than his brother, leaner, and with more moderate hair. He wore clothes better, too. Steve arrived at work in casual clothes and changed at the office, collecting a batch of pristine shirts from the drycleaner on Monday morning. It seemed like too much effort for Jeff who would be afraid he'd forget some vital component of the outfit and have to spend the day in lace-ups but sockless.

Tonight, a warm April evening, Steve looked relaxed while Jeff felt dishevelled. But he was pleased to see his brother. He longed to fill their evening with provocative opinions about cutting-edge concerns but all he had was the minutiae of a week that had passed as unmemorably as the last one, albeit with the holiday day lopped off either end, thanks to Easter. He should have scanned the news websites on the tube but had spent the journey scratching some BluTak off the knee of his trousers.

All he could think to remark on was the way in which the dinner set was the lasting emblem of both his marriage and its demise. It haunted him, even though it now lived in the cupboard under the sink. His culinary repertoire was, as a consequence, restricted.

'I wouldn't say it's a metaphor . . .'

'Would you not?' said his brother, uninflected.

'No. It's not a symbol, either.'

'Not a symbol?'

'But it's there, every time I think about what's happened. In a funny way I'd kind of hate to be without it. I know it's not like keeping a bit of Sarah in the flat.'

'Mate, she isn't dead. Nobody gave you an urn, did they?'

Jeff bristled. 'Of course not! How could you even—'

Steve spread his hands in a don't-shoot-me gesture, and took a gulp of beer. 'Jeff, you've had far too much thinking time of late. I can imagine people wanting to bring you casseroles. People who think you're sad and lonely. People who want to get into your pants—' Jeff looked alarmed, but Steve merely shrugged. 'But that's about food, not what it's served in. Look, Jeff—' He put down his glass, as if to show his full attention was on his brother. 'Everyone's sad but they don't blame you and they certainly don't feel guilty themselves. No need to beat yourself up about it.'

Steve was right. Not all of the friends who'd chosen cookware pieces knew one another, let alone who was adding what to the collection. But when Jeff reflected on the ramekins and baking dishes – he had recall of every detail of his wedding day (gold and silver confetti, rainless clouds, gift bags of sugared almonds; an uncle had broken a crown) – he envisaged the purchasers as linked, like innocent victims drawn together in a natural disaster. But the marriage hadn't failed because someone had selected the sauté pan over the utensil jar. The guests wouldn't blame themselves, for sure.

'Do you think Sarah's secretly beating herself up about it?' Jeff asked. 'Do you think she'd do that?'

Steve shrugged. He had been loyal to them both, but it was his brother he was trying to help. 'Oh, I hope not. I really do. But I can't speak for her, only myself. And Alyx. We're really sad – goes without saying – but there doesn't seem to be a lot of blame going on here. You're lucky, really.'

Steve might have had a point but it was Jeff's instinct to query, '*Lucky?*'

His brother nodded. 'Sure. The opposite would be so much worse,' he proposed.

Jeff inhaled some crumbs from the crisp packets that lay prone on the table before them. Empty calories, which matched his head at that moment. 'What do you mean?'

'You say that Sarah stripped everything back – said there was nothing left. As if all the years together amounted to nothing.'

The words were stark but Jeff couldn't feel savaged because they were his, more or less. He nodded. 'That's right.'

'Think how it would have been worse if she'd done the opposite.'

Jeff felt drained. He was drunk. 'I'm not with you.'

'Imagine Sarah had invented things in order to make herself look good or to make you look bad. In the old days, you had to cite pretty heavy reasons for divorce.'

'Like what?'

'Desertion. Violence. Neglect. That's what happened to Nan and Grandad.'

'I thought they split because he never put the bins out.'

'Think about it. They lived in a tower block. There would

have been a rubbish chute. Mum invented the bins story when we were little and asked why our grandparents didn't live together.'

Jeff pondered. 'I don't understand the point you're making.'

But Steve, as ever, was only trying to help.

'All I'm saying, mate,' Steve continued, 'is that Sarah did things pretty cleanly, pretty simply, so you could both move on.'

Why are people so fond of that phrase? It must be liberating, so long as you've no recourse to it yourself.

'Are you saying I should have *moved on* by now? It's not even been a year.'

'Maybe it doesn't sound long to you, mate, but does the timing really matter? Can't you just *decide* to pick yourself up and move on? There's no benefit in waiting. It's not like getting a month's redundancy pay for every year you work.'

It sounded harsh. 'Maybe I don't want to move on.' For one thing, Jeff felt reluctant to ease the burden of the le Creuset.

'That's just stubbornness. Think of all the opportunities out there for a fresh start.'

'I'm not seeing them.'

'That's because you're not looking.'

'The thing is,' said Jeff. 'I don't want new opportunities. I just want what I had before.'

'Well, Jeff, your problem there is it's not yours any more to have. So why not start looking for something else?'

*   *   *

A common link with cookware on one side of the family should be of no consequence when a mania is eroding the other – *your own side*. If anyone were to ask, however, Jeff wasn't much interested in his mother's pursuit of family history. Oh sure, he was happy to support Celia, not just because nobody else was. He admired her enterprise. But the reason he'd begun to spend so much time with his parents was his thirst for snippets of Sarah. Just as Jeff communicated with Vivien and Ken, Sarah had retained links with her former parents-in-law. Did that mean she couldn't quite let go of Jeff?

'She asked after you, of course,' Celia had told him, just after the sale of his and Sarah's flat had gone through. Jeff was renting a flat in Peckham, not far from where he and Sarah had lived. His parents were in Harpenden, having downsized out of London a decade ago.

He didn't want to try to wring meaning from Sarah's words that wasn't there. But he wanted more. 'What did you tell her?' he asked.

'I said you were well, which is true, isn't it?'

'Yes.' He had to admit it. 'Yes, I am.'

'I said you were busy with work.'

'That's true, also.'

'I said that you probably missed her. Which I'm sure is true, also.'

Silently, he said: *I owe you, Mum.* 'Yes, it's true,' he said, his voice unsteady.

'She said she'd give you a ring sometime,' said Celia. 'Said it would be nice to catch up. Now that things have quietened down.'

But wasn't it because their lives had become too quiet, too uneventful, that Sarah had left? Maybe she'd had a spell amongst the rapids, but now was craving smoother waters. Or was it just something people say? And, so far, Sarah *hadn't* phoned, nor did she pick up Jeff's messages, and respond to them.

Celia's quest had begun in innocence late last summer, when Nigel received a copy of a letter from a woman called Grace who said Nigel's grandfather had been her own father. Grace had been born, illegitimately, before Nigel's grandparents had met and married. She was, effectively, Nigel's great aunt. Apparently, all this was known to everyone at the time but it came as a surprise to Jeff's branch of the Sullivans. Grace's mother had brought her up herself, and she had no other family. Grace was long married but had no children of her own. Now that she'd retired, she wanted to get to know her father's descendants.

'What a great story!' The team at work sounded envious when Jeff shared the basic details. Until that point, Jeff had envied them. He'd noted every one of them was in a relationship. One since university; another had had a quick remarriage after divorce and so had been almost continuously wed for thirty years; there was a recent pairing off and one woman was in a long-distance union in which she was incredibly happy. But perhaps, secretly, they longed for scandal to be unearthed in their own families.

One of Jeff's own aunts declared a lack of interest in Grace from the outset. Another sounded affronted at the intrusion.

A third said nothing – or perhaps she hadn't been consulted. She wasn't someone the Sullivans heard from very often, and was the spouse of the uncle who'd followed Jeff's wedding with expensive dental work. Nigel positioned himself somewhere between the first two.

It was Celia who retrieved the letter from some potential recycling, and asked if Nigel intended to make contact with his new great aunt. He hadn't and the matter could have rested there. But Celia picked up the gauntlet, and ran.

'We ought to get in touch,' she said. 'It was brave of her to reach out like that – it would be awful if we just ignored her. We'll just write back and say, how lovely to hear from her, and that we'd be happy to get to know her. If she wants to.' Celia reflected. 'She might not want to.'

'Why wouldn't she?' Nigel sounded affronted. 'What's wrong with my family?'

'So it's your family, is it?' said Celia, who handled the Christmas card list.

'Sorry. Our family. Let me speak to Sue and Kate again and see what they think.'

Celia shrugged, and said she'd wait to hear more from Nigel's sisters. She didn't provide a deadline, but after a week, she started to prod.

'Oh, Sue's calmed down, which is good, but basically, they've no objection if we follow it up. They haven't got time themselves. Busy lives.'

Celia affected a yawn. 'Lucky them. I'm going to take the car in for its service, and then I'm going to collect my new glasses. Do I mention the windscreen wipers or not?' The conversation moved on.

It was in the depths of winter when Celia picked it up again. By now, the dreariness of the place Jeff was renting depressed him, so he escaped as often as he could at weekends to his parents'. There was no news from Sarah – he wondered if she'd bought somewhere by now, or was still lodging with her friend? – so Jeff asked about his long-lost relative, to please Celia.

'Grace isn't on e-mail,' said Celia, slapping down a handful of envelopes which had been securely fastened by a rubber band. 'So we've been exchanging letters.'

'Keeping the Royal Mail alive,' said Steve, who'd dropped in on the way back from watching an away game, and had offered Jeff a lift back to London later on. 'That's so cool, Mum.'

'Who wants to read them?' said Celia, rhetorically.

Both her sons dutifully took a couple of letters each, scanned and exchanged them.

'She sounds nice enough,' Jeff concluded. 'A bit lonely, perhaps. Needy.'

'Did you actually read what she wrote?' Celia demanded.

'Well, sure . . . yes. I gleaned the basics.' Jeff looked to his brother.

Steve placed the envelopes on the table in front of him. 'She's retired now, but she worked as an orthodontist – no, an optometrist. We're more than welcome to visit any time we're in the north. They don't make it to London very often but they'd love to come down for the Proms again one day. They'd planned to, but her husband snapped a tendon.' Steve added, 'Nasty business.'

Steve never needed to impress, but at least their mother was pacified.

'You asked what's new?' Celia prompted over Sunday lunch, several weeks later. She put down her knife and fork. She said, 'I've discovered that Grace is practically royalty.'

'Come again, Mum?' Steve encouraged, although since he was still in credit from the letters episode he could have afforded to sit this one out.

'Grace married Lord something and inherited a considerable chunk of Yorkshire. There's a profile of them in *Country Life*. Beautiful house and furnishings, lots of paintings. Another world. Fancy it being part of our family?'

'Those estates are all practically bankrupt,' Nigel noted, sourly. 'They can barely manage the upkeep. Better watch out, Cee – she might ask for a loan.'

Was that the first reference to money? Looking back, Jeff decided that it was. He'd never seen pound signs swirl before his mother's eyes before.

'She didn't mention the assets,' Celia said, thoughtfully. 'I read about them, like I said.'

'Just by chance?' Jeff wondered. 'As in, a magazine at the doctor's?'

'Have you been to the doctor's, Mum?' Steve asked, with an appropriate degree of concern.

'No,' said Celia firmly. 'I saw it on the internet. I was looking for something else – not a medical complaint – when I logged on to an old search and came up with *Country Life*. They've got Constables, apparently. As in the painter.'

'It's not really our family,' said Nigel, as if urgently wanting to distance himself from his wife's enterprise. He went revisionist. 'This is our family.' He nodded with satisfaction, as if it were a walled city.

Celia looked wounded, and left the table, as if, damned by Nigel's words, she had taken herself into exile. Jeff felt protective towards his mother but ill-equipped to turn that feeling into words or actions. He knew that you couldn't speak of people as if they were property. But sometimes it was difficult to find the right words to describe people who weren't you. Then again, it's hard enough to find words to explain yourself. Celia swiftly returned with a crumble, saying she supposed 'our family' wanted dessert.

Money recurred as a prevalent theme when Celia's clothes shopping began. Shoes and a jacket, to start with, when in fact the only new item of clothing Celia appeared to need was a flak jacket.

Nigel explained it to each of his sons individually, because Celia was too busy to chat herself. 'She's out to impress someone.'

'She's angling for a promotion at work,' Steve suggested.

Nigel said, 'Or maybe she's gearing up to meet Grace so she can impress her and benefit in the long run. It stands to reason. Grace must be in her seventies. No children. Time's running out . . .'

'Spending Grace's money already . . .' Steve added.

'Spending your inheritance, that's for sure.' Nigel laughed. Why do parents always think that's such a funny thing to joke about?

Steve gave a philosophical shrug. 'You can't miss what you never had.'

'Good, son, because you won't have it the rate it's slipping through your mother's fingers.'

We've all had to crouch down and retrieve our reputations from the gutter but there is seldom the need to salvage our parents'. Jeff knew he ought to try, but he became distracted by thinking of the Constables. So he said nothing, just settled on relief that Celia hadn't overheard the conversation. For a woman who'd been called a fox by her teenage sons' mates, it would be a major comedown to be labelled a gold digger.

Things got worse. On an otherwise ordinary Saturday afternoon, Nigel disappeared to take a phone call in the study. He returned looking wan, as if he'd had some bad news. Both his wife and younger son regarded him with concern.

Jeff said, 'Dad, what . . .'

'That was Kate on the phone,' said Nigel. 'She was livid. She says you've been talking to Phoebe.' Clearly, he was addressing Celia. Jeff hadn't spoken to, let alone seen, his cousin since Christmas. There were so many of them to keep up with. (This brokered an insight: all Jeff's cousins were female. At once, doubt was cast on Jeff's theory on the perceived value to Celia of daughters-in-law. On both sides of her family, Celia had a huge supply of younger female company, if she wanted it.

Which she didn't, much. Jeff felt a little sorry for Sarah, as if realising too late she had missed out.)

Despite her husband's cool but cautionary tone, Celia was unabashed. 'Yes, that's right. I was asking about the family archives, for Grace.'

'But why did you call Phoebe?'

'I didn't think her mother – either of your sisters, in fact – was interested in helping. Are they interested now?' Celia's voice rose, as if she had the potential to be delighted and surprised.

It was a dream unrealised. Nigel said, 'They're not. But they are interested in the fact that you went behind their backs to nose around.'

Sounding reasonable, Celia replied, 'I was simply cutting out the middlemen. Or women. Phoebe's always been nostalgic – well, she's a bit soppy, if we're honest – and she was only too happy to ask her gran . . .'

'You've got my *mother* involved? You rubbed her nose in her own father's . . .' His face wrinkled in disgust. 'Infidelity?'

'Let's not be precious about the past, Nigel. Your mother certainly isn't.' She turned frosty. 'It wasn't as if she helped under duress. Nobody was coerced. Everyone offered.'

'Shouldn't you have asked me?' he said.

Celia looked amazed. 'You've made no effort to be helpful whatsoever. Have you changed your mind?'

'Look, Cee, I couldn't give a fig about this so-called cousin. It's just that you should have asked me before you started stirring.'

'For pity's sake, why? Why should I have asked you?'

'Because ... because ...' He was foundering.

Jeff, anxiously looking on, felt mired in anguish. He'd feared his mum and dad would be embarrassed to argue in his presence but it was apparent that they hadn't even clocked that he was there.

'That's *brilliant*!' Celia shrieked. 'Pardon me for thinking this was a marriage of equals, a partnership. I didn't realise I had to kowtow to my husband.'

Nigel hardened. 'Don't exaggerate, Celia. You're blowing this out of proportion.'

'You're the one who came steaming in here to have a go at me!'

'I had to say something. My sisters are upset. They feel ...'

'How do *I* feel, do you suppose?' Celia bellowed. 'Or doesn't that matter any more? Oh, why bother asking!'

She stormed out and locked herself in her bedroom. She didn't emerge for half an hour, and Jeff feared that she might never come out, or that she'd appear with a packed bag. His parents used to argue quite a lot, but normally one would make the other laugh and the tension would diffuse. But that was years ago, in the old house, in London. Were there recent developments of which he should be aware? Had perceptive Steve said something that Jeff, steeped in self-absorption, had missed? But what *business* was it of his? Jeff knew only that it would be a craven act to depart in her absence – possibly hurtful – so spent a silent, tense thirty minutes while his father pretended to be glued to SkySports.

*　　*　　*

Just *why* was Celia so obsessed with Grace? What did she truly want out of it? Jeff gave it a lot of thought, breaking into new territory that he hadn't dared traverse in his own life. Perhaps it invigorated her in a way that her work and family life could not. Or had a loss of satisfaction with these everyday concerns sent her in search of new enthusiasms? He'd considered that Grace might tear the family apart but perhaps the opposite was true. Thank heavens for Grace, they might all be saying in a year's time. She saved us. Was Celia looking that far ahead? Had she done a proper risk assessment or was she coasting along, potentially imperilling them all?

Jeff began calling his parents at least once – sometimes twice – a week. Today was Sunday in late April: the call was the day's only enterprise.

Nigel picked up, almost as the answering machine took over. 'Jeff! You've just caught us. We only got back twenty minutes ago. Haven't even had a cuppa.'

'Oh, right. Sorry, Dad. Do you want me to call back later? Nothing urgent.'

'No. You can console your mother,' said Nigel after a quick hello to his younger son. As if he had tried and failed himself? Or not been moved to try?

It began promisingly. 'Hi, Mum, it's me. How are you?'

'Oh, I'm all right, really, just pissed off at those vipers up in Hemel Hempstead.'

'What do you mean?'

'It was a wasted day. Someone Kate put me in touch with – albeit grudgingly. Should have known it would be a fool's errand designed to teach me a lesson. Petrol money, the hideous traffic. All we were offered was a cup of tea and the loo. All that way for nothing.'

It was disappointment, rather than frustration, that he heard and was moved by. Jeff's own spirits were sufficiently lowered that his guard went down and he was able to close in on the heart of the matter – to ask the question on which they had all speculated, but been too coy or just cowardly to have answered. What were they afraid of? 'Mum, what were you expecting?'

'I had a lead that they'd had some baby's clothes passed on to them years ago that might have belonged to Grace. They denied all knowledge of it. Seemed more interested in ferreting out what I knew. Probably they'll be diving head first into mothballed bin bags in search of hidden treasure. I hope they get poisoned by the fumes.' She chuckled crudely, but she was injured, he could tell. She added, 'And they've the cheek to claim *I'm* on the make.'

He tried to be objective. 'But what if you don't find anything, Mum? You won't be upset, will you?'

'Upset? I'll be furious, Jeffrey.'

'But you'll have spent time with other branches of the family, made connections.' Behaviours he was unlikely to pursue himself, but he could admire them vicariously. 'Won't that be something?'

'For heaven's sake, don't try to tell me that it's all about the *journey*.' Her voice dripped scorn.

That floored him. It wasn't the tone, for Jeff had to accept that was now characteristic of his mother, albeit hopefully for a limited duration. It was the sentiment that caught him out. You were meant to embrace the journey, weren't you? The experience was everything; its own reward.

But Jeff didn't believe that. Wouldn't he have invested more in his own journey if he did? Instead of sloping between the flat he didn't much like and the office (where he coasted along, unchallenged), and the pub where he met his brother, he'd *do* more, meet different people, have other experiences. He'd embrace change. But he had changed nothing.

Why would he? Jeff wanted to be partnered to Sarah, pure and simple. He hadn't forgotten Steve's advice: a wise recommendation from a practical person who loved him. But still he could not take it.

So it was odd that he completely missed the anniversary of Sarah's departure. At first, he thought he'd got the date wrong, but no – today had been the day: Sunday, 5 May. Jeff should have felt wretched but surprisingly, it felt like any other day. He finished all his chores by mid-morning, so devised a second tier of tasks which he narrowed down to filleting out unwearable shirts from his wardrobe. He culled four, with frayed collars and worn elbows, and put two aside for decorating – he'd have to move, eventually, and chances were, he'd want to paint ceilings and re-tile walls. After stowing the shirts in the cupboard where he'd have kept tins of paint and glue-guns if he possessed them, Jeff decided he ought to go shopping to replace what he had jettisoned.

Did Jeff come across as a man making strides in the world? The kind lady who had folded his purchases and stowed them in a stiff cardboard bag had offered no evaluation, even though it was a quiet afternoon. Jeff decided that years on the shop floor had instilled discretion in her. He wondered if the same applied to his colleagues. Nobody commented on the crisp white shirt he wore to the office on Monday morning. But he told himself he didn't come to work to have his personal progress measured, and set about his tasks.

Jeff had a job within a job, like a Russian Babushka doll. For nearly a decade, he'd been employed by a licensing firm called Go Aware. He'd got into the industry through a school friend, with whom he'd had a brief but successful stint producing T-shirts for local festivals. Jeff had been the brawn of the operation, being fast and accurate with screen printing. Jeff's old pal had apprenticed himself to a printer and was now a leading light in font design. He lived in Berlin but on a trip to London – three years ago? Longer, maybe – he'd elected to catch up with old friends. Jeff supposed the first choices weren't available, so he'd been approached. He'd invited the friend round to dinner.

Sarah hadn't been pleased because it had come in the middle of a stretch of twelve-hour days, but the unexpected tale of Jeff's entrepreneurial streak enthralled her. 'That's amazing!' she glowed, grabbing her husband's hand across the table. It was an insight Jeff had never thought worthy of relating, because it had never led to anything, beyond a business degree, and then, for the past eight years, this run-of-the-mill, but until now safe job.

For a while afterwards, Sarah suggested Jeff renew his skills. He'd considered it, he'd even looked into buying equipment on eBay, but he lacked the passion. Sarah dropped the subject soon enough; her own career provided enough to engage with. Jeff stayed at Go Aware, and saw his stock briefly rise when Guy took the helm, and turned to Jeff for continuity. New people joined, in time, and stole a march on him.

There had been flashes of potential. Deals pulled out of the bag without cutting corners. Jeff's focus on ethics had led to a shortlisting for an award (but no further). In his time, he'd written some cracking copy. He'd slapped down straplines that made workaday products irresistible. Oh yes. Jeff was no genius, but he'd never been a liability.

Jeff's day-to-day report was to one of their clients, a sports charity. How had he become such a specialist? He'd had all kinds of clients, to start with – everyone did in the early days of the company. The change happened in the build-up to the London Olympics, when everyone was being encouraged to be more active. Had Jeff casually enthused about swimming? For years, it had been his exercise of choice, mostly at Brockwell Lido, after work and at weekends. He liked the fact that you didn't need to cart much stuff around, especially since he'd discovered those towels you can wring dry so they weigh hardly anything. Guy, the CEO, had a special connection to the charity because of a personal tragedy concerning a nephew or niece – it wasn't much talked about – so he encouraged Jeff's involvement.

The charity proved to be especially needy, because it was as short of strategy as it was of funds, and its merchandising to date had not been profitable. The fact that this client was far from lucrative for Go Aware didn't seem to matter to Guy, who was happy to let the work absorb Jeff, who, in turn, could find no reason not to give it all the time it required. And he *was* making a difference, it had to be said. His focus had shifted from solely charitable aims to embrace the ethical. Last summer, a clothing partnership had taken Devon by storm. There was talk of launching top-quality umbrellas and deck chairs. Things were looking up. He'd begun to like channelling his energies so narrowly. Did that make him a one-trick pony? Well, commitment was not to be sneered at. Although he hardly swam these days – he must get back into it.

Sarah had derided his 'aid work'. She was a high-flyer, a self-starter, whose business card was as bare as the shiny name plate outside a shop on New Bond Street – as if everyone knew what she did, which they probably did. Sarah felt that Jeff wasn't pushing himself, and therefore inhibiting their potential as a couple. True, he could have striven for promotion or at least sought some higher-profile enterprise. With more money, a childless couple could have indulgent holidays and nicer cars. But did he really think living the high life would have helped Sarah sail over forty?

Actually, *derided* was too harsh. Sarah hadn't ever been

nasty about it. So she hadn't been moved by Guy's personal tale of tragedy, but she didn't know Guy or any of his family. (She'd actually discovered the background – a niece, barely six, had drowned on a summer holiday, because no one else present could swim.) To be fair, Sarah was more frustrated that Jeff never tried to use the facts to benefit the cause. He could see her point – he knew she'd find a way not to exploit the family. Probably, he'd sounded ungrateful, he might even have accused her (wrongly) of exploitative intentions. It was shameful. Now he wondered: if he'd asked for her advice, perhaps they would still be together?

Routine carried Jeff through the days. But within the space of a fortnight, the world had three surprises in store. First, he received an e-mail with an invitation to a summer party from Tara who had always been more a friend to Sarah than to Jeff – in the early days, at least. It seemed she didn't know that they were no longer together. Jeff hadn't said anything; and he knew she wouldn't have forgotten. Perhaps it was one of the relationships Sarah had left to Jeff to update. Not that they'd sat down to divvy up the list. It was rude to ignore Tara's invitation, but Jeff wanted his response to be measured, so he delayed. And then the week's other innovations swept it from his mind.

On Wednesday afternoon, Jeff's mobile rang. It was Steve, who'd finished a site meeting and therefore finished the day early.

'Mate,' Steve began, 'don't mean to be funny or anything,

but what's with all the messages you've been sending my wife?'

'What messages?'

'Last night – lateish. Alyx didn't pick them up till this morning. So good to speak with you. Just following up our conversation. Wednesday at 4. Then the other one, which was a bit bizarre, saying would she mind if you brought along someone called Tom. Brought along *where*, exactly, we wondered.'

'Oh, sorry, those messages weren't for Alyx. I must have called her by mistake.'

'Really?' Steve sounded doubtful.

Jeff began to gabble. 'Yes, really! Of course they weren't. Why would I be calling Alyx late at night?'

'That's what we wanted to know ourselves, little brother.'

'I was phoning someone in New York. She's called Alison – she's coming over next week for business. I was just making arrangements.' No wonder she hadn't followed up herself. He'd promised to confirm Wednesday. Would she be annoyed?

'You gave my Alyx driving lessons,' said Steve. 'Years ago.'

'I know. You were working up in Leeds at the time. She thought it would be less stressful with you out of the way.'

'You gave her all those raunchy films. Erotic dancing.'

'They were Sarah's Pilates' DVDs. She never used them. Alyx sounded interested.'

'You got her that great big case of make-up with the padded lid.'

'It was a free sample from work. Sarah hates make-up – she doesn't need it – not that Alyx does, I'm not saying that –' he was getting himself tangled '—the point is it, it was while I was married. All those things happened while I was married. It wasn't . . . inappropriate behaviour.'

'Did I suggest it was?'

Jeff burned. His older brother knew how to rile him, but somehow, beneath the joke, a point was being made. Had Sarah thought he'd been too close to Alyx – to other women? When married, Jeff had noticed other women. Naturally he had. He'd gone along with Steve's jokes and those of colleagues. But he never acted, never wanted to.

'What about this American lass?' queried Steve.

'Alison. She set up our parent company's new office in Boston. I don't know very much about her.'

'But you must know a bit? Age, height, hair colour, marital status . . .'

'She's about forty. I don't know if she's married. Judging by her photo on the staff intranet, she's pretty.'

'And you've been chosen to look after her while she's here?'

As someone who predominantly kept to himself, Jeff had no concept of other people's lives and commitments so it didn't occur to him that no one fancied having their weekend interrupted by what would be, effectively, a work commitment. He got the gig.

'I volunteered. It's just the weekend. She's off to a conference in Leeds on Tuesday, then back to the States on Thursday.'

'Most laudable!'

'It's not as if I've got much on.'

'You'll show her the sights, then. Give her a good time. Something to remember?'

'We're doing the V&A. I did suggest the Shard or the Eye but apparently she's not too keen on heights.'

His brother sighed. 'Oh, mate. You can do better than that. You can do so much better.'

Alison's flight arrived late on the bank holiday Monday and she had all day Tuesday to catch up on e-mails and recover. Her Wednesday was filled with meetings – the 4 o'clock was Jeff's first introduction, but there had been no time for more than a friendly handshake and welcome. He hadn't seen her again till Friday, when there'd been a lunch meeting, at which he'd managed to confirm arrangements for Saturday. Tom, who worked with Jeff, came to lunch but was unavailable at the weekend. Jeff would meet Alison at her hotel near Gloucester Road at two. She was happy to spend the morning mooching about by herself. This suited Jeff, who easily enough crammed his weekend chores into four brisk hours.

She was waiting for him when he arrived at the hotel on that first day of June – a breezy, sunny day. All her clothes were stylish and expensive-looking, even her walking shoes. She was prepared for some serious tramping. Jeff had taken care with his appearance, but he felt shabby in what would have been his dress-down Friday look, if only the company had adopted dress-down Friday. The heel of one of his loafers quickly began trying to work itself free.

'I left my guidebook in my room,' she told him, making a hands-free gesture, and he offered assurance that it would not be needed. And, to Jeff's relief, it wasn't. Although it had been a while since he'd explored this part of town (he had no nephews and nieces to take to the Science or Natural History museums), the network of streets soon came back to him, linked by the obvious positioning of landmarks.

Early on, Jeff tumbled to the fact Alison's interest in his specific portfolio was almost non-existent. Perhaps she had no time for charities, or maybe Jeff's priorities did not correlate to the areas of the business with which her visit was concerned. Wouldn't you have thought (he wondered) she'd have sought a more appropriate companion for the weekend? Because she must have asked about her chaperone. She must, to some degree, have been able to vet the volunteers.

Cultural territory was safer ground. Once inside the V&A, they would drift apart to explore a specific room, knowing the other was close by. Sometimes they shared observations. Talk never dried up. Afterwards, they walked along the Brompton Road, so Alison could make a quick inspection of Harrods, although it was such a fine day she was keen to be outside again. From Hyde Park Corner, they accessed Constitution Hill, through the parks, stopping for photos at the Palace.

As the afternoon dwindled, they lapsed into silence, but it wasn't awkward. Alison was sporting large sunglasses, so it was impossible to read her expression. So Jeff allowed himself to retreat. In that state, on this route, he was completely anonymous – no one paid him any attention, or picked up on what he said. The language he spoke was just one of many; perhaps as inaccessible to the people around Jeff as their multiplicity of languages was to him. It was a state he enjoyed very much. It was one he could get used to.

The only downside – which did not escape him – was the fact that he might not see Sarah, unless she too, by miraculous coincidence, was showing a tourist the sights. The coincidence would generate fresh common ground, which in turn would rekindle the familiarity they had once taken for granted. Of course it didn't happen. It hadn't even happened when Jeff shifted his weekend routine a couple of miles back towards their old stomping ground, nearer to the friend with whom Sarah was sharing, hoping to catch sight of her, and fall into familiar patterns.

He wasn't done with the fantasy. If something happened to him, suddenly and inexplicably, what would happen? Alison, with no knowledge of his medical history, might panic and flee. She might misdiagnose. If he did suffer some kind of trauma, the only person to notice would be Sarah who – no matter where she was – would become alert to his distress by some instant sonar sensation, and drop everything and come to his aid, finding him by yet another instinct. As no one else could. As he had rescued her, once, long ago. Ah, but that was only a myth, wasn't it? Again, it wouldn't happen.

(Anyway, never having been cursed by so much as a peanut intolerance, the only possible affliction he could think of was a delayed reaction to the trauma of the anniversary of the break-up. Sarah wouldn't be prepared to assist him with that.)

Alison and Jeff resumed their conversation at the top of the Mall, as if alerted to the thrust of continuous motion in Trafalgar Square. She wanted to know where he hung out at the weekends – which cafés and bars, which indie cinemas and theatres. Where he went dancing. Where he bought books and, maybe, music. She was only here for a week: what was she planning to do with all this knowledge? Anyway, there wasn't much to describe these days, so he started to talk about what it had been like growing up in the capital, which in conversation always turns out to be more of a novelty than you'd expect. But she wanted details of the here and now.

Tired and hot a few hours in, sharing a drink and a meal was obvious. It was paid for on her company credit card at her insistence. What did they talk about? Jeff wasn't sure, but it was dark by the time they left. He guided her to Piccadilly Circus station, because she wanted to walk off her food, which had been excellent but rich, and to clear her head of the wine, which had also been good. Jeff shook her hand in farewell and asked when she wanted to meet tomorrow.

Alison looked aghast, but gushed, 'Oh, no, Jeff, I couldn't possibly intrude on any more of your time. You've already been more than generous.'

'It's been a total pleasure, I promise you. There's so much more to show you.'

'You've given me loads of great ideas. I think I could probably find my own way around.'

'But you might not know short cuts. No offence, but public transport can be confusing.'

'Then it'll be an adventure, won't it?' She offered a fleeting smile. 'But thank you,' she said. It sounded final.

'But I enjoyed it. Really. I'd be happy to meet again.'

He remembered her response, the way puzzlement flickered across her face, as if she might be changing her mind. His heart lifted, then it sank, when she said, 'No, really, it's OK. But thank you.'

Jeff felt flattened, but rose again, already contemplating the bonus of a day free of obligation. But how would he fill it? Jeff felt deflated again but not because of that, he realised; it was another feeling, which was all too familiar but still painful. Rejection.

Jeff replayed the afternoon in his head as if it were scenes from a film with the dialogue overlaid by music. He didn't immediately recognise it as a rom-com, but once he did, he felt a flare of excitement.

Such sequences end in one of two ways – heartbreak and parting, or the release of sexual tension, and bed. Oh, he thought about sex a lot. It had been *so* long since he'd felt another person's touch. He longed for the curve of a shoulder. The shape of a leg. More. Much more than that. He missed it, but the idea of going out and getting it seemed like treachery. Besides, you heard such awful things about 'the rebound' – never mind that half his bed had been cold for fourteen months. Maybe Jeff didn't feel single enough, which was surely a pre-requisite for falling in love again. There was also the question of expertise. Before Sarah, he hadn't had what you'd call a consistent girlfriend. Sometimes, there were girls, plural, none of whom expected or offered exclusivity. At least no former lovers were likely to emerge from the woodwork and set his heart aflutter anew. Why would they, unless they'd been in hibernation for the length of Jeff's unavailability? As if.

In any case, sex – or love – had no bearing on his afternoon with Alison. The e-mail hadn't even specified a male chaperone, let alone a single male chaperone. If it had, would Jeff had applied? It might just have sailed over his head. Because he was still in love with Sarah.

He thought about love. It's such a robust word, which is heartening. So decisive, too: it was either or, hot or cold: if you weren't in love there was no pretending you were. If you were there was equally no doubt – and woe betide anyone who tried to dissuade you. Jeff had spent the past year unswerving in his own faith. Only now . . .

Jeff, who had been frozen for a year, felt the first stirrings of a thaw. He shuddered with possibility, with expectation. He remembered, in fact, feeling the sharp tang of excitement when he keyed Alison's number into his phone. Had he been similarly skittish when he called her, stumbling on to Alyx's number, too nervous to calmly press the right key? Too excited? Even though it was work. Even though it intruded upon his precious free time. Then he remembered the tang of Alison's perfume. That didn't feel like work at all. Her eyes, when she removed the dark glasses, conveying a flicker of surprise. A dry rasp in her laugh that sounded harsh at first, but was actually warm. One after the other, impressions swept into his head and quickened his heart.

Jeff hadn't expected to have to share an account of his weekend. He had always actively discouraged people's interest in his life. He and Sarah had never accompanied each other to work functions. He would make excuses about a clash of events at weekends and evenings, when really he'd just gone home to his wife (or to wait in her for) which was what he'd liked best. For Sarah, it was more policy than preference to keep work and social life separate.

It had taken nearly six weeks for Jeff to report that Sarah had left. He hadn't expected a response. The sympathy was surprising, but he'd found it excruciating. People who barely knew him – or whom he considered to be only acquaintances – had treated him like a private patient. He was bought lunch and had drinks replenished. He'd responded with ingratitude and had worn his victimhood like a badge of honour, like an excuse note barring him from normal conduct. Guy, with targets to exceed and budgets to curtail, had had to cut him some slack, but noted: 'The lad needs to get his house in order.' A time limit hadn't been imposed but Jeff knew he couldn't afford to be complacent.

The team had a right to be interested in Alison, however. Jeff might have considered his American colleague's introduction to London in isolation, but for everyone else it was an episode in the history of relations at Go Aware. Why hadn't he seen that?

It was the CEO's PA who delivered the consensus. 'So Alison assumed you liked men.'

Jeff pressed 'save' on his current document. 'She what?'

'Well, the V&A was a bit of a giveaway.'

'Everyone goes to the V&A,' he said. 'It's famous. *What* did she—'

'Well, it wasn't just that. She said you were very sympatico with her difficulties concerning poaching staff.'

'Did she say that?' Jeff smiled. It had been a rare moment when he'd managed to steer the chat back to professional concerns.

'Oh yes. Of course, what Guy *actually* wanted was for someone to give the third degree over her overspend on IT and get her to revise her Q3 forecast upwards.'

'He never said that to me . . .'

'Didn't he? Perhaps I was meant to brief you. Strictly speaking, though, that's not your remit, is it?'

Jeff shook his head. 'It isn't. No.'

'Oh well. Alison had a very pleasant visit, don't get me wrong. She was singing your praises. But I think next time, Guy will do it the other way round, and go to Boston himself. Throw his weight around a bit.'

Oh God. There had been a serious fuck-up. Someone else had been meant to go instead of Jeff. Consequently, he hadn't fulfilled the role as expected. But nor had he behaved as expected within the unexpectedness of his placement.

It seemed churlish to blurt 'I'm not gay!' but he did feel he'd been overlooked in the summation of the day. He had been misrepresented. But first, he needed to be clear about the agenda he felt he might be required to refute. 'Are you saying this because . . . because she . . . well, *liked* me?'

'Don't be coy, Jeff. She fancied the pants of you.' Then she lowered her voice and offered, *sotto voce*, 'Women do.' Then she added, brushing a staple that had embedded itself in her sleeve. 'Not me, of course. And not Mary, either.'

'Well, no,' agreed Jeff. 'Not Mary.' They'd had run-ins, over treats brought back from holiday or, from Jeff's side, the lack of them. But the conversation had gone off-piste. 'So you're saying, Alison fancied me. She wanted—' His head swam.

'Keep it down, Casanova. No need to brag. She was waiting for you to make a move and was very disappointed when you didn't.'

'She told you this? When?'

'Well, you'd have probably noticed if it had been a live commentary during your date. Or maybe you wouldn't. We caught up in the loos.'

'Oh. I see,' said Jeff, but everything seemed opaque, like the bottom rows of an eye test chart. Except for the question that he had temporarily parked. 'She thinks I'm gay?'

She nodded. 'Uh-huh. Now everyone does. It's no big deal, of course. You can sleep with whomever you want. But Alison was a little disappointed that it wasn't her. The fact you didn't keeps the expenses down a bit, I guess. Don't forget to put your claim through. I think there's a payment run on Thursday. I'm off on Wednesday afternoon, remember, so I'll need all paperwork first thing. Actually, I've got the dentist then. I'll give you till eleven.'

So his brother thought he was a home-wrecking wife-stealer. Now half the office thought he'd turned gay. So that's why his marriage broke up. No one mentioned Sarah any more. Nor, since the weekend, had Jeff thought much about her. This final point consumed him more than any speculation about his sexuality, so his denial came as a parting shot, last minute, perhaps desperate. 'I'm not gay, by the way.'

She preened. 'Nothing would surprise me in this crazy world we live in.'

Jeff paused to consider what his next move should be. He wondered if any action on his part would brook influence. 'Do you think I ought to check in with Guy?'

With a shake of the head, his doubts were confirmed. 'I wouldn't bother. He probably didn't expect you to deliver anyway.'

'Oh. Right. Well, then. No harm done, I suppose. I think I'll sort my receipts out while it's fresh in my mind.'

'Yes. You do that, Jeff. See you around.'

Never mind Guy, it was Alison Jeff must seek out, and offer an explanation. But it was Tuesday – it had taken a day for the rumour mill to work its way around the floor, and then scuttle back to him – and she was now in Leeds at the conference. He checked her schedule and saw it was unlikely that he'd see her again before she flew back to Boston. If this were a movie, he'd hop on a train to Leeds. He thought you could catch one from

Kings Cross. But that was too desperate, and unprofessional (although he wouldn't expense it). Should he e-mail her – perhaps from his personal account? Would that also be deemed inappropriate?

What would he say to Alison? Was it preferable to let her think he wasn't interested because he preferred men or because he was still in love with his wife – ex-wife – and refused to move on? Mentally, he composed the message but the words wouldn't settle – they pulled away, as if repelled, like iron filings. Why was that? Weren't they true?

He knew so little about Alison, because in his efforts to ward off her questions, he had failed to extract her own story. So he began an investigation. Not just on the company and networking sites. He found a talk she had given in Chicago. There was an interview with her in a management magazine.

In the space of a lunch hour, he blitzed the internet to find more about her than he had gleaned during their afternoon together. He felt a sudden, urgent need to put his findings into words, and to share them. (Jeff realised that he did, after all, care, about the opinions of others.) He was relieved to coincide with Guy's PA in the post room.

'It wouldn't have worked,' he said, relieved partly because he wasn't saddled with the burden of knowledge alone. 'Alison and me.'

'Oh really?' She was measuring folded documents against envelopes. 'Why is that, Jeff?'

'We're completely different people. For example, Alison is slow to make decisions, and I tend to jump in.'

An eyebrow was arched. 'She seemed to make her mind up pretty fast about you.'

'I was right not to encourage it,' he said. 'You can't be impulsive one minute, then slow to act afterwards. It just messes people up. Alison is methodical, whereas I'm not very patient. I'd get frustrated, and then *she* would.'

'Jeff, how do you know all this? Have you been having heart to hearts over the teleconferencing?'

'No,' he admitted, glumly. 'We haven't been in touch. I've just been reading about her.' Surely not *all* his impressions had been drawn from an internet search? But Jeff was too late to restore his standing and was met with a frown of disapproval.

'*Reading* about her?' As if this in itself was a deplorable act.

'Yes, she blogs about her management style.'

'But Jeff, that's work talk. She's probably totally different in real life. You saw her in between work and leisure. I thought she was fun, myself.'

Jeff wondered, 'Do you seriously think people have a work self and a home self?' It sounded exhausting.

'Of course they do.'

'Like Jekyll and Hyde!'

'Jeff!' That was a warning. She grabbed her envelopes, ready to depart. 'Everyone has to strike a work/life balance. Anyway, that's getting off the point. It sounds like you're trying to talk yourself out of fancying her. Fine, if that's your decision.'

Jeff didn't want to be spoken for and protested at once. 'No, I'm ...' He stopped. Sarah had made a lot of decisions for them both and he'd found it soothing. Usually they'd been the right ones. But that belonged to another time. Another life. He didn't know what to say next. He no longer felt reassured.

'Anyway, you've neglected the biggest obstacle to your planets being in blissful alignment just when Cupid shoots his arrow.'

'Oh? What's that?'

'She lives in Boston. So you're off the hook.'

Jeff let out a sigh. *That* was the chief reason why he and Alison couldn't have got together. They might have intended to stay in touch, but that would have fizzled out, and he'd be bereft again. Despite all Alison's questions about London life, she hadn't hinted that she might move here. He'd saved himself a lot of bother.

Eyes were rolled. 'So you're ready for your next victim – oops, I mean, for the next lucky lady who takes a shine to you. Do let me know how you get on.' With a smirk, she exited the room.

There never were days of days – no wonder he'd missed the anniversary – and today, a Wednesday, was no exception, because until that morning, he'd had three eggs in the fridge, all within their use-by date. Somehow Jeff had knocked the box off the shelf and they'd fallen from fridge to the floor, and smashed. Jeff wasn't usually clumsy, and he hadn't even been hungover (although he'd drunk last night, as he did most nights, whether in company or alone, as his waistline had begun to reveal). He'd had black coffee for breakfast – Sarah was lactose intolerant so he was OK to go without milk – and tripped off to work, grabbing two bananas from the café across the road.

Back at home, reality bit when Jeff realised his fridge was empty. How had it come to that? He wasn't too poor to buy food, nor too busy. He passed enough shops on the way back from the station to pick up any number of staples. He was hungry, usually, when he left work, and ravenous by the time he passed through the ticket barrier at Peckham Rye. So how come tonight's only comestible was a stiff half loaf?

As he sat munching toast – it was a miracle; he found Lurpak – Jeff found himself drifting from facts to philosophy. (He'd steered clear of it, since being rounded on by Steve.) There wasn't even a can of soup in the cupboard. No packet sauces – had he thrown them out? Nothing, anywhere, you could quickly warm up in a pan, let alone cook. Oh, *pans*. Pots and pans. Was he consciously *boycotting* the le Creuset?

For fuck's sake, enough was enough. The dishes had a lifetime guarantee but surely the metaphor (or whatever it was) had a shelf-life? It was a week off the summer solstice (was the longest day, the shortest night significant to a singleton like Jeff?). Enough was *enough*. But the fear that he had smashed the eggs accidentally on purpose lingered. Eggs were indefatigable and could be prepared in any number of ways, in any receptacle – of which Jeff, of course, had an endless supply. But there he was, alone, eating toast.

In silence. Wasn't *silence* taking this repression too far? Normally Jeff switched on the TV as he deposited his keys and wallet on the bookcase. Somehow, today he'd managed to shed his shoes, socks and trousers and donned shorts, but he was still in his work shirt, which was crumpled and unpleasant around the armpits. He sat on the bar stool, swinging his legs. (The flat was airless but he hadn't bothered to open a window.) And he realised that he was horrifically bored, and lonely.

Jeff faced the fact that, easy though it was to lose friends, making new ones was far from simple. It seemed you had to be gregarious, or else engaged in current crazes or issues which Jeff, frankly, wasn't. He'd never been a joiner-in, never been any cause's advocate. He'd just been married. Until he'd met Sarah, Jeff had told himself he didn't care what people thought, and therefore resisted any kind of public scrutiny. It wasn't a lethargic indifference, it wasn't idleness. He hoped it hadn't started off as arrogance, but somehow a little confidence had bloomed in him. Well, that had been his gift from Sarah, wasn't it? Had she meant to take it away in her suitcases?

He couldn't go on like this. Summer would be ideal for looking to buy a flat and put down new roots, if only he'd sorted out his finances. Jeff had intended to move some money around at the start of the year but had failed to achieve that, or very much else. He might sign up to some property sites and leave his details with a few local agents at the weekend. In all likelihood, however, he'd be stuck here until the autumn, possibly the winter. His heart sank deeper.

Jeff had been so occupied thinking about Alison, and then not thinking about her, that he hadn't noticed another question sneak in and demand his attention. Coldly, darkly – just like an abyss – it stared him in the face. *Was* he still in love with Sarah?

What a question! Jeff wouldn't have spent the past year in this state of suspended animation if he hadn't been. For so long, Jeff had invested all his energies into his marriage – even after it ended – actually holding the divorce papers in his hand – his world view was channelled through the lens of being Sarah's partner. Even now it seemed a wonderful cause to adhere to. He certainly wasn't going to throw it away on a whim.

And yet now he saw his strategy was flimsy. It was only because Sarah hadn't blamed him that Jeff had allowed himself to think that they could wake from any slumbering lapses, repair whatever cracks had opened up, and fall violently in love all over again.

Sarah had indulged him. Was that a special privilege of a marriage at its amicable end? The preservation of privacy, an unwillingness to leak harsh truths to the outside world. Like the fact that their marriage had been running on empty for some time – months, maybe even years. And he had simply been too blind – too stubborn, as Steve suggested – to notice. Which meant that if Jeff had succeeded in persuading Sarah to stay, he would be failing her a second time. She would be trapped, like an insect in amber. She would be incandescent, like he'd never seen her when she realised the truth. 'Utter *shite*! You kept saying you loved me, Jeff, that there's never been anyone else and never will be, but it's all *shite*! Why did you string me along? Did you think I'd be *flattered*?'

How could he have got it so wrong? Was he the ultimate fool? Were other people as careless, as imperceptive, as blind? Surely they knew better. *Which* people, exactly?

He'd known them at work – not just individuals, but entire businesses. It was amazing how some companies laboured under confused identities and contradictory messages. Jeff relished such accounts because so much could be achieved, and the results were always visible. It fascinated him how mistakes got made. Sometimes, firms outgrow an existing identity or, having trundled competently along, they find themselves at a standstill: they've suddenly realised the persona they've been operating under isn't them after all. You have to ask them basic questions. Do they want a stepping stone or a complete reinvention? Where do they want to be in five years' time, ten, fifteen? Then there's the market, most important of all. Jeff had long had it drummed into him that you shouldn't expect people to flock to you just because your brand is shit hot (or you think it is). You have to look at people's needs, to make sure that you're not limiting your appeal. Are you leading or following? What are your rivals offering?

Could he apply these questions to his own life, so he could start afresh?

The idea excited him – *this* was striking the work/life balance. Besides, Jeff hadn't had the opportunity to take on new business for ages. In the parlance of his profession, Jeff was about to undergo a rebrand. But he stalled at a fundamental question. Actually, he'd avoided it. You have to ask the client: who do you want to care?

Jeff gave it some thought, but drew a blank. Who was looking?

Jeff felt the pressing need for engagement. He was wary of expecting too much from his family – well, why approach Alyx just to confirm that he had no romantic designs on her? His parents had enough to deal with so he wouldn't impose, although he might be able to learn from Celia's experience. Not that anyone had mentioned Grace for weeks. It seemed less of a risk to join a gym, until he heard a horror story about hamstrings in the lift. He checked his e-mails to see if he'd missed any invitations for forthcoming parties. Maybe targeted, tailored approaches could be made. 'Jeff, have you met X? I have a feeling you'll get along brilliantly.' Nothing doing, anywhere. People said London was an unfriendly place and although he'd never believed it – Jeff was a Londoner himself – perhaps there was truth in the claim.

But he wanted *someone*. There was room enough for other people. Jeff wasn't talking about friends, after all, because he was lucky enough to have his brother as his best mate and Steve, fortunately, had a lot of time for him. What Jeff wanted was the company of women. Another woman, that is. It came down to sex, again – but this time, he didn't clam shut. The imprint of Sarah on his mind had faded – there was no point pretending otherwise. The same was true of Alison, who really had gone. (He'd let her.) But he didn't want to *exclude* people. He could summon a surfeit of beauty: models, film stars who made him perk up when he saw them on ads or magazine covers, newsreaders. There were people he exchanged glances with on escalators or in queues at the supermarket. Every opportunity seemed like starting from scratch, and nobody made an impression. It was as if he had a particular image in mind which he'd failed to locate.

There *was* someone. No surprise it was the singular, because Jeff was a one-trick pony. And he *wasn't* surprised, but he was excited to retrieve feelings he had pushed away. Suddenly, he made her step from the shadows and engulf his mind, and in turn, the very thought of her engulfed his heart. It happened so quickly that Jeff knew that for him, she had never really gone away.

Minna, who worked at Macsamphire Strutt, a few floors down – not that she seemed to know what she did there. He'd even wondered if Minna had invented her job. He'd heard of people who dress for work, leave the house at eight, but spend the day riding public transport, back and forth all day. But no, of course not. Jeff had Googled Macsamphire Strutt: digital advertising, basically. There was probably some overlap in his and Minna's day-to-day tasks, though he couldn't find any record of Go Aware employing their neighbour's services. Minna's work wasn't at all difficult to describe, so he must have knocked her off her stride. *Damn.* Oh, and he might even have used the Babushka reference. *That* was unlikely to impress.

In any case, it was Minna's legs Jeff thought about. Lovely legs, not long but shapely – *oh*, and gorgeous ankles. Amazing cheek bones and those sharp green eyes! Or were they grey? Could grey be beautiful? Minna's eyes were. Blond hair, like

Sarah's, he admitted, but a bit more savagely chopped, which he liked. Personality wise, he'd clocked that Minna was urgent, ambitious, cautious, optimistic, easily thwarted, naive but hungry for understanding, sociable but reserved. Jeff had experienced them in various combinations himself. To juggle them all seemed to him extraordinary.

If Sarah was, or had been, any of these things – it was more than likely, for Jeff found them attractive, as well as familiar – then she'd have adopted them singularly, serially, as if to mix them was asking for a lawless ambiguity. Not that Jeff was trying to chip away his estimation of Sarah. Or – God forbid – strike a comparison. Minna was not Sarah. He no longer needed to turn to thoughts of his ex-wife. Sarah's life just wasn't his business.

But what right did he have to think of Minna?

Slow down. Slow . . . down.

There had been plenty of cautious smiles between Minna and Jeff – polite, friendly, but definitely flirty. How long had that been going on for? When had Minna joined Macsamphire Strutt? Could it have been before Sarah left? Could the smiles have begun – innocently? Inappropriately? – during the marriage? Jeff knew that he had spoken to Minna only once, which had led to their date – their drink – a couple of months ago. Their disastrous date.

Ridiculously, he'd spent so much time speaking of his former wife, not that he'd cast Sarah in a flattering light. 'Crash and burn' made her sound like Carrie from the film. It conjured a pyre of choking black smoke, noxious fumes, a smothering blanket of ash, and wreckage. It wasn't even true! Anyone would attest that Sarah's extrication from his life had been clean and – pans apart – traceless. Jeff's baggage, his misery, was his own creation. So how dare he try to blame it, and then dump it on someone else? Minna must have been insulted. At best, she must have felt that her time had been wasted.

Jeff could only hope that her expectations had been low. Maybe she'd seen it as a possible networking opportunity. Perhaps it was a drink just because she was bored, disappointed by Valentine's hopes that remained unfulfilled. (Jeff hadn't even made the connection.) Well, he can't have troubled her tedium threshold because he hadn't heard from her since.

He'd done nothing to follow up the date. He'd assumed he'd see Minna, but they hadn't bumped into each other, possibly because discounting those who got disorientated during fire drills, there was little interaction between the companies in the building. Each floor had its own security system, so you couldn't wander in and out. Based on the ninth, Jeff had no reason to pass through the second and third floors – and he could think of no legitimate cause to venture now, aside from searching for Minna. Missing a stop in the lift wouldn't cut it. He considered posting himself a parcel to his work address, only putting the wrong floor number on it, so he would have to retrieve it. No, the helpful, all-seeing eyes in the post room would intercept and ensure it reached the correct destination first time. Could the guys on the front desk be bribed to give a tip-off on Minna's movements? Could he sit in the café across the road and watch for her? All these seemed tawdry, implausible suggestions.

Could she have changed jobs? Could Macsamphire Strutt have moved out of the building? The other day, he'd noticed a lot of old furniture being hauled through reception on the ground floor.

Perhaps she was avoiding him. Wasn't that a sensible tactic?

Jeff felt the hot flush of shame. If there'd been a lost opportunity, it was this. Was all now lost for good? Jeff *hated* feeling sorry for himself. Despite the evidence to the contrary – a whole year's worth – it really didn't suit him.

He started investing energy at home. Someone might come for a meal, not necessarily a woman – not someone just for sex, but, *well* . . . Jeff wanted the place to look less temporary. He invested in new bedding and bought a throw and new cushions for the tired sofa. He hung some of the pictures he'd brought from the old flat – how different they looked; the light was so much better here. He'd buy lamp shades and cushions, when he got round to it. In the kitchen he tidied and streamlined, starting with the le Creuset. Because it really was time for it to go.

Steve seemed aware of a change in Jeff the next time they met. They'd missed a couple of weeks – because Steve and Alyx had been away and – well, the following week, Jeff hadn't needed his brother's company to drown his sorrows. He'd been to the gym instead of the pub. Steve hadn't seemed to mind. 'You look good,' he said, tipping his pint in approval.

Steve and Alyx's holiday had actually been a long weekend, for a wedding in the Dordogne. (Still Steve refused to admit he was a Francophile.) The brothers could have met in the week, as usual, and it was a big deal that they hadn't. As if by way of compensation, Steve handed over a bottle of very good wine and a lump of cheese.

The French theme endured for much of the evening. Jeff was interested to hear about the mini-break, so Steve described the olde world feel of the region, likening it to Tuscany, where Jeff had been (with Sarah, of course). They talked about farms and hills and rivers and market days. They talked about *Bergerac*, which segued into reminiscence about childhood TV programmes, and then got back on track to speak of vineyards and markets and prehistoric caves.

They were in a pub a few streets west of Marylebone Station, because Steve had been based that day in Paddington. It was busy already and took ages for Steve to fetch pints from the bar. When he came back, he said to his brother, 'Can you even say *the* le Creuset. Doesn't "le" mean "the"?'

It might have grated. It might have regressed Jeff to those dark weeks and months which now, he hoped, were over. Jeff aimed to be dismissive, rather than rude. He said, 'It doesn't really matter. I've got rid of them.'

'You what?'

'I've got rid of them. They were giving me grief. Someone at work's kitchen caught fire, so they've got the saucepans. End of. Your point?'

'Oh? Really?' Steve shivered.

'Sorry, did *you* want them?' It hadn't occurred to Jeff to offer them. Wouldn't that have been the perfect solution from the day Sarah moved out? 'You never said . . .'

'No, no, no, it's fine.'

Still Steve looked spooked. Jeff said, 'Something's not right. What it is?'

'Kitchen fires,' said Steve, thoughtfully. 'Nasty. You hear about them. Chip pan?'

'Apparently. They've had to move out. The other hazard, I heard, is the tumble dryer. It gets so hot, you see. Then there's lint . . .'

Steve squirmed but also shook his head. 'I'm always saying that to Alyx. Never leave the dryer on when you go out. Asking for trouble.'

After thirty-seven years, Jeff discovered an insecurity lurking inside his indefatigable brother. Who knew?

Steve had been such a brick, so Jeff tactfully steered the conversation away from his insecurities. They ended up back at the wedding Steve and Alyx had attended, which perhaps was not tactful – only it wasn't fair to ask Steve to avoid all potentially tender topics of conversation, especially when they'd lost their capacity to wound. He really should have filled Steve in about that development.

'If you had to go to a wedding now, who would you take?' Steve asked. 'Or would you go on your own?'

Jeff considered. He wouldn't want to go alone. 'One of our cousins, maybe,' he said.

Steve smiled. 'Phoebe? God, she'd be in her element. She's always loved dressing up like a princess. D'you remember what she wore to your wedding? She almost upstaged the bride. As for her sister, she looked like she'd just come from the gym. What about Mum's side of the family? There's Ell—'

Jeff felt suddenly light-headed. Was it the alcohol? Adrenaline poured faster than any beer pump. He said, in almost a gabble, 'Actually, I wouldn't invite Phoebe. Or any of them. I've got someone else in mind.'

Steve looked momentarily surprised, and then intrigued. 'Oh really? Who's the lucky lady?'

Jeff longed to say her name. He hadn't yet spoken it aloud. *Minna*. But he knew it was too soon. He just said, 'Look, it's very early days. Very early. I don't want to jinx it.'

Steve accepted his answer. 'Fair enough, mate. Good news, though. Once you're feeling more confident about it all, let us know when we can be introduced. I'm very much looking forward to meeting her.'

Despite his tentative progress, Jeff continued to be outpaced by developments in the wider world. Tara, who'd issued the summer party invitation, got in touch again, having failed to hear from either Jeff or Sarah. Once again her e-mail was addressed to them both:

I'm SO, SO sorry. You must think I'm incredibly insensitive or just stupid. But I didn't realise you'd separated. How crass of me to send the e-mail. It goes without saying, you would both be more than welcome – and please do bring other people if you'd like. If you can't make the party, why not suggest some other dates? We're not away until September. Much love . . .

Jeff had forgotten to reply, but it was Tara who felt guilty. That wasn't right. He messaged his ex-wife: *Do you want to reply? If you want to go, I'm happy not to.* He signed it with a *Jx*, then removed the *x*, and then the *J*. Until recently, he'd have longed for the chance to see her more than the friends, but it was easy to pull away. He wasn't being chivalrous.

It was a watershed moment. Sad, but reassuring, too. Jeff *was* single, so he might as well acknowledge it. He should let people know. He should find Minna. Jeff intended no delay. He certainly wasn't waiting for Sarah's endorsement of his plan. He decided to give her forty-eight hours to respond to his e-mail, then he'd write to Tara himself.

Somehow, Celia had detected Jeff's hiatus, and elected to fill it. At least she didn't admonish him for a lapse in contact. Her instruction was clear.

'First thing to do is get in touch with your cousin Niamh.'

'I didn't know we had a cousin Niamh.'

'Of course you do. One of Dad's brother's kids.'

'We haven't seen Roger in years. Didn't they move away?'

'Yes – it was tricky – but that was a long time ago. Niamh was sweet on you when you were younger, so she's bound to want to help.'

Jeff reflected. He was sure he'd remember, given the paucity of attention he'd received. 'Sorry, Mum, I can't place her.'

'Maybe it was Steve. Yes, now I come to think about it, it was Steve she fancied.'

'So wouldn't it make more sense for—'

Celia paused to let the – clearly implausible – proposition

slip away. 'Now, Niamh lives in Balham, so not far away from you at all. Which is handy. It'll seem casual. It needs to seem casual.'

'What needs to seem casual, Mum?'

'Your visit, of course. Your grandmother sent her some photo albums which I need to get my hands on, only I don't want Jane and Sue finding out.' 'Or your father' was the unspoken postscript. 'Though God knows why they've all made such a fuss.'

'This has got something to do with Grace, hasn't it?' Jeff asked warily. He really didn't want to know, but he might need to justify his actions to Niamh.

'Partly, yes. When I asked if there were any keepsakes – any family collateral – your gran was so forthcoming. It seems she's been wanting to de-clutter her flat for ages and this has given her the motivation to start.'

'So it's a win-win situation,' hazarded Jeff.

Celia hesitated. 'Well, yes, I hope everyone sees it that way, eventually.'

'What about Niamh? How come she's involved?'

'Niamh's been spending quite a lot of time at your gran's, apparently. She's taken it upon herself to co-ordinate the clearance, even though it's quite a trek from out to Hammersmith for her.'

'What's in it for Niamh?'

'Jeff! She's being a dutiful grandchild, that's all. When was the last time you did anything for any of your grandparents?'

'Whenever I called, Gran was always out, and if I got

through, she was always too busy to meet. Perhaps Niamh is her favourite.'

'Or just makes more effort,' suggested Celia. 'There are lots of grandchildren – it can't be easy making time for you all. Now, Niamh won't want to hang on to the albums for ever, so I suggest you call quite soon.'

Jeff muttered, 'You don't want to give her too much time to think of questions to ask, I suppose.'

Celia was sharp. 'Now what do you mean by that?'

'Sorry, Mum,' said Jeff. 'OK. I'll phone Niamh in the week, and let you know how I get on. Then I suppose we'd better make a plan for me to get the albums up to you.' It seemed unnecessarily circuitous, but Jeff assumed there was no room for negotiation. Or should he make one last attempt to co-opt Steve to the arrangement? No! Don't be such a wimp.

'Son, that's excellent.' Jeff couldn't recall the last time he'd enjoyed his mother's approval, and brightened for a moment. 'I know you won't let me down.'

When Jeff identified himself as a Sullivan son, Niamh asked, 'Which one are you?'

Names would not suffice. 'I'm the younger one. Steve is my bro—'

'Steve!' she fairly spat. 'God, he ruined my life!'

'He what?'

'I was in love with him for five years but did he even acknowledge me? No he did not. Bastard. Sorry. You're the other one. What is it you want?'

She was brusque, but not wounding, thankfully. Jeff stumbled over an explanation which to him seemed full of holes he'd be unable to fill in.

'Have you spoken to our grandmother?' Niamh wanted to know.

'Well . . . no, but my mother has.' Was he giving too much away? 'I think it sort of emerged in casual conversation.'

'I didn't know they were in touch. Your mother certainly hasn't spoken to mine in more than a decade. Since the rift.'

Celia hadn't mentioned that. Jeff decided to play it cool. 'Oh, the rift. Yes. Well, we don't talk about that, do we? It just makes everyone feel . . . upset.'

'*Upset?* That's putting it mildly. So, our parents don't speak, we don't speak, but you want to come to my flat. Is that what you're saying?'

He couldn't deny it. 'Yes. When it's convenient. I'm fairly local.'

Niamh considered, as if she were scanning a calendar. 'Come on Saturday at three. I assume you know the address already?'

'Actually, I don't,' said Jeff, relieved to be humbled. 'I've got a pen and pad right here . . .'

Niamh spoke the address slowly – perhaps grudgingly, or maybe just to eliminate the risk of error – and confirmed the appointment. Jeff knew it was one that he'd be unwise to miss.

The last weekend of July was the year's hottest so far, and Jeff was glad to have an excuse to escape the flat, much improved though it was these days. He put on new flip-flops – he hadn't had far to travel – but his feet were sliding around in them and he felt blisters form. He longed to sit down with a cool drink but couldn't expect such an offer from Niamh, who seemed anxious, like a caged bird waiting to flee. Celia had told him that Niamh was a teacher, so he was equipped with small talk about long summer holidays and questions about how she was keeping busy. But it was clear Niamh was in no mood for chat.

'I'm glad you're on time,' she said. 'I'm desperate to get to the park and lie in the sun.'

'I won't keep you,' he said. 'I'll just grab the albums and go.'

She assessed him, suspiciously. He didn't look like Steve, so she wasn't confronting a ghost from her past. Maybe she'd sourced a recent photograph and so had already dealt with any disappointment. Jeff had done no research but Niamh did seem vaguely familiar.

'Then I'd better get them,' she said. 'Won't be a moment. Stay where you are.'

In her temporary absence, Jeff leaned against the dining table, and slid one foot from his sandal. The relief was intense. But the silence was unnerving. The whole building seemed deserted. 'Do you live on your own?' he called.

'By myself in a three bed flat in Zone 2? What do you reckon?'

'Sorry, no, of course not. None of my business.'

'I've got two flatmates,' she replied. 'They're both out. It's a nice day, after all.' Almost immediately, she reappeared. 'Actually, I'm glad to be rid of them.'

At first, Jeff assumed she meant the flatmates. Because he didn't instantly clock the heavy weight in his arms until they dropped involuntarily, and he almost let go of the albums Niamh had burdened him with. He righted them just in time.

Niamh said, 'There's no storage space.' She gestured at what seemed to Jeff like an airy living area, tastefully decorated. 'I really don't know why Gran wanted me to take them but she was pretty insistent. Do you know why?'

Jeff looked at Niamh, then at the volumes he was holding. Tooled leather, a thin film of dust. He suspected they'd spent their recent life in a plastic bag. He could smell polythene. But all that consumed him was a second stolen glance at the feature which had struck him suddenly, thrillingly, the moment before Niamh had re-entered the room. He daren't snatch a third look, even fleetingly, for fear that she'd consider him nosy, and terminate the visit. But he had to look again. *He had to.*

'No,' he lied, trying not to appear flustered. 'I don't know – well, I didn't really ask Mum.'

Niamh gave a thin smile. 'Well, that's my end of the bargain fulfilled. Is there anything else?'

He slid his feet back into his shoes. 'No, no. Not at all. Thanks, Niamh. Thanks very much.'

She guided him towards the door, picking up a canvas bag on the way. 'We'll leave together, shall we?' She put on big sunglasses. 'After you.'

It was the weirdest coincidence, but was it also a perfect gift? Of all the furnishings – a brightly coloured throw, an

Anglepoise lamp, a quirky-shaped shoe rack – what he'd noticed was the framed photos on the mantelpiece. One photo, in particular. Niamh and two other girls. Women. One of them was Minna. *Jeff's* Minna – except she was Niamh's, obviously. One of her flatmates. Fuck! What were the chances? (But if your world is small, it stands to reason that if coincidences happen they're on a tiny canvas.)

What did not seem random was that the first chance to come Jeff's way to make a fresh impression on Niamh saw him dressed down in T-shirt and shorts and bloody flip-flops. Jeff was of the school that you wore them on the beach or on holiday – he hadn't even worn them to the lido. He'd put them on today to be casual, and unassuming. He hadn't applied himself the last time he saw Minna, and today, in preparation for seeing Niamh, he hadn't bothered again.

Imagine what Niamh would say about him! (If she spoke of him at all.) 'God, he was so nervous. And he looked like some wannabe surfer. Pathetic.' She might go further, and evoke her resentment of Steve, tarring Jeff with the same brush of bitterness. 'Steer clear of that family,' she'd warn Minna. Jeff felt despair. Acting as Celia's bitch was shameful enough – dare he sink lower? (Why *had* his mother picked on him? Was he just a Mummy's boy? Was that one of the many detractions that had prompted Sarah to pare herself away? He couldn't help being younger than Steve.)

But later, Jeff dared to see a ray of light and reconsidered. In his new scenario Niamh and Minna were not close friends, but bonded only by the expense of London rentals. Was Jeff alone in perceiving Niamh to be a little on the frosty side? What if Minna felt the same way? What if – should he and Minna ever get it together – she had to smuggle him into the flat under cover of darkness, for fear of Niamh's blanket disapproval? (It was possible that Niamh shuddered at love, having been rejected herself.) Should he have looked for drainpipes that he could shin up? Would it be a relationship based on snatched opportunities? On fear?

Oh, chill, he told himself. Even if he had to risk life and limb on his external ascent, Minna would be inside to welcome him. Minna would make anything worthwhile.

Work was quiet in the first week of August, which was just as well because the enduring heat made everybody listless. It was the excuse Jeff employed to remain inactive. He'd worked out Minna's e-mail but he did not message her. Nor did he try to track her movements – easy enough, since everyone runs on clockwork. Couldn't they accidentally on purpose coincide? She might have been on holiday, of course.

Fortunately, he was not completely inert. When the weather broke, violently, a week later, Jeff was galvanised into action. He made the call he'd been putting off for fear of failure.

'Oh, hey there, Niamh. It's your cousin Jeff.'

'I know who you are. You came round the other Saturday.'

'Well, yes, of course. That's why I'm ringing. I just wanted to thank you for the albums.'

'They're what you wanted?'

He hadn't looked. He'd handed them over to Celia, who'd met him at lunchtime on Tuesday. 'Perfect, thank you. Mum's delighted. Actually, she wanted to thank you herself.'

'That's nice.'

'But I said I'd do it.'

'Right. Well, appreciation noted.'

'There's one other thing . . .' He looked out the window. It was tipping it down. He'd have to speak up or his voice would be lost. (His opportunity.) What a contrast to last weekend. The temperature had dropped. He'd left his socks on after changing from the office. Well, it was a bit more formal, which seemed appropriate.

'What's that?' asked Niamh, but not coldly, not briskly. Was it warm in Balham? Couldn't be. Perhaps she'd had a change of heart. About what?

'I noticed a photo on your mantelpiece. Three women. One of them was you and one of them was someone I work with.'

'*You work with Minna?*'

She'd practically screeched it and Jeff recoiled. The rain got louder, so he had to speak up. 'Well, not work, exactly. Our companies are based in the same building. Coincidence, isn't it?'

In a steely voice, Niamh said only, 'Yes.'

Jeff, however, was driven by inertia. He braked to check his words. 'Hang on, Niamh, when I said I worked with one of the women – your flatmates, I assumed – you knew it was Minna. How did you know that?'

'Our other flatmate is a teacher, so it couldn't be her.' Niamh sounded indifferent. Then, 'And Minna mentioned she'd had a date with someone called Jeff. I just put two and two together.'

'Just now? She didn't show you a photo of me?'

'Do you really think she'd have done that, Jeff?'

Although she could not see it, he hung his head. 'Well, no. It wasn't a successful date. I went on far too much about my ex-wife. Sarah. Did you ever meet her?'

'Afraid not. No. But you can see why Minna might not have savoured the story.'

'She told you about it, I assume?'

'Enough.'

He paused, listened to the rain, which had eased. He said, 'The thing is, I'd really like a second chance. I'd like to see her again.'

'Don't you work in the same building?'

'Well, yes. We do. I told you that.'

'So aren't you well placed to organise another meeting?'

'You'd think so, I agree, but it never seems to happen. So I just wondered if you'd . . . well . . .' How ludicrous it seemed to seek help from Niamh whom he knew even less well than Minna.

'If I'd put in a good word for you?'

Was she putting words into his mouth? Jeff wanted help but he did not want to feel coerced. 'Well, it might help. You never know.'

She sighed, perhaps sympathetically. 'Look, Jeff, I'd like to help, really I would. You're family, after all. And so, I'll tell you this: I'd leave Minna alone for now. Not just because of your previous form, but because of where she's at. Not a good place, in a word. She tried to see someone a couple of months ago but it didn't work out. I think she was quite cut up by it. And she's got two exes who she doesn't quite know how to deal with. She's got her hands full. Do you see what I'm saying?'

Jeff understood perfectly, but it was only Niamh's interpretation, filtered through her own experience. Jeff suddenly resented what he saw as Niamh's intrusion. He had loads of cousins – others might offer more compatible points of view, more palatable guidance. But they weren't here now. And they didn't know Minna. Like it or not, he needed Niamh.

He said, 'Well, put like that. She seems—' He let the question fall away.

Niamh offered, 'Troubled.' But not harshly. 'Ask yourself,' she went on, 'is someone like that really what *you* need?'

Perhaps Niamh knew about his own messy life. Perhaps she thought she was doing Jeff a favour. He wanted to say, *You're just bitter because you can't have Steve.* But that was uncalled for, and Niamh sounded so reasonable. So he said, 'No, I suppose not. I should thank you for the warning, I guess.'

'It's no problem. Like I said, we're family. And to save any further awkwardness, I won't mention this conversation. It's in nobody's interest to do that. Agreed?'

'Yes. Sure,' said Jeff. He thanked her, and ended the call as fast as was polite.

He could warn Celia that Niamh was difficult and to be avoided – whatever the demands of Celia's next request might entail. Maybe Jeff's own next enterprise was to wean Celia off the family-at-large, and focus on the four of them. Take things back to the way they had been. The way it *had* been, once. (He wouldn't exclude Alyx, of course.) Jeff felt the stirrings of a bold plan to steer his family back on course. Nobody would expect this accomplishment from him but no doubt they'd all approve, eventually. Well, as a plan it was a way to salvage something from his encounter with Niamh.

Jeff genuinely intended to take action. This was a moment in which the narrow boundaries of his world had expanded. But quite soon – and through no fault of his own – he felt the walls narrow once again.

Jeff finally heard from Sarah, who'd caught up with Tara and 'filled her in'. Well, fine, he'd thought – your right, I guess. But then, days later, clearing spam, Jeff reread the original correspondence. And decided that no, it wasn't all right. Sarah had got there first, but Jeff had also been a friend for seven years. Sarah had taken things offline, and had pulled the conversation out from underneath him. Why had she done that? What had she written that she didn't want Jeff to see? Allegations against him, or news of her emergent life away from him? Perhaps Sarah had told Tara not to contact Jeff. Or implied that Jeff wasn't interested in their old acquaintance. Why hadn't he just hit reply straight away?

As Jeff lay in bed, unable to sleep, it was as if nothing else mattered. He mentally composed an e-mail to Sarah outlining his irritation. He'd never been confrontational but his words were spoiling for a fight. Was it a quality Sarah might have appreciated seeing? Well, now she'd just punish his tirade with a simple one-liner to make him want to shrivel and crawl into a hole. (She'd sent more than a few like that, professionally, over the years – she'd joke about it with him. It wouldn't be funny now.) Jeff gave up.

Steve sent a text at the end of August. *'Mate, I know I had a go at you for making a pest of yourself to Alyx but you didn't have to take it to the opposite extreme and TOTALLY FORGET HER BIRTHDAY. (It was Tuesday.) Luckily, she's a very popular lady – you're not going to disagree, right? – and it's no big deal. Just thought I'd mention it. Catch you soon.'* Jeff was horrified. It wasn't that Sarah had handled family birthdays – each had taken care of their own side. Jeff was sure he hadn't missed last year's, even when he could have been forgiven his neglect. He had no excuse this year. Nothing excused his behaviour.

And then, in mid-September, Jeff suddenly lost his job. His results were to blame, Guy explained. They were down on other people's, although, to be fair, in positive growth. 'But look at the targets,' Jeff had dared to challenge Guy's ruling. 'Look at the budget.' If the budget hadn't been ambitious enough surely something ought to have been said months ago. Someone else was to blame for that. They'd practically deceived him! Jeff's words had cut no ice. They hadn't convinced him, much, either.

A junior in marketing and an analyst on a fixed contract were also given the flick so it can't have been personal. Five per cent of the workforce, so the minuscule headline in the industry bulletin would claim. And then it would be yesterday's news but still Jeff's future. Apparently, it was widely known that the business had had a dismal July, a sluggish August and do-not-ask September. More heads were sure to roll. Guy's PA offered Jeff a taxi voucher 'for your day of reckoning, whenever that is. They're like gold dust so don't tell a soul. By the way, we're a month in arrears with the recycling firm so if you could take your rubbish down to lower ground when you leave, it'd be an enormous help to Facilities.' Proof that the writing was on the wall for all concerned.

Nevertheless, Jeff couldn't shake the suspicion that his dismissal had everything to do with the way he'd completely cocked up Alison's visit in the summer. Would she have given him such a bad press that the London office felt obliged to remove him from the payroll? Was it within her power to send trans-Atlantic edicts? It was entirely possible Jeff had had it coming to him even then.

The first person Jeff told was Steve. On the fateful day, they'd arranged to meet, although Jeff had been given leave to finish early – on the proviso that he would return the following morning, as if all his anxiety about the future would dry up overnight. He decided to walk to their meeting place at the top of Haverstock Hill but still had time for two drinks before Steve arrived.

'You look wrecked,' his brother greeted him. 'What's up?'

Already light-headed, Jeff let rip and repeated what Guy, in

HR's presence, had told him. The official line was that it all came down to efficiency and streamlining.

Steve said, 'Losing your job is on that list of stressful events, isn't it?' Helpfully, he summoned the information on his phone. 'It's called the Holmes and Rahe stress scale.' He nodded, thoughtfully. 'Interesting. It's six down from divorce and one above marriage. But there are forty-three in total.'

'I'm not planning to collect them all,' Jeff said.

Steve grimaced. 'Glad to hear it. Seriously, how much shit can a person take? Who wants to find out?' He shook his head. 'So, what sort of timeframe are you facing? They'll pay you off, presumably, since you've been there so long?'

The plan was that Jeff would work until the end of the year – and thank God it wasn't sooner. The shops had already begun to gear up for Christmas but like most other citizens, Jeff was far from ready to accept its close proximity. His unemployment would only bring its insidious artificial industry nearer, leaving him feeling even more indolent and cheerless.

Steve must have forgotten his offhand comparison between the proceeds of redundancy and divorce, because he linked the two only in topping and tailing Jeff's 'shit year'. It had been seventeen months now, in fact, but even Jeff had stopped counting.

If Steve seemed to be lacking in sympathy, it might have been because he'd been self-employed for so long. He couldn't imagine what it was like to be dismissed. Jeff could have furnished an answer: it was humiliating, once the resentment faded. Or, perhaps, Steve was simply fed up with Jeff's ongoing passivity and was waiting for him to take control of his life, unaided. Did Steve feel he'd been carrying his younger brother all these years? Would Steve finally have enough and cast Jeff aside? Families fall out all the time.

This was the fear that prompted Jeff's declaration: 'I'm OK about it, really.' He added, for good measure: 'Maybe it just hasn't sunk in.'

But he knew it had; he just had no idea how to handle it.

It had been some time since Celia mentioned her search for collateral for Grace, but did anyone think her pursuit had been abandoned? Jeff had willingly let himself be distracted by other concerns, even though he'd been instrumental in executing Celia's plan. He was disquieted to think he'd inherited Celia's instinct for subterfuge and skulduggery, assuming discretion was the watchword without needing it confirmed. Now he had a reason to keep his participation under wraps. It kept Niamh at bay. Now he'd lost his job, he really hadn't the will for another encounter with his embittered cousin.

Jeff hadn't been around to celebrate Celia's results when she'd finally met Grace, who had acquired last-minute tickets to one of the late Proms for herself and a friend. The two women had had an afternoon strolling in the grounds around the Albert Hall. They'd got on famously. Celia handed over a small selection of photos which she'd culled from the albums Niamh had provided. 'Grace was *thrilled*, so it was all worthwhile,' his mother phoned to say (when he did not call to ask).

Jeff intended to call now, once he'd slept on the news of his dismissal and had come closer to knowing how he really felt, but Celia and Nigel pre-empted with a text which conveyed sympathy but not practical assistance. Steve must have fed back Jeff's glimmer of optimism about the future, and they'd seized it. Jeff imagined it: press send, lights off, head under the pillow, problem dismissed. Had life for the Sullivans really come to that?

For several days after Jeff's meeting with Guy and HR, life went on, as if nothing had happened. Jeff wasn't excluded from meetings or relieved of any duties. He'd been asked not to tell clients, so remained diligent and helpful.

Then he made the mistake of letting the post room know his news. They'd never been close associates, but always offered a smile and a chat if Jeff stopped by. Apparently, discussing the situation contravened the terms of his consultation period. Unwittingly, they'd tipped off other people – who actually cared? – and the news firecrackered up to HR, and his leaving date was hastily brought forward to next week; not quite the end of October. (Was the saving in salary the reason? Did they think Jeff would act irresponsibly as he worked on borrowed time? If that were the case, then they didn't know him at all. He doubted it would trouble them too deeply.)

A dive near the office called Monroe's was booked for Jeff's farewell. The shortening of his notice period was the reason given for the limited attendance. A whole floor hadn't even known he was going. It meant the small group could chat informally about any subject other than Jeff's superfluity. He came away with a lavish bunch of flowers and a generous clump of theatre tokens – apparently, Jeff never missed a West End debut. 'Keep in touch,' they insisted, checking LinkedIn connections before the night was out and jotting down his personal e-mail and phone numbers on the backs of coasters. Jeff had been given some lovely farewell cards, too. People wished him luck in 'moving on' and in the 'next stage of his career' as if guaranteeing continuity. He was moved by his colleagues' affection.

Jeff wondered what might be his lasting impression of this year's final quarter. He wasn't *grateful* for what had happened, obviously. He knew the relief that comes of being spared actions, and had found it wanting. He was pleased to have gone out with dignity – he'd challenged Guy, but he hadn't exploded, or imploded. Had they *assumed* he'd be fine with their decision? Had they thought: Well, we need to lose people – who can cope with it best? Jeff won't starve. He has no dependents, to say nothing of key accounts. Jeff's our man. It wasn't often Jeff heard acclaim of any kind, so in a funny sort of way he could live with this.

But he couldn't deal with Niamh's corrosive influence. Suddenly, Jeff longed to suppress her miserly, debilitating actions. How dare she dissuade him from pursuing Minna! How dare she discourage Minna!

Jeff ought to find Niamh's weak spot. He could investigate Steve's version of their back story. It might require underhand tactics undreamed of in a day job – but it was the right way to play the work/life balance. Except, could family be treated like that? Wasn't it easier to be ruthless with colleagues who you didn't need to like in the first place?

But Jeff wasn't, and had never been, confrontational. Niamh was best avoided. As soon as he reached this conclusion, his case against her crumbled. Could he *really* believe that Niamh had impaired his chances of getting together with Minna? Wasn't it actually the case that when the doors of Go Aware closed behind him, so did his access to the woman he felt sure he could grow to love?

PART THREE
A MISTY
START TO
THURSDAY

Whether crossing a corridor or a county, an office move is always unsettling. Macsamphire Strutt's – which finally took place in the first week of July – was no exception. For weeks Minna's team had been subdued by a raft of e-mails that threatened the purge of possessions not boxed and labelled before the end of June. These menacing messages were followed by days of unnerving silence. Four new names were added to the distribution list for the 'Redeployment' missives. None of them was known to Minna and her colleagues, although Kerry suggested they were dummy addresses, planted only to monitor bitching about senior management. Adam suggested organising a meet-up, but then reconsidered. 'What if it turns out they're being moved for being agitators? Do we really want to be linked by association?' Steph accused Adam of scaremongering. He pointed out that *he* wasn't to blame for the disruption. Minna feared the addresses belonged to real people, whose welfare was as undetermined as her own.

There had been moments when a tide surged towards objection. Minna joined the rallying, wanting nothing more than to be part of this enduring team, but a little voice halted her: *can* it be stopped? The voice went further. Would it be so terrible if it weren't? Minna took a nefarious look at another life with different colleagues – with the current team reassigned to the status of friends to chat to in the corridor, to meet now and then for lunch. She shuddered at her treachery.

Astrid gave the heads-up that Steph's new desk would be south-facing, but Steph needed no inducement to blossom. Minna noticed that several of the global e-mails came from Steph, all announcing good news or positive initiatives. Normally, Minna gave such messages a barely cursory inspection but of course she read Steph's. She began to see that she'd missed this stream of encouragement from on high, this brave belief in the integrity and skills of the company. Minna noticed also that many of the tasks Steph performed were part of her own remit. Common words cropped up in reports. So did specialist programmes and client profiles, even names. Reading these reports had been like mastering a new language, until she realised it employed the one she already had. Perhaps it was time for Minna to lift her game?

Her grasp on Kerry's new situation was hazy. Minna was reluctant to make a direct enquiry; and if she asked Steph and Steph fed back to Kerry, it might generate undue tension. (Minna had heard that Kerry and Steph had bonded, so the old quartet had become a pair. The maths would have suited Steph, for sure.) Adam remained available, so Minna leapt on the chance when they found themselves in the kitchen – their old kitchen – on her way to a meeting. 'How do you think Kerry's getting on?' she asked.

Adam pondered. 'I think she's reserving judgement. From what I hear, she set down a few conditions for the redeployment and she's waiting to hear when they'll be ... well, you know ... Ratified.'

'Ratified?'

'Maybe implemented is a better word. Yes. Implemented.'

Minna said, 'I didn't know we were allowed to make ... conditions.'

'We're not,' Adam agreed. 'But Kerry's good at contracts. It's the landlord in her, I suppose. In fact, I heard they were considering farming her out to the legal team one or two days a week when Colette goes on maternity leave.'

Adam himself quickly cultivated optimism. One bright morning, he returned from a meeting with his new manager looking gleeful.

'What happened?' asked Kerry, severely.

'We went through my appraisal,' Adam explained. 'You know how Carol used to get us to fill them in because she didn't have time for one-to-ones?' His colleagues nodded, but committed nothing further. Adam continued, 'Well, apparently it's against company policy. But Charlie – my new boss – just tore mine up. I'm glad, because my brother-in-law wrote it, in return for the Glastonbury tickets Laura and I had to give up when the girls got chicken pox. It sounded impressive but it's not really me. I've got new objectives, now. I'm really chuffed.' Denied any kind of endorsement, he forged ahead. 'Look, it's important for your career to have focus. Sometimes you have to branch out to achieve that. Don't you think?'

Adam had gone out on a limb, and Minna's heart thudded. Would he go as far as saying he couldn't wait to move on?

He said, 'I realise now if this hadn't happened I probably would have had to leave in order to get ahead. I mean, I've got a family to support.'

As if this reality were not startling in itself, Adam appeared amazed that he'd arrived at it in advance of a crisis. Minna was full of admiration. Was now the moment to ask what had led him to this job in the first place? It might seem a backward step when there was so much to say of the present and what lay ahead.

Unsurprisingly, Minna lacked clarity on her own feelings. Suffice to say, it had been odd to front up to a new workspace on a new floor – it turned out that the space she'd occupied with Adam, Stephanie and Kerry had been known as 'the coffin', and was speedily converted into a massage suite – only to log in to the familiar system with the old password. There were extra software privileges, but Minna was denied access to certain folders and shared documents. For a fortnight or so she felt nostalgic for the L drive.

A week into her new role, Minna glanced at the corner of her screen, and allowed herself a luxurious stretch. It was 3.47 pm, a Tuesday. Her day had been devoted to reformatting a spreadsheet which needed further tweaks before being mailed onwards. That'd take her comfortably to six. (She needed her own schedule, in lieu of prompts from Steph.) Minna opened a fresh e-mail, and almost immediately the telephone rang.

'Minna! Hi.'

'Ju—!' she burst out, but became hideously self-conscious. '—lian,' she whispered. 'It's great to hear from you.' She took a quick glance around. No one had stirred. Well, why *would* they?

'Sorry I haven't been in touch,' said Julian. 'I've been a bit busy. I remembered your birthday, though. Just didn't manage to get the card sent in time.'

'Don't worry,' she said, swamped by raw affection which had seemingly come from nowhere. 'So what's new?'

'Mostly, long hours on a job in Clerkenwell. The money's good, because I've been up against a deadline, you see. I've decided to go abroad.'

Minna thought, You've said that before. But you didn't go anywhere. She wasn't being critical. But it seemed unfair – and unproductive – to delve into the past.

Julian called her bluff. 'I've said that before, I know, but this time I mean it.'

'So what's the plan?' asked Minna, trying to keep her voice low but needing to compete with the background babble which had broken out.

'I'm going to Sydney,' he said. 'I'll be working with Ady. Got a visa sorted, and everything. I leave next Monday.'

'Wow,' said Minna. 'That's soon. And it's . . . exciting.'

'Is it?' Julian wondered. 'I don't know. It's not like travelling but it's a bit different. I'll be doing all the things I'm doing here, basically. Only there.'

You won't be meeting up with me while you're there, Minna thought. That'll be different. But she did not let it needle her.

'You will come back . . .?' she said.

'I might have to, but I'll stay if I can. Anyway . . . it would be great to see you before I go. My evenings are a bit booked up, and I expect you've got lots on too. But I've got to be in Islington on Thursday, so I could swing by the office, sort of mid-afternoon. If that suited you and . . . well, everyone.'

'That sounds good,' she said. 'Only, I need to warn you. Well, it isn't anything, really. But we've had a bit of a move around. We're not all at the same desks.'

'Oh, right. Well, in that case, had you better check with the others before we make a plan? I mean, there might be meetings . . .' He was suddenly nervous, as if the new office arrangement was the final frontier.

'It'll be fine,' she assured him. 'Just let us know what time you're coming, OK, and I'll let everyone know.'

'Well, OK. If you're sure. That'll be . . . nice. See you Thursday, Minna.'

'Look forward to it,' she said. 'Bye.'

She put down the phone and picked it up again. She phoned Steph, to check her availability later in the week.

'Oh, Julian! That'll be nice,' said Steph.

Kerry was thrilled. 'Oh! Terrific. Julian! Dear Julian!'

Adam said: 'Great stuff, Minna. Thanks for organising.'

She nodded, and set about deleting old e-mails, reflecting that not long ago she would have said, 'You're welcome,' as if she'd set out to do them all a favour.

* * *

168

Minna's new colleagues were friendly and accommodating. 'Not that you'd expect them to be baying for your blood,' said Sharmila. 'Don't you?' offered Niamh, by way of a counter-argument. 'Have you deposed someone who's been shunted aside?' Minna hadn't asked who had occupied her desk before her, because there was a half-empty bottle of Benylin at the back of her pedestal drawer. It belonged to a fixed contract temp, who'd gone on to score a fantastic permanent role in her home town in the south-west. Minna hoped, therefore, that her desk harboured no bad karma. She wondered about asking for an address so she could send the elixir on, but decided not to mess between the present and the past.

Her colleague Andi – two desks away – loomed above her desk the Thursday afternoon of Minna's third week. Despite the cautious approach the padded bag was clearly identifiable as a farewell collection.

'It's for FT,' Andi said, almost apologetically. 'She leaves tomorrow.' She shook the envelope, meaningfully. 'This got trapped for a couple of days in Creative.'

'FT?' Minna queried, thinking of the newspaper.

'Felicia Townsend. Visual merchandising analysis.'

'So you won't be the new girl for much longer, Minna!' came a reassuring cry across the partition.

Andi said, 'Yes she will. They won't be seeking a replacement.'

'Is there another recruitment freeze?' asked Minna, casting her mind back to the start of her first incarnation at Macsamphire Strutt. She wondered, thrillingly, if she were perhaps a pawn in some clandestine game played at the heart of management.

'Not that I know of.' Andi dived in. 'Word is, FT's leaving under a bit of a cloud. But she was much liked – years of service, ran the Wimbledon sweepstake – so the least we can do is spare a pound or two.' She shook the padded bag again. 'Those of us who knew her. I don't suppose you did, Minna? So no need to feel obliged.'

The choice was simple. FT, who was leaving – which meant Minna might never encounter her – wouldn't care what she did. But if she signed the card, popped in a few coins, she'd be viewed by her colleagues as a team player and a joiner-in.

'I haven't met her,' said Minna, 'but I'm happy to contribute.'

At least she didn't have to set the bar by beginning the collection. When she peered in, which was a bit like staring into the back of an ambulance, she saw a pair of tenners and four IOUs. She suspected that people had taken change, because there were more signatures than banknotes – she didn't interpret this as a measure of FT's standing. Job done, she checked her name off the list, and passed it on, not expecting to see it again. But come Friday morning, there it sat in her in-tray. Minna double-checked: yes, she *had* ticked her name off. Well. It must have come from someone who hadn't yet clocked who she was. She married the unmarked names with the secret floor plan she'd winkled out of Astrid and handed on the packet with conviction to someone called Della.

'I didn't know you knew FT.' Della's tone was laced with accusation.

'Felicia?' said Minna lightly, hoping it inspired familiarity rather than contempt. 'Well, we haven't met, but I'm all for wishing her the best.'

'Fiona,' said Della. 'It's Fiona. She's FT because there was another Fiona in her class at school and she was forced to change. Apparently, it came to Chinese burns in the end.'

'Oh?' said Minna. 'Really.'

'Yes, and our good wishes aren't really going to help very much. But I put a fiver in, to show willing.'

The collection seemed no heavier than yesterday, but still Minna declined to read anything into it. She was confused about the name, still, but she didn't pursue it. She said, 'Have they found evidence against her?'

Della's eyes bulged. 'What do you mean?'

'Well, Andi said—' No, she must not name names so early in her placement; it might lead to false alliances. 'I mean, I heard, there were ... unresolved issues concerning her departure.'

Della rolled her eyes. 'Her mother's got dementia and there isn't a care home in London that she'll settle in for longer than a week!'

Minna blanched. 'Oh, I thought ...'

'Yes, it's a crying shame. I mean, she's only been working here for nine months—'

'Isn't it years?'

'Her mother's been on the slide for years, that's for sure, but it's got worse since Christmas. Things looked on the up in the autumn – they'd chosen a fabulous care home in Surbiton – which is why FT went back to full-time work.'

Fiona. Felicia. A long-timer. A recent incumbent. Minna wondered if her candid colleagues were speaking of the same person. Or was the fault with Minna? Had she had too much new information to absorb, and had suffered an overload? That seemed more likely.

Minna went along to the drinks in the boardroom, because she could afford to wind down near the end of a full-on week, and because she was keen to see just who actually was leaving. She deserved some clarity: after all, she'd invested three-fifty.

She was surprised and relieved to see Steph in the corner, casting her gaze about, as if looking for friendly faces. Minna made a beeline for her. 'Steph! It's so good to see you.'

'Very nice to see you, too, Minna,' said Steph, still looking round. 'How's tricks?'

'Oh fine, fine thanks. Think I'm getting the hang of things. Slowly. Hey, I didn't know you knew Felicia. Or Fiona.'

'Is it Felicia? I'm not sure. I'm here for the snacks, to tell you the truth. I was on my way to the shops and caught the whiff of Twiglets. Now I'm here I'm not sure I wouldn't prefer something sweet.'

'Stay for the speeches, at least,' said Minna, as she was handed a glass of fizz. Steph accepted one also and said, 'Oh, just for a bit.'

There was more mingling and banter, and bowls of snacks

were passed round, and glasses refreshed. The black-and-charcoal brigade coolly snickered in one corner. Minna saw Astrid, but she was on the unreachable far side of the room, so she didn't bother to fight her way across to join her. Besides, she had Steph for company. No one else from her old team was present – had they received invitations? Had they even *heard* of FT?

Twenty minutes later, the deputy CEO swanned in. This struck Minna as odd: if FT really *was* leaving under a cloud wouldn't she have been instantly removed and not accorded a celebration with quite nice prosecco and plainly non-own-brand crisps? The speech delivered a major surprise because it emerged that FT was actually Fenella. (Her parents were not named in evidence against her leaving.) Finally, FT spoke herself. She thanked everyone for the 'amazingly rewarding experience' of working at Macsamphire Strutt – which probably explained why she and Minna had failed to cross paths – and begged everyone to stay in touch. There followed a few more jokes and laughs, and everyone was encouraged to 'Drink on.'

Minna longed to confront Andi and Della to challenge their descriptions, but inconveniently, neither of them seemed to be in the room. Had she imagined their conversations? Then she thought about the mad scrabble they'd had in their old team to try to work out what may have happened to Steph that day. Steph – who was solidly here beside her, apparently happy with savoury, after all. And Minna thought: no one knows very much about anyone, really. We hardly ever get beyond names and roles. What a setback at the end of such a cheerful party.

Minna was delighted to catch Adam in the first-floor kitchen, on Monday, which was his first day back at work from a week in the Lake District. It was a vacation he seemed reluctant to be drawn to discuss.

Sniffing Friday's milk, he asked, 'Have you heard from Julian recently?'

'He sent a postcard from Sydney,' Minna replied, guardedly. 'Didn't I mention it?'

Adam shook his head. 'Perhaps you did. You must have done.'

But his tone suggested that Minna's reply was inadequate. The only thing she could think to ask was, 'Have you?'

'No, but the girls were asking after him,' said Adam.

Minna had never heard her former team mates so described. 'Steph and Kerry?'

'No, my daughters!' Adam's eyes lit up. 'They saw quite a bit of him at Christmas, you see, and—'

'Julian came to you for Christmas?' She almost added, You never said—

'Yes, he didn't really have anywhere to go so we invited him round to ours.'

Minna's voice cracked. 'Julian was alone on Christmas Day?'

'No, by then he'd arranged a lift so he could visit his parents. Getting there sounded like quite an ordeal but he was insistent. You have to go home for Christmas, don't you?'

Minna nodded. 'Of course. But you saw him over the holiday?' Don't be jealous of Adam, she warned herself. It isn't nice.

'Christmas Eve,' he said. 'He came round to deliver some presents for the girls. You see, they'd really liked the yak story, so Julian somehow found two toy versions.'

'Toy yaks?'

'Yes. Identical, except one had a green tie and the other's was red.'

'Yaks?' said Minna. 'With ties?'

Adam laughed. 'Yes. Tibetan yaks. Surely he told you about the yaks in Tibet.' It rang a bell, vaguely. Adam was eager. 'Didn't he tell you what happened in Tibet?'

The story had unfolded in her head, and was almost over. Minna did her best to slow it down. 'Yes! Of course. Brilliant, wasn't it?'

Adam beamed. 'The girls were spellbound. It was yak, yak, yacketty yak in our house for weeks after Julian's first visit. I think they mostly liked the sound of it. Then, when he came back—'

Minna needed to slow down. 'His first visit? He came *before* Christmas Eve?'

'Yes. After you came back from Australia, but before he left work. And after. At one time, you could say he was a regular visitor. Of course, Laura and I weren't deceived.'

'You weren't?'

'No way! It was the girls he came for. They adore him. In fact, Josie referred to him as Uncle Julian on bonfire night which pissed off my brother and Laura's sister. Funny, I can't remember him saying he even *liked* children.'

'No. Not to me, either,' said Minna.

Adam laughed. 'But those toy yaks . . . Don't get me wrong, Minna, they're hideous. Impossible to keep clean – all that . . . hair.' Adam sniffed. 'Even though they've been in the bath. Several times. You almost feel sorry for them. Like they're real.'

What was Adam getting at? Was he saying he was *jealous* of his daughters? Wasn't that absurd? Minna had lost her hold on Julian to Adam, so maybe logic prescribed Adam's would be passed on too. But they'd all lost him to Australia, and his recent visit had proven to be something of a wake. How they'd grieved. But was the inference now that Adam's loss was deeper than Minna's own? She bridled. Even if it were true, she didn't think the point needed to be made.

The kettle started to whistle. Minna was so absorbed in her own thoughts that she'd practically forgotten Adam was there, until he tapped her elbow and suggested she pour water into the mugs.

It could have ended there, an awkward, off-the-record conversation, but Adam wanted more. 'So, Minna . . . are you seeing anyone at the moment?'

'Sorry?'

Adam faltered, 'I mean, I was just wondering – tell me if it's none of my business, which of course it isn't but – well, I suppose I did *wonder*, did you finish with Julian because you fancied someone else?'

It wasn't an accusation, but it stung. In a panic, Minna flared. 'Is that because no one in their right mind would dump Julian?'

Adam saw he'd caused offence, and backed down. 'Absolutely not. I'm sure it was six of one, half a dozen of the other.' Minna's look made it clear he was not helping himself. Or her. He spread his hands. 'Look, I'm sorry, like I said, it's none of my business.'

But Minna's defence was crumbling. She said, 'Has Julian been seeing anyone?'

'I wouldn't know. Like I said, I haven't spoken to him for ages.'

'So he didn't ask you to find out if I was?'

Adam shook his head. '*You* were in touch with him most recently.'

He had a point, of course. 'Perhaps he wouldn't tell us if he were,' she said. 'He has no obligation to, I guess.'

Adam considered this. 'It just wouldn't occur to him.'

'To tell us?' Minna queried.

'No, to start a new relationship. I think he's sort of given up on doing very much at all. When he was at ours, Laura was asking him all these really interesting questions about the things he'd done, the places he'd been. All he wanted to do was talk to the kids. We might as well not have been there. Odd, don't you think?'

Minna nodded, recognising her own experience. She said, 'Maybe he just doesn't know what he wants. All *I* know is, it just didn't work out between us. That happens sometimes.'

He smiled. 'True, but it's a shame. You're both terrific people. You deserve to be happy. I hope you will be.'

'Thanks, Adam,' said Minna. But it felt wrong to rise to the compliment.

'We all think so. Steph and Kerry and me. We're all in agreement about that.'

Minna smiled. 'We'd better get back. People will start to talk ...'

Adam rolled his eyes, and laughed. 'No offence, Minna, but office romance isn't really my bag. Aside from the fact that Laura would kill me, I'd be too bloody knackered to do anything. Fact is, I generally come in to work for a rest.'

As if the changes at work hadn't been enough to contend with, all was far from well in Minna's shared Balham flat. Minna and her flatmates were disturbed by the prospect of homelessness. Their landlord had made noises about selling the property. Niamh, allegedly friendly with the landlord's niece, promised to obtain a reprieve, but never managed the necessary conversations.

When Minna referred to her anxiety in the office – her new office – she wasn't expecting assistance, just updating news. She had mentioned it to Andi, who must have passed it on, because before the day was out, an e-mail came in from Kerry – who now worked two floors below – to say that one of the flats she and Dave owned was empty. It was in Stockwell, so brilliantly close to where they were now.

'It's been repainted and had new flooring put down,' Kerry wrote. 'We had a couple all set to move in but they've withdrawn unexpectedly. Let me know if you and your mates are interested.'

Even in this new age of friendship, the notion of Kerry as landlady was alarming. Her rigorous policing of tenants was legendary; she'd often make repairs in advance of damage done. But to reject the offer outright would be ungrateful, and perhaps churlish. So after work one evening, Minna made her maiden motorcycle voyage on the back of Kerry's Kawasaki and inspected the apartment.

Of course it was immaculate, despite the catalogue of disasters that had befallen its recent tenants. 'I'd trust *you*, Minna, to look after it,' said Kerry. 'So what do you think?'

The pressure was maddening. Minna managed to express her gratitude and said she'd let Kerry know.

She told Niamh and Sharmila. So far, it was her only contribution to their housing crisis, which was causing a degree of tension around shared bottles of wine.

Sharmila alighted on the offer, coolly. 'Our problem solved!'

But Niamh was circumspect. 'Maybe it's not such a good idea ...'

'Why not?'

'Minna might not want to live with her boss.'

'She isn't my boss,' Minna clarified.

Niamh said, 'Sounds worse than a boss, from all that you've said about her.'

Minna felt instant remorse. Had she really depicted such an unflattering image?

Sharmila closed the cover of this week's Sunday supplement. 'Loads of colleagues live and work together. But your team are an exception, aren't they? In many ways.'

'They are?' asked Minna. Of course it was true. Wouldn't it have been more useful to hear the remark months ago? Then she thought, Well, maybe I *had* heard it. She just might not have taken it in, distracted by other things that she perceived to be going on, whether they were happening or not. It sounded likely.

'Yes,' said Sharmila. 'Anyway, my worry would be that this colleague – Kerry, isn't it? – might be trying to keep tabs on you. Or keep hold of you. Not in a sinister way—'

Minna flinched. 'Sinister?'

'No. Not saying she's a bunny boiler. But perhaps she wants to *claim* you. Have you ever thought of that?' With this, she returned to her magazine.

Minna shivered, but felt obliged to defend her friends and former colleagues. 'It wouldn't be like that,' she said. 'They all switch off when they leave the office because they've got more important things to do, and more important people to see.' She added, coolly, 'We all do.' It pleased her to make this assertion.

'Well,' Niamh instructed, 'ultimately it's your decision.'

'But it's not!' Minna objected. 'We'd all have to live there.' At least there had been no talk of living separately, or for Niamh and Sharmila to find somewhere together which would cast Minna adrift.

Niamh spread her hands. 'I don't have a problem with it.'

'Nor me,' said Sharmila, and offered a fleeting smile.

Minna said she would be happy to accept Kerry's offer if everyone was in agreement and nothing better came their way. She added, 'But let's keep our options open, just in case.'

Minna couldn't wait to sign off for a week's vacation in the sun. A single thirty-one year old woman accompanying her parents on a package deal is not an unknown phenomenon, so she had no reason to feel like a failure. Comments at work were forged in envy – 'My parents stopped including me the day I turned eighteen' – and admiration – 'You're so lucky that you get on well enough with your mum. Two nights is the most we manage together. Then it's daggers drawn.' No one thought it showed an inability to devise her own entertainment. Besides, no other offers were forthcoming.

Minna returned to Balham to find there had been no news from their landlord, and no further discussion. Perhaps it was a done deal that they'd live in Kerry's flat. Understandably, Kerry required an answer. A week after Minna's return, she fronted up at Minna's workspace. It was her first visit, so she scrutinised the set-up. She ran her finger along the smooth curve of Minna's rounded desk. It was difficult to perceive approval or otherwise.

She said, 'I'll be frank, I'm losing income, Minna. I can wait another week, and then I'll have to advertise.'

Minna promised to resolve the matter swiftly and determined to broach the issue that night. Sharmila was home early, and Minna felt they could have reached a decision then and there. But they needed Niamh's input. While waiting, Minna reminded Sharmila of the new flat's advantages and Sharmila agreed it sounded like an excellent option.

Minna was nervous by the time Niamh got home. She opened wine, largely for her own benefit. 'We've been talking about the flat . . .' she hazarded. She glanced at Sharmila whose look made it clear that Minna must do all the work. 'The flat that Kerry's offering . . .'

'Oh, we don't need to worry about that,' Niamh said breezily. 'Sorry, meant to e-mail you both at the start of the week but we've had an outbreak of nits and even the head's gone down with it. The family has come into some money so they don't need to sell this place. They're going to draw up a new lease for another twelve months. No increase in rent, either. I demanded that for all the stress we've put up with. So that's a relief, isn't it?'

Relief wasn't the emotion that Minna experienced. In fact, she bristled with indignation. A new feeling. 'Well!' she snapped. 'You could have let me know before now.'

Sharmila and Niamh exchanged looks of surprise. 'Relax, Minna,' said Sharmila. 'There's no harm done.'

Niamh rolled her eyes. 'Don't bother to thank me for sorting it all out . . .'

Minna was about to say more but thought better of it. There was no point in falling out now. Instead, she turned her mind to her new priority: letting Kerry know. She was nervous, of course, but thankfully Kerry handled the rejection with unprecedented grace, and even went so far as to say she was glad that Minna was spared the ordeal of a move. As for herself, Kerry was sure she'd find new tenants by the end of the week. Their friendship was restored, but Minna feared their relations had regressed. Or maybe she'd just never get used to Kerry's special brand of friendliness. For sure, it wouldn't be worse than the coolness that pervaded life at home.

The housing crisis was not the end of Minna's troubles. Callie, her oldest friend in the world, turned to her as never before, for support. Callie had an idyllic marriage, as she was the first to admit. But a potential blight had arisen. So far, Callie let it skim like a dragonfly upon the surface of a swimming pool. Was Minna meant to scoop it up and return it to the wild? There *was* no wild, outside of the world in which they lived. If Callie was truly upset then Minna did not want to risk making her feel worse by doing or saying something wrong.

Cunningly, these new frequent meetings were scheduled randomly. (This would not impress Stephanie one jot.) 'Fancy a quick one after work?' Callie would ask towards the day's end. When Minna hesitated, Callie employed persuasion. 'Oh come on, Min. Just one drink. I need cheering up, to be honest. You haven't got any other plans, have you?' Minna would concede, that no, she did not.

'Is Callie an alcoholic?' mused Adam. 'Minna, are *you?*'

The old team were in Monroe's, the week of Minna's return from Spain. Steph had e-mailed to say she was meeting Janine in Islington at seven-thirty, so had an hour or so to spare and did any of them fancy a drink? Time was precious, but everyone was accorded the chance to relate recent life events. Minna realised she was desperate to unburden herself.

Minna shook her head. 'I don't think Callie has an alcohol problem. It might only be one drink stretched out over a few hours. Hers are non-alcoholic, generally. That's why I've worked out what's going on. She sees me because Todd – that's her husband – is delayed or unavailable – even though his office is just a couple of streets away from Callie's – so there's no point her going home to an empty house when they can't have sex, and she can't get pregnant. Then they do have sex, eventually, but she's still not pregnant, so she meets me to drown her sorrows, with drink. She might as well, I guess.'

'You're absolutely convinced of this?' Kerry wanted to know.

Minna nodded, unwilling to be dissuaded. She said, 'I remember her saying that they had been actively trying for a baby. That was around the time of my birthday. So April. It's their third wedding anniversary next month.'

'What does trying *mean*, exactly?' asked Steph. 'That they've stopped using contraception, or they've acquired a guide to extreme sexual positions?'

Adam shrugged but he offered, 'I agree, it's a strange use of the word. Trying. I mean, I suppose I never realised we were trying for a baby when Laura got pregnant.'

'She must have been,' said Minna. Then, because that was possibly discrimination, amended, 'One of you must have. Or both.'

'Well, Laura was surprised. I heard her tell her mother that.

You know, because of the dates.' He was all too aware that he was speaking to women without the authority of being one. 'Of course, we were both delighted.'

'You would say that,' Steph said. 'Everyone would.'

'We *were*,' Adam said.

'Have you thought of having any more children?' Kerry asked candidly.

Adam appeared to shudder. 'Well, never say never. But we don't want to be greedy, do we? You've got to think of the world's resources.'

'What about Minna's friend's resources?' Steph said, gaining control of the discussion.

'What about her husband? Could be that he's firing blanks.' That was Kerry, and it put Minna uncomfortably in mind of a nail gun.

Minna replied, 'I'm sure she told me they'd both been checked out. Before they got married. I don't think it was a pre-requisite but . . . well, Callie's very organised.'

'Which must make the failure to conceive such a bitter pill to swallow,' said Steph. Then she realised the irony of her words, and everybody laughed.

Adam shifted the discussion forward. 'Is it essential to always meet on Callie's turf?'

Minna considered. 'Not necessarily. On my birthday, I was Callie's guest. She was paying so it was reasonable to go where she chose.'

'She could have let you choose,' Steph said. 'That's what I'd have done.'

'But you know all the places your friends go because you go with them,' Minna said. 'You can budget in advance and know your friends won't be extravagant. They're reliable like that.'

Steph preened beneath the praise, happy to surrender the point. 'That's true.'

'And then, afterwards, well, it made sense to keep meeting in the city,' Minna said.

'A change of scene is good,' said Adam. He added, forestalling criticism, 'Sometimes.'

'I can generally leave work on time,' Minna explained, 'whereas Callie never gets out before six-thirty. I might as well use that time to travel over to her. It means I'm not hanging round waiting, and we have longer together.'

Kerry nodded. 'You can't argue with that. And it's an easy journey home for you from Bank.'

'Sometimes,' Minna added, 'Todd joins us, although usually I head off when he arrives. Callie and I'll have talked enough, and they'll have barely seen each other.'

'That's tactful,' said Adam. 'Gives them a chance to catch up.'

Kerry said, 'They live together, they work a couple of streets from each other, and they don't have time to make a baby. Isn't that a sad reflection on our times?'

'Well, it brings us right back to the central problem,' Steph observed.

'Yes,' said Minna, amazed they were back on message. 'I do feel sorry for them both. Callie says she gets ratty with Todd because he's sometimes too tired to do anything, and that can't help. He's working harder than ever because he's aiming for a promotion which of course would benefit them when and if a baby comes.'

'So that's why you keep agreeing to meet,' said Adam. 'Even though you don't enjoy it.'

'It's not that I don't enjoy it,' Minna said. 'Callie is my best friend. But we don't have a lot in common these days. It's difficult to make conversation, at least it is for me. Callie talks about everything.'

'Except the obvious,' said Steph.

'She hints at it,' said Minna. 'Should I force the issue? Would you?'

Adam and Steph looked away, shielding themselves from scrutiny. Instantly Minna recognised their return to form. *They* wouldn't force any issue.

Kerry said, 'It's pretty thoughtless behaviour on your friend's part, actually. I mean, for all she knows, you might be having the same problem. A lot of people can't have children. It's nothing to be ashamed of.' Noticing everyone's eyes settle on her, then blink away, Kerry added, 'Dave and I decided early on we didn't want children. We've never regretted it.'

'I would.' Adam was wistful. 'Sometimes I wonder what it'd be like if we hadn't had children.' He began to drift. 'But I soon snap out of it. I don't know where Laura and I would be without the girls.'

'You could probably be anywhere you fancied,' said Stephanie. 'Running a guest house in the south of France.

Researching rare breeds of monkey in Bogotà. Building mud-brick houses in Namibia. The choice is endless.'

'Thanks for that, Steph,' was Adam's quiet response.

'Kerry might have a point,' mused Steph. 'Why do you think she's chosen you, Min?'

It was a good question, so Minna considered it. She concluded, 'Because I listen, I suppose. I'm available.' Why did these plus points chip away at her sense of self?

'And not in the same predicament,' added Steph. 'I mean, if you were in a difficult relationship – whether or not you were trying to conceive – then hopefully, Callie would have the decency to stay away. But you're not. Luckily.' She awarded Minna a bright smile.

'When are you seeing her next?' Adam asked.

'Tomorrow night,' Minna answered glumly. 'At least I've had warning. Though maybe it would better if I hadn't. I wouldn't need to dread it then.'

How miserable she'd sounded, not to say grudging. Minna didn't get off on it. The fact is, that witnessing the misfortune of others can only provide a short-lived and limited hit.

You couldn't claim that Minna's summer had been light on interaction. She caught up with friends from her old job, which happened once a year. She mopped up a lot of family: both sets of grandparents, who were visiting London. She saw Lisa, briefly. She contemplated getting in to work half an hour early, as well as staying late, but because of the season, her phone rang less than targets required, and clients she e-mailed responded only when chased, if they offered anything more than an out-of-office bounce-back. Overall – two months into her new role – life had begun to pick up speed.

Even so, every office has slack times and on one such hot August afternoon, Minna was browsing the internet when a glitch took her back to the home page which doubled as the company intranet. It was a facility Minna consulted rarely, unless logging illness or booking leave. *Need to have your eyes checked out? Fancy a massively discounted gym membership? Click here for bereavement counselling* – all of this offered by the company, legitimately pursued between nine and five: untapped opportunities for any voucher-weary woman.

Next Minna browsed the staff directory. She looked at her own profile page, which she vaguely remembered filling in during her induction week. The photo wasn't bad, but it dismayed her somehow. She decided it was her hair. She couldn't remember it ever looking any different. Suddenly, she longed for a change. She arranged a cut for that very evening, with an automatic discount when booking from her work address; no print-outs required, and no mention of vouchers. She went a tone lighter, and instigated a fringe. It wasn't a total transformation, but back in the office, there were compliments.

On another search of the intranet, Minna encountered training courses. A place on 'Confident Conversations – Part One' had become available this very Wednesday. HR confirmed there was budget provision in Minna's team. Her manager approved her choice with an instant e-mail, so Minna applied and was accepted.

It was almost like taking a day off. The course was held in a nondescript office in Covent Garden, and arriving early, Minna bought a coffee and wandered around the piazza. She'd dressed smartly, but not as formally as if attending an interview. The other attendees were similarly attired, and similarly nervous, too. They sat around the table in silence, fiddling with their phones or the crumbs from a pastry taken from the plate in the middle of the table. There was a first day of term mood within the room.

The trainer was much more switched on and assertive than any of Minna's teachers had been. Minna wasn't given to hero worship, nor one for female crushes, but she was entranced by the woman, whose name was Patricia. Fiftyish, Minna presumed, with excellent skin and hair and a beautifully cut suit in yellow, a colour which Minna had never known to be carried off successfully. No frenzied scratching on flipcharts with desiccated felt-tips for Patricia – all her wisdom flashed up, neatly typed, on a screen, with convincing clarity. She purred with wisdom from the moment she opened her mouth to speak.

Patricia effortlessly got the best out of people. Minna volunteered answers she didn't think she knew and even participated in a role play. It was a wrench when Patricia disappeared at lunchtime, to let the attendees mingle. By now, they'd relaxed and had exchanged details of their jobs and lives, so conversation flowed. Business cards were exchanged:

Minna hadn't thought to bring any, so she had to use pages from the complimentary notepads supplied – and pledges to stay in touch were made.

Minna was pleased when the afternoon session began, though it passed too quickly. Had she learned anything? Yes, and was already forming eloquent praise for the feedback forms. Finally, it was time for consolidation and wrapping up.

Then something odd happened. Patricia was standing in front of the screen on which her day's presentation had been projected. Her concluding remarks were bullet pointed succinctly but she was elaborating generously, her audience still rapt. Then the laptop in front of her clicked quietly and the screen went black. No one said anything, fully engaged with their tutor. Her gaze seamlessly roved from one face to another. The screen lit up again, the computer clicked, and a series of images began flashing up on the screen.

They were holiday snaps. Patricia and a young man (quite a bit younger, actually) sitting in a hot tub with palm trees in the background. Patricia and her companion clinking champagne flutes. Patricia in a sarong, leaning over a balcony, waving a joint. Patricia leering at a chocolate fountain with her tongue poking out.

Still no one uttered a word. Minna was torn between admiration for a life lived richly, and a humiliated paralysis on Patricia's behalf at having her privacy breached. Oh, the indignity of it! Minna longed for Patricia to halt the show but also feared the moment when she realised her social life was being splashed before strangers, like a tabloid exposure.

Eventually, mercifully, the showreel stopped. The laptop clicked and the screen cleared to an innocent, unprobing blue.

'So I think that just about wraps things up,' said Patricia, taking a quick glance at the unbetraying wall behind her. She smiled indulgently. Minna realised that the entire room's rapt gaze remained unbroken. There wasn't so much as a snigger. 'Thanks for your company today, people. I hope you've all gained as much as I have. And I hope to see you back for part two. Enjoy your evenings, won't you?'

Inwardly, Minna cheered. You couldn't have called it a save because people like Patricia did not need saving in the first place.

Minna packed up her hand-outs into the folder supplied and when someone suggested heading home via the pub, longed to tag along – except she'd already promised to hook up with Callie, which she of course regretted but could do nothing about. Patricia was also invited (to elaborate on the holiday snaps, possibly), but declined, citing prior engagements. No doubt, there were, but no doubt, also, she was providing tactful distance between student and teacher. Again, this signified her credentials as a true professional. Everyone can learn from someone like that, Minna resolved.

The day had been a triumph. Not only would her conversations gain in confidence; Minna would, herself. By the time she got to work the next day, an invitation to part two was sitting in her inbox and went straight into the diary for the middle of January. It was something to look forward to in what might otherwise be an unpromising new year.

* * *

Consumed by Callie's crisis, it was no wonder that Leo had taken a back seat in Minna's life. Well, that and the fact that he was ensconced in his own relationship. Minna didn't feel neglectful. Even so, she didn't delay in returning the message he'd left on Friday afternoon, angling for a catch-up over the August bank holiday. Minna volunteered Saturday night, thinking Leo would say no – surely he and Darren had plans – but he accepted without hesitation. Same time, same place as usual. They ordered wine and settled back into the padded sofas, toasting the end of the season.

'So,' Minna said, a glass of Pinot Grigio in. 'How's Darren?'

Leo smiled. 'Oh, well, he's ... just fine. He'd want me to send his love, I'm sure – he thought the world of you. But hey! I want to hear about the office move.'

She said, 'It was no big deal.' But she detected that Leo wanted more. About *what*, however? What else was there to say? She could talk about the stresses at home, but that would dull the evening. 'So, have you and Darren had any trips away together?'

With glistening eyes, Leo said, 'He dumped me, Min. Go on. I'm ready for it. Say the obvious words: "I told you so."'

Minna flinched. It *wasn't* obvious. She'd spoken of Darren to buoy them both up. 'I can't believe you think I'd say that,' she retorted.

'*I* can't believe you're thinking about yourself when I'm the one who's been dumped.'

Minna knew when Leo was winding her up. She'd known

it once, at least. But why blame *him*? Darren was at fault; Darren the dumper. She said, 'If you don't want to talk about it . . .'

He appeared mollified. 'OK. I'm sorry I snapped. I *do* want to talk about it, actually.'

'Then we will. So can you tell me why he dumped you?'

Leo made hypothetical parentheses in the air. 'He said I was too "out there".'

'Meaning?'

'In a literal sense, too out. O.U.T. Which is totally unfair because the last time I was on the scene it was with you. I haven't been within a mile of Soho, not since Darren and I started going out. I deliberately kept away, for his sake.'

She ventured, 'I have to say it's pretty ironic that he criticised you for being "out there" given the way he carried on at my place. His comments were pretty "out there".'

Leo nodded miserably. 'We had a row about that. I wasn't sure if I should tell you.'

'Of course you should have told me!'

Leo shrugged. 'It seemed rude – you know, in case you felt guilty about creating pressure, when it was obvious you were just trying to help.'

'I didn't help much by the sound of it,' Minna said. 'Still, I don't suppose that was the only thing the two of you argued about.'

There was a gleam of hope in his eyes. 'It basically *was*, Min. I really thought things were fantastic. Early days, still, but not *that* early. It was almost six months.'

She tried to comfort him. 'You wanted it to work,' Minna said. 'You were being optimistic. That's brilliant.'

'It was *definitely* special, Min. Like nothing I'd ever experienced before.'

Minna kept the ex-girlfriend in her checked, but now she felt obliged to defend her honour. 'We were together for more than a year. Do you mean to say you feel as bad now as you did then?' But did she mean to ask that?

'It wouldn't be fair to make the comparison,' Leo told her. 'It's totally different.'

He could have just said 'no'. Ordinarily, Minna would have taken it on the chin, because he'd mean no harm. But tonight, for some reason, she couldn't.

She said, 'You *do* mean it's worse?' Her cheeks reddened, betraying her. Luckily, Leo had turned away, watching a procession of people down Wardour Street. But he soon returned. He said, 'If it's worse then it's probably because it's harder.'

'Don't qualify it,' Minna flared, thoroughly rattled. 'Either you think this break-up matters more than ours did, or you don't.'

He glowed with affection. 'But you handled it brilliantly. You were a real brick!'

She was astonished at her vehemence. 'Is that meant to be a compliment?'

'But you *told* me, Min. You *assured* me . . .'

'For your benefit. I said what I thought you wanted me to say.'

Was it true? Where had this certainty come from? All she could see was its build-up: before I didn't *want* to know. I'm listening now. I just don't much like what I'm hearing. But she couldn't switch off. Wouldn't.

She exhaled – it was like the cork sliding through a bottle's neck. Her bottleneck. Out poured words that were totally foreign but unmistakeably her own. 'Look, it's fine that you've switched to fancying guys, but it's not so great if you write off what's gone on before. I never thought you had.'

Leo looked pained. 'What are you getting at, Min? You know I don't regret a moment of us being together. You are one of the few truly special people in my life.'

'I hope that's true.' But she had to know, 'Do you really think gay relationships count for more than straight ones?'

He wrinkled his nose, in consideration. 'You have to admit, it means more for a gay couple to make a go of things than it does a straight one. Like, for example, everyone loves a gay wedding. It makes them feel on trend and tolerant. But I'll bet a gay divorce wouldn't be quite so flavour-of-the-month. Worse than a straight divorce. I know this couple—'

Why was he giving her someone else's story? 'It isn't easy for anyone,' she said. 'Which probably explains why we're both single.'

The look on Leo's face was clear: Minna had failed *him*. He wasn't seeking her approval, but assuming her allegiance.

'Actually, it was pretty horrible for me, Min,' he said, his disappointment stark. When *he* had wounded *her*. Only, it hadn't felt like an attack at the time. In Minna's saddest moments, she had felt as if Leo had been taken from her, not that he'd removed himself. That's why they were able to be friends.

She demanded, '*Why*, Leo? Why did you wait until *then* to come out? Why me?'

Abruptly, he looked away. 'I don't know, exactly. I definitely wasn't lying to you before. I hadn't done stuff with guys. It just . . . happened.'

'How is that possible?' Minna wanted to know.

'Maybe it was inevitable. I mean, we don't need to go down the old nature versus nurture argument—'

'Not unless you want to sound like Darren.' Minna was brusque. 'Maybe you've picked up his technique.'

'Better than crabs,' he snorted, then bowed his head. 'Sorry. It's just the last guy I saw tried to end it before I realised he'd given me lice. But you didn't need to know that.'

'So what you're saying . . .' She no longer felt angry but there was nothing in anger's place. She ought to stop, but the urge to work the truth out into the open was unquenchable. 'What you're saying is, you suddenly woke up one day and realised you were gay.'

Leo frowned. 'It wasn't sudden . . . but it happened quickly. I met this guy . . . I swear, Min, a month before – a week, even – I wouldn't have looked at him twice. I was out with work, in Richmond, of all places. I met this guy and then, immediately, I knew.'

'You knew?' She could have been scathing but felt admiration. Envy, even. Leo was describing a moment of clarity. But it was also the moment that foretold the end of their relationship. Her instinct was to reel Leo back in before they parted a second time, but her only tools were her own experience. She said, 'Was it like ... a mist clearing?'

'A mist?' whispered Leo, as if fearing he'd misheard.

Minna inched closer. 'Yes. You know – like everything seemed foggy and then it cleared and the whole world looked different.'

'I think it was sharper than that, Min. Mist sounds a bit ... well ... vague.' He was struggling. But he *was* making an effort, wasn't he?

Suddenly, she said, 'I didn't realise it at the time, but I had a misty start to thirty.'

'You had a *what*?' Leo's gaze was stern, but perhaps underneath he was striving to look deep within her.

'My thirtieth, last year – do you remember? Well, you won't remember this, but I was in the pub after work and the TV was on. It was noisy, but there were subtitles.' As the words began to flow, Minna heard her voice go higher and faster. 'I was watching the news – I don't think anyone else was paying attention – and then the weather forecast came on. The caption said that Tuesday would be fine and mild, Wednesday much cooler with increasing cloud, and Thursday – which was my actual birthday – would begin with widespread mist, quite possibly fog in hilly areas. Only it hadn't read Thursday: they'd got the caption wrong. I thought, Bad news for me. I was joking, of course – but it's been true. This past year – longer, even, I've felt as if I'd been disconnected from my real life. Well, *you* must have been like that when you realised you were gay. I suppose we have that in common.' It was a cheering thought.

Leo flared in response: 'God, Minna! Darren *dumped* me, and you think talking about the bloody weather helps. I *pleaded* with him, Min. I made a fucking *tit* of myself, actually. Luckily, we were at my place, so only my housemates heard. I begged him to stay but it didn't work. He'd made up his mind. And then he left. That was two weeks ago. I haven't heard from him since. Even though I texted him. I suppose that's all there is to say. I just thought you'd be a bit more – well, never mind. Now it really is time for a new subject.'

There was just a drop of wine left; it was Leo's round, but he seemed in no hurry to fetch another bottle. Minna wanted no more. No more of her story, either, which she regretted sharing. A misty start to thirty. It sounded falsely whimsical, not scientific. Surely he'd meant fog, anyway, unless he'd been talking about the sea. Didn't the guy know the difference, or care? Was he only hedging his bets? Why had Minna felt it was a warning?

More importantly – in this moment of genuine clarity – why had she pushed Seb away just before *this* last birthday? It hadn't been Seb on the telly that night. Seb hadn't fudged anything in the hour they'd spent together. He'd laid his cards on the table, and Minna liked the hand he played very much. He'd deserved as much from her.

Leo said, 'I just want what everyone else has.'

'Well, there's nobody stopping you!' she raged. 'Least of all me.' And instantly, she choked on her own words. Attacked not from without, but within. She couldn't blame Leo. She couldn't blame the guy who awakened Leo's self-knowledge. She certainly couldn't blame it on the weatherman. Either of them.

'I have to go,' she said. 'No, Leo – you stay. Stay here. It's where you belong.'

'Minna!'

As she picked her way across the bar, she heard Leo repeat her name a second, and third time. He seemed rooted to his seat. Unhindered, Minna kept walking. She pushed her way through the crowd towards Charing Cross Road. The bright blue lights of Leicester Square station gleamed, the whorls and lines of each letter clear and distinct, as if to taunt her. But for once Minna saw clearly.

She couldn't dump Leo as he'd ditched her. Imagine being abandoned by your boyfriend *and* your best friend in the same month. And she was sobered too, by the memory of that other encounter at a different station. She'd walked away from Seb, which somehow warned her against walking away from Leo now. She might not get another chance to step close to anyone again.

So Minna hesitated before descending into the station. The tide of people made it difficult to hurry. This encouraged her to think that if she was doing the wrong thing, wouldn't she be stopped? But no one accosted her, nor even marked her presence. This dismayed her, a little, but the feeling was gone by the time she tipped on to the platform.

In any case, Minna needed no help to condemn her choice. She just couldn't believe she'd made the same mistake all over again.

*Some*thing was new, at least – though was it anything to celebrate? Just the sorrowful conclusion that acknowledging your own flaws is actually much worse than being told about them.

Monday was routine, which meant that Minna felt entitled to leave the office on time, and do a little shopping in Boots' before she went to the gym. It was a satisfactory session which showed personal improvement, and she showered and dressed casually, reflecting on her achievements. Last thing of all, she checked her phone, as she usually did. A typically forlorn affair was transformed when she saw she had six new messages! This was tarnished, swiftly, on discovering that five of the voicemails were from her mother and Lisa. Disappointed, Minna considered ignoring them all.

When confronted by an inbox full of e-mails with a common message line, it's expedient to read the latest comment for summaries and action points. But Minna took time out to sit in reception and review the messages in chronological order, pressing a finger to one ear to block out the motivational music. An unfamiliar number was dealt with first: just one of her new friends from Patricia's workshop, requesting the details of another group member.

It was a model of economy, and conveyed both information and kind concern. Minna replied at once and deleted the voice message.

Maureen's first communication relayed word from Minna's grandmother about an old film she had mentioned to Minna but whose title she'd been unable to retrieve. The plot meant nothing to Minna, but she noted it down and would feed back.

The third call was from Lisa. It conveyed no urgency, but then Minna had never scored high on the list of her sister's priorities – usually around the mark of a five-pound donor on a Just Giving tally. Cryptically, Lisa said, 'When you get the chance,' but also 'I'll be home by ten.' To phone after ten on a week night was something undertaken only in pressing circumstances. (Lisa was an early riser, to make room for her extensive training programmes.)

Maureen's next call was aborted – presumably by her, though she'd blame O2 – but the fifth was clear. 'Minna. I suppose you've heard from your sister. Call me as soon as you can.'

Then, Lisa: 'No doubt you've heard from Mum. Min, I really wanted you to hear the news from me. Sorry about that. Anyway, we'll speak when we can.'

Both sounded exercised, but neither had disclosed so much as a topic line, or conveyed a hierarchy of inconvenience. Surely they would have been explicit in a crisis. That wasn't too much to ask. You couldn't rely on colleagues or exes or even some friends, but family was a different matter. Family owed and was owed an obligation.

Should Minna have picked up on a vibe? She considered her last meeting with Lisa. It had been no different to others in that Minna could have scrolled through her sister's schedule herself and missed out on nothing. They didn't talk about things like . . . feelings. They never had. Did 'sibling intuition' exist? She'd read about identical twins who shared pain – one vicariously, one in actual bodily torment. But maybe that was just a myth. You only ever heard it from the one who was suffering already.

It was nine o'clock when Minna got home, thanks to a burst water main causing a pedestrian diversion on the high road. Too early to call Lisa, but possibly too late to phone Maureen, who was known to pull the phone from its socket after the watershed. Minna conceded that she mightn't get through to either of them, of course, which would mean going to bed with a troubled mind. She ought to make an effort, at least.

She heated up and played with last night's leftovers, then carried a fortifying glass of wine to her room, where she telephoned Farnham.

Maureen answered at once and cut to the chase. 'Lisa's getting married.'

So that was what the calls were about. Minna leaped to no conclusions, but she conveyed her immediate reaction: 'That's fast work! Even by Lisa's standards—'

'Minna . . .'

'Although she would have had someone new in mind. She always does—'

'Minna, if you'd let me continue . . .'

She reflected. 'You have to admire her, don't you, Mum? She never seems to fall out with any of her exes. It's as if she's done them a good turn by setting them free. Do you suppose that's how it works?'

Her mother hissed with exasperation. 'Minna! Just be quiet and let me explain.'

'Explain what? I liked Craig. More than a lot of the others. I just hope he's OK with being an ex.' Minna sounded haughty, but with reason. Lisa's pattern was established, but if Minna chose to sympathise with the cause of the abandoned, she was entitled to do so.

Maureen said, 'He's not.'

Minna sighed. 'He's taken it badly?'

'It's Craig Lisa is marrying.'

Minna did a double take. '*She's what?*'

Maureen cleared her throat. 'Craig asked Lisa to marry him and she said yes.'

Minna, startled, marshalled the available facts. 'I thought the reason Lisa didn't come on holiday with us was because she was going through a break-up. Mum, you said—'

Minna cast her mind back to a conversation prior to the family holiday. She asked Maureen why Lisa had decided not to join them, and her mother explained that Lisa had had things to sort out.

'It's her love life,' Maureen had said. 'She's in the process of dumping her boyfriend.'

Minna asked, 'Which one's this?'

'Craig. It's been about seven months, so not a bad run. I don't know what went wrong.'

'Does it matter? They never last, do they?' Minna hadn't wanted to sound caustic; she wasn't jealous. 'I wouldn't be surprised to find that by the time we touch down she'll be loved up with someone new and it was as if Craig was never on the scene.'

'Not this time, Minna. I don't think she wants to separate. That's the trouble.'

'So why is she doing it? Do we *know* that she is?'

'She hasn't said so. For once, I just don't know what's going through her mind.'

'Well, there's nothing we can do, is there? We'll just have to wait until the transition period is over and she launches the new model.'

'I suppose so,' conceded Maureen, with a sigh. 'You know, I had this brainwave that she could send Craig a text from the plane just before they ask you to switch off your electronic devices. Then she could enjoy the flight and then the holiday, and not think about the consequences.'

'And what would the text say?'

'Well, you can guess, can't you? Everyone gets dumped by text message these days.'

'As it turns out,' Maureen explained to Minna in the present, 'your sister was reeling from this shock proposal of marriage. Obviously, Lisa needed time to mull it over. Not nearly enough time, if you ask me.'

'Have they set a date?'

'Yes. The beginning of December.'

'So soon!' Minna exclaimed. And then, 'But they're not even living together.'

'Oh, that's their little project for November.' Her mother clucked reprovingly. 'Lisa says the wedding won't be an elaborate affair so there's no need to spend months planning. I ask you, wouldn't she want all bells and whistles if she was really committed to the idea?'

'Did you ask her that?'

'No, but I might have wondered if she was going to bother with a dress or if she'd just turn up in a leotard.'

'What did she say?'

'She just laughed. See – she thinks it's all a joke. Not to be taken seriously.'

Constantly measuring her intake of carbs, her heart rate, her miles walked (and setting targets for everything else), Lisa had never been one for flippancy. She was hardly likely to start now.

'That doesn't sound like Lisa,' said Minna.

Maureen was vehement. '*I* wasn't amused, I can assure you of that. And I don't believe the line about a lack of fuss. The reason the wedding is so soon is so she doesn't have lots of time to wriggle out of it.'

Minna said, 'Mum, what makes you think it's a mistake?'

'*Because she's cancelled Japan!*' Maureen fairly screeched. 'The eisteddfod she's been training for all year. Just pulled out to focus on her wedding. She's let the whole squad down. You have to admit that is not typical behaviour for Lisa.'

Minna was on the back foot. She knew nothing of Japan. But what was Maureen's problem? 'Mum, I don't understand why you're so opposed to the idea.'

'I've already explained myself. Lisa is being rushed into a marriage she's bound to regret and we need to help her to see the error of her ways. That's what families are for.'

Is that official? Minna wondered. 'What if we're wrong?' You're wrong, she silently amended, with a wrench of disloyalty.

'We're not. She'll come to thank us.'

'She might not. She might want nothing to do with us.' The wrench this time was worse.

'That would never happen in our family,' said Maureen confidently.

Minna said, 'What does Dad think of it all?' It was purely an academic enquiry and wouldn't add fuel to any flames.

'Naturally, he agrees with me. So, Minna, what are you going to do about it?'

'I could have a chat to Lisa,' she said, carefully. 'I need to phone her back, anyway. It'll just be chat, though, Mum.'

'Good girl. And do report back as soon as you've done that, won't you?'

'Yes, I will. Of course.'

Wednesday was noteworthy for its stationery cupboard reckonings with Astrid. It was as if they had entered a different dimension, because no one else ever seemed to be around at the same time.

'Hi, Astrid. How are you?' Minna offered.

'Very well indeed, thank you,' said Astrid brightly. 'Just back from an extended weekend in Paris for the horse racing. You know, I came looking for you other day, Minna. Must have been last Wednesday. You weren't there.' The brightness vanished, as if sucked into a black hole.

'Oh, that's a shame. Did the others help you out?'

'No. Someone mentioned a hospital appointment. Is everything all right?'

'What, *me*?' Minna was horrified. 'I'm fine, thanks, Astrid. I was on a training course, actually. I did set up an out-of-office *and* changed my voicemail.'

This cut no ice with Astrid. 'What was the course?'

'Confident conversations,' said Minna, which felt ironic in the circumstances.

'Who led it?'

'Patricia McCorqu—'

Astrid rolled her eyes and heaved a peal of laughter. 'Oh, Patronising Pat. They're still wheeling her out in lieu of someone who knows what they're talking about.'

Minna saw Astrid for what she was: a reality broker. Or was that breaker? She said, 'I thought she was excellent. Very professional.'

'Oh, *please*, Minna. No need to be diplomatic. We've all endured Patricia's sycophantic encouragement in our time. There's nothing she can't spend a whole day wittering on about.'

'Seriously, I enjoyed it. I learned a lot.' None of which

presently served her, but that was no reflection on Patricia's skill.

'Can you imagine what she's like to live with?' More cool laughter. 'Impossible, I should think.'

'I hadn't really thought about it,' said Minna. There'd been no need to do that.

'Every decision from whether to change brand of washing powder to how late to cut the roses back being preceded by endless calm mediation and discussion. Probably with handouts and flipcharts.'

'She didn't use a flipchart.'

'Marker pen on every wall of the house. Can you *imagine*?'

'Not really, Astrid,' Minna said calmly. 'But I'm sure it isn't like that at all.'

'*Impossible*. Actually, I heard her husband left the moment their youngest child went off to university.'

'It's not really anyone's business, I guess,' said Minna, remembering the young man in the holiday snaps. Patricia had seemed in good spirits then, so she hoped the separation had had a happy outcome. She didn't feel the need to say this to Astrid, however. She was glad, too, she hadn't already shared the Powerpoint story. It was innocuous itself, but in the wrong hands could be twisted and maligned throughout the building.

'I hear he ended up in San Paulo, briefly,' Astrid said. 'Maybe Patricia wasn't the problem after all. Perhaps it was a mid-life crisis. Sounds likely, don't you think?'

Minna would be drawn to neither disclosure or speculation.

She grabbed the packet of plastic sleeves for which she'd come. 'I've got to go, Astrid. Nice to bump into you.' Then she added, 'What did you want to see me about?'

'I just wondered if you wanted to go for lunch. That's all.'

'Oh, that was nice. I'm free tomorrow. We could go back to that nice Italian place.'

Astrid sniffed. 'Can't do tomorrow. Tell you what, I'll check my diary and see when I'm free.'

'OK, give me a buzz when you know,' said Minna casually, as she turned to leave. And privately added: But no hurry.

Lisa had a spare half hour before a spinning class that evening, and consented to meet Minna for coffee, although Lisa drank only water. Aware of time constraints, Minna corralled questions as fast as she could, but Lisa cut to the chase.

'So,' she said. 'You've come here to make me change my mind.'

A howl escaped from Minna's lips. 'Mum *told* you I was going to do that?'

Lisa shook her head. 'Not exactly. She told me I really ought to listen to what you had to say. So what do you have to say, Min?'

Lisa's tone was more severe than Maureen's had been, so that the family seemed more at fault than Lisa. Minna had not accounted for this reversal. Not that she wanted to be critical of anyone. She strove for an even-handed approach. 'What do you want me to say?'

Lisa still had the upper hand. She smiled. 'Ah, nice try, Min. But you can't wriggle out of it that way.'

But it's the opposite I want! Minna thought, desperate to be understood.

Lisa said, 'OK, I'll help you out. You ask me questions and I'll supply the answers.'

'I guess I want to know why it's all happened so fast.'

Lisa nodded, as if in approval. 'OK. So Craig and I were dating. It was going really well. Better than usual – easier, somehow, which kind of inspired us to put in more effort. Not because we were frightened of running out of steam. There was more to play for. You know what that's like, don't you?'

Minna thought of Adam. 'I can imagine how you felt, yes.' I must *try* to imagine.

'Then he asked me to marry him. Out of the blue, Min, only, it wasn't, exactly. I can see we were both leading up to it. Well, *something* was going to happen. I've been practically living at Craig's for the last three months, and well, we sort of knew that there was a deadline looming – nothing bad, you understand. Just the natural point where you need to stop and consider where you're going.'

The last deadline Minna had set herself had been her birthday. As landmarks go, it hadn't been a watershed. 'And what was the deadline?'

Minna held her breath. She hoped it wasn't the spectre of illness. Or financial ruin. Could it be pregnancy? Surely Maureen would have reached that conclusion and probed accordingly. What about deportation? No, didn't Craig hail from Horsham? Minna braced herself for the answer.

'Craig's mum goes back to Canada on New Year's Eve.

She's been here the last six months or so. We want her to be there when we marry, of course.'

'Does our mum know that?'

Lisa placed her hands flat on the table and studied them closely. 'Mum knows she lives in Canada. They've met. All the parents have met each other. They got on well.'

It wasn't quite an answer, so Minna repeated the question, applying the gentlest pressure.

'Well, I *tried* to tell Mum, of course. But she kept interrupting, going on about making decisions in haste and repenting at leisure. So I thought, well, if she doesn't want to listen now, *she* can repent at leisure.'

'Lisa!' But it sounded wrong to remonstrate. Minna took another tack. 'So Mum doesn't know that it's got to be December so Craig's mother can attend?'

Lisa said, 'No. That's one piece of knowledge you can offer her if you like.'

Knowledge is power. It depends on the knowledge, of course, as Minna had discovered. She had no appetite for gaining the upper hand over her mother. Or Lisa. She felt certain of this, and it pleased her.

She wondered: was this what was *really* meant by 'what other people have'?

'So now you know the facts,' said Lisa, when her sister failed to rise to the bait (if in fact Lisa had been baiting her). 'Now you can answer *my* question.' She paused to pour water into their glasses. 'Will you be my bridesmaid?' A hopeful, striving look was fixed to Lisa's face.

Minna was floored. But if she'd misjudged or been misjudged the feeling was swiftly replaced by sheer delight. '*Yes, please!* Thanks for asking.'

Lisa rolled her eyes. 'Don't be mad. As far as I'm concerned, you're the only woman for the job.' She checked her watch. 'Look, Minna, I hate to rush, but . . .'

'No, it's fine,' said Minna. It would be selfish to take up more of Lisa's time when she had just been bestowed with this special honour. But she couldn't abandon her responsibility. 'But what about Mum?'

'She'll be mother of the bride, of course.'

'No, I mean, will you fill her on what you've just told me? Will you put her mind at rest?'

Lisa looked away, and Minna anticipated rejection. Lisa owed her older sister nothing, yet Minna desperately sought her sister's compliance. Not to pull rank – it was too late to start that. Minna simply wanted something constructive to emerge from this conversation. It didn't seem to happen very often in her family. Or maybe anywhere.

Minna held her sister's gaze as long as she dared, which worked, in the end.

'All right, I'll call,' Lisa conceded, with a hint of irritation. But when the sisters parted, Lisa held Minna just a little bit closer than usual, as if reluctant to completely let go.

Leo left a message while Minna was out. 'Oh, hi, it's me . . . Look, I'm really sorry about the other night. I guess I was in a worse way over Darren than I thought but – well, it was no excuse. I'm so sorry. I'm better now. Well, I hope you got home safely. And I hope you'll forgive me. Catch you soon. Lots of love.'

Having missed one call made it so much easier to miss the call that followed, days later.

'Minna it's me again. Sorry, I meant to phone on Sunday but then the week got crazy. I presume you got my message. So ... give us a bell when you can. And I really am sorry for the weekend. I was a twat.'

Minna didn't phone back because of Seb. Remember him?

One evening, the following week, Minna fell in step with a couple of colleagues who were discussing anniversaries, and partners generally. At the time, Minna felt excluded (no surprise there) but back in the flat, after catch-up TV and wine, she began to brood in a melancholy fashion.

She'd dialled Seb's number, which she had stowed carefully in her purse. She'd actually cried, so that the message she left was the most ridiculous garble. In the cold light of day, Minna hoped Seb wouldn't guess the caller's identity. Their brief meeting had been months ago, and she hadn't provided her number. He'd probably met lots of girls since.

But he'd phoned her the morning after. 'Oh, hello – this is Seb, wondering if this number belongs to Minna? We met earlier in the year. Easter Sunday, I think it was. Anyway, I had a missed call late last night. It wasn't a message, exactly. I only heard a few words. A woman's voice. And I thought – well, I wondered – I mean it's probably irrational but I wondered if it was you? I did give you my number. Well, here I am so do get in touch if you'd like to. It would be very nice to hear from you.'

Thereafter, for the rest of September, Leo and Seb's messages alternated so neatly that they might have been colluding.

'God, I keep missing you,' said Leo. 'Mad! Hope it's because you're having fun. Anyway, phone me when you can.'

'Oh, hi – it's Seb here, again. Still hoping this is Minna's phone. Apologies for persisting, but thinking on it, I'm pretty sure it *was* you, Minna. Maybe you pressed my number by accident. Which means you stored it in your phone. That's a good sign! Except ... well, I'm just a bit concerned about the ... well, inconclusiveness of the message. I hope nothing is wrong? I mean, I don't suppose I'd be the first person you'd call if you were in a bit of difficulty, but if I could help in any way ... Probably too late by now. But ... Well, I'm here, if that's not too ... presumptuous. OK, bye.'

Leo said, 'Um ... am I being slow on the uptake here? I know I was an idiot but ... well, it's been a while now. So I hope I'm forgiven. I want to see you and make it up to you. Dinner. Dancing. You choose the date and venue. Love you.'

'Minna, it's Seb here. Yes, again! I've decided it must be you, because no one has contacted me to say that it isn't. I live in hope, you see. Because I really enjoyed our meeting. I hope this doesn't seem too ... well, *stalker-y*. The thing is, I've sort of got used to leaving messages for you. I look forward to it, even. Not that I know you're there. But, as I say, I hope you are. All best ... Seb.'

'OK, Minna. Don't you think this has gone on long enough?

I'm not sure what you're trying to prove, so I really don't know how I'm meant to respond. If you've set out to punish me, then you've succeeded. Hope that's enough. Hope it means you'll feel able to get in touch. Bye for now.'

Each time, Minna had so nearly picked up, but held back, with a strength that was as inexplicable as the need to keep the two men in separate compartments. Not that they were alike. (It wasn't a revival of the White Company incident.) *None* of Minna's boyfriends had been like the others, until each had become an ex. Not that Seb had been a boyfriend.

Besides, it had been different with Leo. At first, his messages had sounded puzzled, but then they'd been tinged with mild frustration. They had become more assertive after that. Irritation soon turned into injury. Next, anger. Then Leo's calls had stopped.

Seb's stopped, too, but with resignation, it seemed. No doubt, his friends had advised against it. Seb would have his own version of Kerry, Adam and Steph, working through problems in their well-meaning but circuitous way. Or perhaps his confidantes were ruthless like Astrid, stripping bare the facts, as carrion picks a carcass clean. Or like Callie, who'd listen but with her mind on her own dilemma.

They might say: 'She's missed her chance. It serves her right for playing hard to get.'

'Maybe she doesn't know *what* she wants. She's probably only going after you because she's worried she'll end up with nothing. You've got enough going on. You don't need that kind of window dressing.'

216

Ouch. Would Seb's friends be so harsh? They would if he needed protecting.

Minna put faces to the voices that might have offered Leo comfort, because she'd met enough of his friends to identify the likely suspects.

'Why do you care if she never phoned you back? She's your past.'

'It's decent of you to want to hang on, so she doesn't feel totally rejected. But, in the long term, what's the point?'

Minna blinked away these imagined voices, but they wouldn't abate, as if offended at her dismissal. Not that she'd dismissed them. She'd just hoped that someone might dispose of them for her. But wasn't that the lesson of the summer? Nobody would do that for you, because nobody knew any better. That's why people don't look.

At least there seemed no reason to hang on to Julian. Since arriving in Australia, he'd sent only the postcard Minna had mentioned to Adam, to which she'd replied by e-mail, lacking a physical address. Nothing since. She had to assume he was fine. There were even some days she didn't think of him at all.

Minna was delighted to join the full complement of former coffin-dwellers for an evening catch-up on the first Thursday of October. She seized the chance to share Lisa's happy news, which somehow she'd not found the chance to share.

'Older or younger?' asked Adam, when Minna had been hoping for, 'Congratulations!'

'I think Craig is more or less the same age as Lisa. So, twenty-seven.'

'No, I meant, is she older or younger than you,' said Adam. 'I'm presuming younger.'

Was a judgement brewing? Minna said, 'Yes. That's right. She'll be twenty-eight in January.'

'Well, it's generous of you to be so enthusiastic,' said Kerry. 'Given your own status.' (Why does the word 'status' always come calling with the prefix 'lack of'?)

Minna said, 'I haven't really been thinking about myself.'

'No?' Kerry queried. 'Well, I expect you'll be a bridesmaid. That'll be a nice compensation, I'm sure.'

'Oh yes,' Minna agreed. 'I'm in training to catch the bouquet. Look!'

She tossed a bag of crisps into the air, not realising it had already been opened. Her friends were covered in crumbs.

Minna rose to her feet. 'Shall I get some more?'

Stephanie started stabbing crumbs with a moistened fingertip. 'Don't worry, Minna, we'll make do.'

After some quiet sipping and crunching, and some general wedding conversation – questions directed to Adam, in the main – Minna mused, 'It's funny to think that by Christmas, I'll have a brother-in-law. He'll sort of *belong* to me.'

'You might come to regret that sentiment,' Kerry intoned. When Minna looked quizzical, she explained. 'In-laws can be a blessing and a curse. I've seen both sides.'

Minna was divided by a longing for Kerry's true-life scenarios and resistance, as if she might be sullied by them.

'Do you fancy him, Minna?' asked Adam, randomly. 'Craig, I mean.'

'Of course not, Adam. The clue's in the title – *brother*-in-law.'

Adam said, 'I quite fancy Laura's sister. Actually, their mum is pretty hot. They're a family of fantastically attractive women.'

'So if you'd met her first, before Laura would you have gone for it?' asked Stephanie.

'Laura's mum?' Adam wrinkled his nose. 'Well, no. She was already married.'

'I meant her sister,' said Steph.

'Oh. Well. Possibly. But I didn't, so it's not an issue. Let's talk about Minna.'

Minna had little to offer so could only disappoint them, though they pumped her for information. All except Steph who, Minna noticed, had a faraway look. Oh, she'd seemed engaged, and had asked questions. Smiled and laughed in the right places. But was she secretly seething at her colleagues' insensitive indulgence in a discussion to which she – being single – could not contribute? Or was she limbering up to disclose a long-withheld revelation? Perhaps Steph had been in a relationship for years with someone in the royal family or MI5, requiring secrecy. Oh, no good would come of hypothesising. Minna could open the door for her, but really – and this was not unkindness – it was up to Steph to speak out if she wanted. Then again, perhaps she was happier knowing that in the present company, she need not say anything at all.

*　　*　　*

The light drizzle that had begun to fall that evening was now a steady downpour, so Minna felt a little battered as she made her way home. It was not an unpleasant feeling, because it countered a deep hollowness she felt inside. She couldn't explain the void but she hoped it was a short-term reaction to leaving the pub and her friends. She would have been happy to stay there longer, if it weren't for work in the morning.

From the street, she saw that the flat was lit up; it would be welcoming and warm. She knew that Sharmila was stopping over at her boyfriend's in Stanmore, so Niamh must be in. She wasn't Minna's preferred flatmate, at the moment. All summer long, Niamh had been distinctly cool, as if Minna had been solely responsible for the housing crisis.

Minna's greeting from the hallway was met with silence. Perhaps Niamh was plugged into headphones. Minna didn't try again but stopped to pull off her wet boots. Then she made her way to the living room, to find her flatmate lying on the sofa, annotating exercise books.

'Hi!' said Minna, as loud as she dared. And then she noticed the large bunch of flowers standing in a jug on the mantelpiece. For some reason, she thought of Darren, which made her think of Leo. She gulped, and extinguished the thought.

Niamh put down her pen. 'You're soaked. Is it raining?'

'Yes,' said Minna. 'It's chucking it down. You had the right idea staying in.'

'Funny, I didn't notice it before. The rain, I mean. Leo wasn't even wearing a coat.'

At once, Minna looked at the flowers. The stems were still

tied. They were still wrapped in tissue paper. Was there no water in the vase? She looked back to Niamh. '*Leo?*'

'Yes. He was just wearing a T-shirt, I think. He'll be drenched by now.'

'You saw Leo? Leo was *here?*'

Niamh gestured idly. 'Yes. He popped round with the flowers about an hour ago. He was sorry to miss you. Well, he didn't say that, exactly. He didn't actually ask if you were in. I think he hoped to drop them on the mat. I guess he waited till someone left the downstairs doors open.'

'But the flowers are for me?' Minna asked.

'Yes – there was a card. It said *For Minna from Leo*. It wasn't in an envelope so I wasn't prying.'

Minna snatched the card away. 'Didn't you think it was a bit odd?'

'Odd that Leo brought you flowers? Well, no. I just thought it was . . . nice.' Niamh looked so calm, so inviolable.

Minna herself felt brittle, as if she herself might shatter. She said, 'Is *nice* the best you can do?'

But was it any worse than *sweet*? Minna stopped, struck by the cold slap of *déjà vu*. She was immune to Astrid's intrusion. It was Niamh who angered her. Unrequired to take a stance, Niamh had chosen to disapprove of Minna's estrangement from Leo.

Niamh looked up, bewildered. 'What?'

'I thought you'd be interested.'

'In what?'

'Me seeing Leo.'

'He's your best friend.'

'I haven't seen him for weeks!' Niamh said nothing. 'You *know* that!' Minna glowered, thinking, I won't let you pretend you didn't. I won't let you decide – after the event – that it never really mattered.

Niamh placed her red pen on the edge of the table, and watched it roll back, then forth, but not, miraculously fall off. 'What do I know?' she mused. 'To be honest, Minna, what's been uppermost in my mind all through the summer – practically ruining the long break that fills everyone who isn't a teacher with deep resentment – was the fact that we might've had to find somewhere new to live, which isn't easy these days.'

Minna held her rage. 'Don't use that excuse with me!'

Niamh flared. 'It's not an excuse. It happened.' She blinked, as if she might extinguish Minna in the process. 'Anyway, let's not make a big deal out of it.' She yawned and stretched, before closing the cover of one of the workbooks and placing the pile on the floor at her feet. 'It must nearly be time to turn in.'

Minna wouldn't rest. She sat down beside her flatmate, forcing Niamh to squish up. '*I'm* not the one who's made an issue of it. You did, Niamh. You've had the hump with me on a permanent basis for ages.'

A beat passed. 'Minna, I assure you,' lilted Niamh, in a patronising tone, 'I don't have an opinion about Leo.'

'But what about all those weeks when we were worrying about having to move? You blamed me.'

Suddenly, Niamh's face seemed to twitch. She turned away. 'It wasn't about the house move.'

Minna hesitated. 'Or Leo?'

Niamh shook her head, dolefully. 'Neither, actually.'

'Then *what's* it all about?'

'It's all about Jeff.'

It had come out as a whisper, but that wasn't why Minna said, 'Who?'

'My cousin Jeff.'

'I've never met him. So what's he got to do with me?' Yet the name stirred a memory.

Niamh uncurled and put her feet flat on the floor. And that was where she looked, studiously avoiding Minna. Quietly, she said, 'Yes, you have. He works in your building.'

Violently, Minna subsided into the cushions. 'Jeff from Go Aware.'

Niamh nodded. 'Yes. He's my cousin.'

'He's . . . what?' Minna felt like someone on a TV show who had just been informed that her sister is really her gran.

Niamh affected a laugh. 'What a coincidence, hey? Anyway, Jeff dropped by, back in the summer, and recognised you in one of the photos on the mantelpiece.'

Minna said, 'We used to smile at each other. We went for a drink. Around Valentine's Day.'

Now Niamh faced her. 'Jeff wanted more than that. He . . . really fancied you, I think. Still does. Only, I told him not to do anything about it.'

Minna took a breath, which was shallow and raspy. She

couldn't have roared in anger if she'd tried (not that it was her style). It occurred to her to seek as much information as possible. Not everyone did that, she knew, so it might for once give her an advantage. She asked, 'Why did you say that?'

'I didn't think you were ready. You know, after Julian. You were really in a bad way when that ended.'

'I was?' *Yes*, I was. Thank you for noticing. It wasn't meant grudgingly, but it didn't count for as much as it might have done once.

'And to be blunt about it, neither was Jeff. He told you about his divorce, presumably? It nearly destroyed him. I just thought it would be bad combination.'

'You did?' asked Minna, weakly.

'The third reason is, I was jealous.' Minna felt her heart plunge into her stomach. But still she just listened. 'It all seemed too easy – too convenient. The coincidence of me knowing you both, and being able to bring you together. No one's ever done that for *me*.'

'Oh.' It felt wrong to sympathise, but Minna permitted this reaction, thanks to the old nagging need to oblige.

Niamh said, 'Why didn't *he* do anything about it? That's what you need to ask. And, to be fair, you didn't exactly push the envelope, either.'

Stationery made her think of Astrid, but Minna overruled. She said, 'No, but I didn't reject him, exactly.'

That seemed to hit a nerve. 'No,' Niamh admitted. 'Jeff didn't think you had.'

For a long, hard moment Minna managed to hold Niamh's gaze. But to what effect?

Minna said, 'I just didn't follow it up. And now, he won't either.'

'No. Probably not.'

Minna asked, 'Does he know that you never told me about the visit? Does he know you never told me he was interested?'

Niamh bowed her head. 'No.' *No* and *know*. Those homophones sounded as limiting as each other. Niamh added, 'I haven't spoken to Jeff since the end of the summer.'

'You're not particularly close?'

'Not at all!' Niamh seized her defence. 'I have no influence over him, Minna.' Far from being an admission of defeat it provided the rudiments of a brand-new venture: 'So we can't for one minute assume that I've caused any permanent damage. Since when has anyone ever listened to *me*, that's what *I'd* like to know!' she roared, then added, quietly: 'Needless to say, if there's anything I can do to help things along, then I'll try my best. I mean, I could give you his number if you don't have it already, but well . . . *you* know where to find him, Minna, don't you?'

'Yes,' asserted Minna. She asked, 'So why have you decided to tell me now?'

Niamh tossed her hair. 'I just couldn't live with myself any longer.'

The remark hadn't exactly oozed contrition, and deserved Minna's sceptical, 'Really?'

'Yes,' sighed Niamh. Job done.

'Well,' said Minna, redundantly. 'I'm sure you'll get over it quickly enough.'

In Minna's experience, revelations tended to thunder down like falling masonry, but Niamh's had sort of flittered, like a white feather dropped at the feet of a man who refused to enlist for war. But it wasn't about being the last to know. No, *this* was a clear deception. A stark withholding. Premeditated. Patently targeted. Minna had every right to be furious.

Minna found it impossible to concentrate on work, despite the fact that she preferred to be in the office than at home, where she tried to avoid her flatmates. But she kept being distracted by thoughts of Jeff Sullivan. Specifically, the fact that he was *here*, a few floors above at Go Aware. Only Minna wasn't thinking of him in a work context.

She conjured a Saturday in an otherwise lost summer. Jeff was in the flat; her home. Would Jeff have been in shorts? Or always jeans? A trainers guy when not wearing brogues? Would he have shaved? Brushed his hair? Was he happy to see Niamh or had the family sent him under duress? What had been his reaction on seeing Minna in the photograph? Did he know that Niamh had filled Minna in? Was he waiting for her to get in touch?

Minna thought about their drink back in February. She had dismissed him because he was off limits. But then Minna had been too, she supposed, because of Leo. Yes, she knew (but only just admitted), as others had told her, that her attachment to Leo made it hard to commit to someone new. *Am* I still in love with Leo? she wondered. She would prefer not to be. The alternative seemed rather desperate: the subject of a letter in a problems page, when Minna tried to keep her interaction with magazines at the competition level.

It surprised, and pleased Minna to retrieve quite clear details of her evening with Jeff. The memory had jarred at first but it didn't now. She *might* fancy him, she decided. And not because she knew he was keen on her. Not only that, anyway. What about all those times they'd smiled at each other? They can't have counted for nothing. They counted for a great deal now. But what was the point in trying to pick up where they'd left off? Anyway, she was meant to be thinking of Seb. Jeff she could do without.

Minna conjured a whimsical *Sliding Doors* scenario, or perhaps just any rewound film, in which she backed out of the flat (in and out of the rain), to return and find Sharmila not Niamh, remote but not reckless. No word about Jeff, or anyone. Wouldn't *that* have been preferable?

At once she knew: *no*. Because you can't go back.

Or maybe this was closer to the truth: why would you *want* to unknow something when knowledge is so hard to acquire in the first place? Self-knowledge, that is, as opposed to the truths that people force on to you. But could *know* be as inhibitive as *no*? Could it be worse? Surely it made a difference if it was yours. You could do more with it, like move beyond it, instead of rehashing the same old theories about the world and your place in it.

Suddenly, the idea of 'what other people had' lost its lustre.

Minna wondered: Can I do it my own way? She knew she still wanted Leo in her life. But she knew, also, that she wanted someone new in her life. It was an urgent need, unshackled to any precedent or prescription.

Would that person be Seb? Would it be Jeff? Regardless of how Leo fitted in, Minna knew there wasn't space for them both.

Minna hoped that escaping London would offer a fresh perspective on her dilemma, followed up by the means to resolve it. She called her parents to suggest she might come for lunch at the weekend. Maureen said they'd be thrilled to see her, and why not stay till Monday morning? (No other guests were expected.) Maureen would book a restaurant for Saturday night and on Sunday they could go for a walk. The plan was music to Minna's ears, until she realised she didn't know if Lisa had had the promised conversation with Maureen. Would the absence of knowledge cloud the weekend? Would it be easier to deal with the fallout? Minna didn't know. 'Let's play it by ear,' she said, cravenly, and ended the call before she registered her mother's disappointment.

Minna found she had the flat to herself on Friday night. She changed, poured a glass of wine, and settled comfortably in the living room to call her sister.

'Oh hi,' said Lisa, warmly.

'Hey there.' How good it was to hear her sister's voice. 'Can you talk?'

Lisa paused, but only briefly. 'Sure. I've just come out of the shower but I don't need to get ready for a bit.'

'Have you spoken to Mum again about the wedding?'

'God, Min, you don't hang about, do you? Not yet but I will. Anyway, it looks like the pressure's off re the timing. Craig's Mum broke her leg last week. In three places. She's postponed her travels.'

'Oh. Sorry to hear that. It gives you more time, I guess.'

'Yes, and it means I might still make Japan. Do you know about Kyoto?'

'Just the basics . . .' Minna said, hoping for more.

'So that saves a lot of hassle,' Lisa confirmed. 'Anyway . . . Was there anything else, Min? What's new with you?'

In the quiet of the flat, the question seemed huge. But exciting too, because Lisa always shared so much, and for once Minna found that she had a lot to share. Only – where to start? How far back could she go?

She spoke of Leo, of this year's developments. Lisa offered sympathetic murmurs, right up to Minna's description of the night of perhaps her last evening with her former boyfriend.

'It can't have been easy,' Lisa said, 'but you probably did the right thing. It probably is time to let go.'

'You always stay friends with your exes,' Minna pointed out.

Lisa said, 'Well, I think that's about to change. It already has, actually. So what *else* has been happening?'

Minna took a deep breath, marshalled her words, and told Lisa about Seb, about her Easter journey from Farnham. And after.

'I like the sound of him,' said Lisa. 'Maybe he's a bit old-fashioned, but in a good way. A real gentleman.'

'You'd expect that of a weatherman, I guess. It's a conservative profession.'

'Is it? Global warming's skewed the picture,' said Lisa. 'I like the way he kept ringing you, even when you ... well, ignored his calls.'

'I missed them,' said Minna, without adding, 'deliberately'. 'And then they stopped. I have no idea where he is now.'

'Have you listened to his programmes? Followed him on Twitter?'

'No ...' And Minna had always thought she'd gone the extra mile in her relationships!

'So you could track him down, if you wanted. Quite easily. Before his legion of fans from Land's End to John O'Groats get there.'

'Yes, but he works funny hours.' It sounded like a poor excuse. 'And he doesn't even live in London. At least, I don't think he does.' She said, 'Jeff is more accessible.'

'Who's Jeff?' Lisa asked.

Jeff's name had leapt out, but now it felt like a regression. Minna was careful to let the words unfurl, but not gad away.

'So you're saying that your date with Jeff was hopeless?' was Lisa's evaluation.

'But so was meeting Seb,' Minna opined. That had been Minna's fault. Hadn't the mishap with Jeff been spurred as much by his awkwardness as Minna's?

'Physical proximity is one thing. What about *emotionally*?

It sounds as if Jeff's break-up was much worse than Seb's. He's damaged goods.'

'But he doesn't have a child.'

'Does Seb's daughter live with him all the time?' When Minna said no, Lisa reasoned, 'So the family schedule is probably organised to the nearest minute. You wouldn't feel like a spare part. Even so, it wouldn't hurt any prospective partner to be flexible.'

'I can be flexible,' Minna proposed. 'Of course I can . . . It's just . . . Easter was such a long time ago.'

'Some couples lose each other for decades, and then get together. You read about it.'

Was there a Cathy Kelly that she'd missed? 'I'm not sure, Lisa. I think it would be easier to have another go with Jeff.'

'How do you know I wasn't talking about Jeff?'

'Because—' She stopped. She *didn't*.

Lisa said, 'Who do you fancy most?'

Minna blurted, 'As if that helps!' Knowing that it should. Knowing that it was all that really mattered.

Gently, Lisa said, 'It sounds like Seb's forgiven you. Like he really cares. Has Jeff been in touch?'

'No, but he probably thinks we'll bump into each other. We're bound to.'

'Won't that be awkward?'

'Maybe not.' Oh, God! It had never been so difficult before. Perhaps it hadn't ever mattered so much? 'Or he might be waiting for me to call him.'

'But you'd really like him to phone you, right?'

Minna felt herself subside with longing. 'Yes.'

Lisa leaned across the table. 'Minna, you sound as if you're keener on Jeff than Seb.'

'What makes you say that?'

'You keep coming back to him. You haven't made up your mind already?'

'Of course not. I wouldn't be wasting your time if I had.'

Lisa sighed. 'It's not wasting my time, Min. I just want you to be sure what you think. I don't want to influence you.'

So it was simple. Still, she said, 'But you think I should go after Seb?'

'You don't have to go after either of them,' Lisa pointed out. 'Just because a guy snaps his fingers and says "You've pulled", doesn't mean you have to dig out your Oyster card.'

'I know that!' Minna wailed, although she suspected Seb's gentlemanliness would run to taxis.

Lisa repeated her prompt. 'Then decide.'

Minna closed her eyes briefly, as if the right answer would reveal itself on a dark screen. 'OK, then. I'll go for Seb.' It didn't feel right, or wrong.

'Ah. Why Seb?'

She took a deep breath. 'You told me to make a choice. I have.' Seb had been part of her original plan. So Seb took priority. But was that a good enough reason?

Lisa was splendidly implacable. 'And if Seb doesn't want to know?'

'I'll phone Jeff,' said Minna. 'But he won't be second best.' She added, for conviction: 'He won't be a consolation prize.'

'He'll be thrilled to know that, I'm sure,' said Lisa. 'So when are you going to put them out of their misery? When are you going to call?'

Minna phoned Seb straight away. She clung on for several hopeful moments, but then the line snapped to voicemail.

She said, 'Oh! Hi, Seb . . . this is Minna, just returning your call . . . I expect you've been crazy busy since we met at Easter . . . but I hope everything's going well. I'm just calling . . . because you suggested meeting up. Now's a really good time for me – much better than . . . well, before – so *if* it's good for you – which I *hope* it is – well, we could, if you'd *like* to. Meet up, that is. Because I would. Really. OK. Well, maybe you could let me – I mean, I'll wait to hear from you . . . Bye for now.'

Seb's message hadn't exactly purred with fuel efficiency, but then Minna's own performance was derisory. Her confidence withered. What if Seb *had* picked up? Minna would have prattled on, no doubt, waffled the way she had when she'd tried to explain to Jeff what she did for a living.

Minna tried to forget about it. All of it. Couldn't. She didn't want to let go and have another failure on her hands. For days she wrestled with her conscience. And then she did forget, as simple as that. She stopped thinking about Seb. (He hadn't responded, which helped.) It was the weirdest thing – how an obsession can just leave you, like it was only temporary to begin with. Jeff remained, but she put the thoughts on hold . . .

*   *   *

When Minna arrived in Farnham on Saturday morning, she found Lisa had called ahead (as she said she would), and not only allayed Maureen's concern but reported that Abigail Gillespie had heard her news and was fishing for information.

'So I phoned her mother,' Maureen reported, 'and filled her in. Took the wind right out of her sails to have a new wedding to chat about instead of banging on about Abbie's.'

Minna agreed this was a happy development, but she elected to end the day on a high, and returned late afternoon.

At Waterloo, she had a twinge of regret. The weather had turned grey and cold, with a bitter wind blowing. It was the kind of autumnal afternoon you want to spend at home with tea and catch-up telly. But Minna wasn't yet ready to go to the flat. There was any number of things to do instead. Galleries and museums. Shops and cafés. As she began to consider her options, her mobile began to ring.

'Minna?' Niamh, who never phoned, sounded wary. 'Are you at the flat?'

'No,' Minna replied, in a far from receptive tone. 'I'm at Waterloo.' As if lending support to her case, a platform alteration notice crackled throughout the station.

'Damn!'

'I've been at my parents',' said Minna, as if she needed to justify her behaviour.

'But you're on your way home?' Niamh was friendlier now.

'I only just got off the train.'

'But you'll be back in say, half an hour?'

'I might go shopping while I'm here.' She fancied a coffee,

at least. She might need something stronger by the end of this conversation, which had already begun to weary her.

'At Waterloo station? It's hardly Oxford Street.'

'I might wander along to the National Theatre. See what's on.'

'Minna, it's four o'clock. Any play will have started by now.'

'I could go in at the interval.' She hurtled towards the nearest exit, where she huddled in a draughty alcove, piled high with bundles of weekday papers. She pulled her coat around her with her one free hand. 'Look, Niamh, what's the problem?'

'I can't speak for long, my phone is running out of battery.'

'Is that what you've rung to tell me?'

Witheringly, Niamh explained, 'I've left my keys at home.' As if it might have been the fault of absent flatmates.

'Oh. When did you realise that?'

'This morning. I was in a bit of a hurry on my way to lunch.'

Minna said, 'If you'd phoned this morning, we could have sorted something before I'd made my plans.'

'But I'm phoning now. *What* time will you be home?'

'I don't know!' Minna was exasperated. 'Where's Sharmila? Can't she help?'

'She's not answering her phone.' Niamh paused. 'You're my only hope.' This was clearly an invidious position in which to find oneself.

'Well, you've been out all day so sure you can keep yourself amused a bit longer. I'll let you know when I'm on my way.'

Niamh was firm. 'That's not good enough. I need to be home within the hour. Someone's coming around at half-past five and I need to get ready.'

'Who's that?' Minna barked. 'Another cousin?' The words, dripping acid, sizzled as they left her lips. Minna was stunned at her own bitchiness.

Niamh gasped. '*Minna*! That was low!'

Minna hadn't regretted her tone until it struck her that by saying the word 'cousin', Jeff had become ensnared in the crossfire. Minna had done that, but Niamh had started it – Niamh had employed him as a pawn in her game.

Minna's heart was beating fast; she need to calm down. Jeff, I'm sorry. 'So where are you?'

Niamh was brisk. Or still injured. 'I'm in a jeweller's. On the Strand. Very near you.'

It was a point of fact. 'Yes. That isn't far away.'

'So you could pop across the river, couldn't you, and lend me your keys?'

'Or you could pop across and come to me.'

'I can't do that. They're fixing my watch. I daren't leave.'

'How long will it take?'

Niamh sighed. 'They've had it a week but swore it would be ready for collection today. I said I wouldn't leave without it. Still, there's free coffee on tap and no end of glossy mags.'

'You sound very comfortable. It's pretty bleak where I'm standing.'

'Well, come on over.' Niamh said, cosily. 'Since it's gone four, we could ask for wine.'

Stiffly, Minna said, 'No. No thanks. I don't need to go into town. I want to have an afternoon around the South Bank.'

'Minna, you're making this very difficult!'

No, you are! Minna couldn't believe Niamh's arrogance. But all Minna cared about was the fact that Jeff seemed lost. Service announcements filled the tense air, teasing it as far as Portsmouth and Southampton. Taking Jeff further away.

Minna didn't know what to do. If she angered Niamh, no doubt she'd incur Sharmila's wrath, and life in the flat could become even more difficult than when they'd confronted potential eviction. They'd outlived that threat, however, and anyway, since Minna had shared with Niamh and Sharmila for four years perhaps a change was overdue. Finding a new flat was preferable to seeking a new job. She'd faced *that* fear, too, and overcome it. And life at work these days was pretty good.

But here Minna was, at Waterloo Station again, so that settling *déjà vu* felt appropriate. Was she making the same mistake again? Then she wondered: *what* mistakes had she made before, exactly? And with whom? Seb? Julian? Leo? None of them was alike so how could the result be the same? What about Jeff? It felt right that in Minna's mind and heart he stood apart from the others. Just too far away from Minna herself at this present point in time.

She said, '*I'm just trying to get off the phone!*'

Niamh hounded: '*Why* won't you help me?'

'I didn't say I wouldn't!' But she hadn't said yes, had she?

Niamh said, 'This is revenge, isn't it? Oh, don't deny it,

Minna. It's revenge against me for not telling you about Jeff. Only, I was actually doing you a favour, wasn't I? Because he's turned you down, hasn't he?'

'Niamh, that's not true!' And don't you dare speak of Jeff now when you said nothing for so long.

Niamh purred, 'Frankly, I'm not surprised. I wouldn't give him another moment's thought if I were you.'

Minna took a deep breath. Words had suddenly sprung into her head. She might as well use them, if Niamh was so insistent on sustaining the tortured conversation. 'That might be difficult, because I'm actually on my way to see him.'

'*You're what?*'

'Yes. We're meeting. Later on this afternoon. I'm actually expecting his call so we'd better finish up. I'm sorry I can't help you.'

'Minna! *Don't you dare pretend*— You never mentioned Jeff until *I* mentioned him.'

'You mean he's yours not mine? Hands off? Are you jealous, Niamh?' Being bitchy delivered the most amazing high.

'*Don't* put words into my mouth. Just tell the truth. You've no plans to see Jeff. You're just getting back at me!'

'Niamh, I've got more in my life to think about than upsetting you. Jeff and I arranged this in the week.'

'Minna, I never realised you were such an absolute—'

And then the line went dead. Niamh vanished, and with her – to Minna's astonishment – went weeks and months of disdain and disappointment. How could it be so simple?

Minna dropped her hot phone into her bag, and zipped it

up. She pulled her coat around her; she'd forgotten how cold it had become this afternoon. What to do now? She had devised the meeting with Jeff to spite Niamh, it was quite true. There was no need for it now – only, it was an opportunity too good to miss. She didn't have Jeff's contact details, of course, but she knew where he'd be once the weekend was over. After all this time, surely she could last till Monday morning.

PART FOUR
SOMETHING TO SHOW

Back in the summer, Jeff overheard the phrase 'a catalogue of errors'. It referred to the failure of a launch which had been doomed from the start – a clear case of ill-conceived branding. It hadn't been Jeff's project, but he'd sympathised with the colleague concerned. The expression stayed with him until he realised it was actually a contradiction. Catalogues are tidy affairs, neatly bound between covers, consistent in style, time-sensitive, and often indexed. The problem with the campaign was that its design was haphazard, unstrategised, and showed no sign of expiration, because there was a lot of stock lingering in back rooms before making its way to a warehouse someplace.

It could have been me, Jeff thought ruefully. They're all the mistakes I've made. Luckily, I haven't been caught out, workwise. And then he was.

Jeff had a lot of catalogues to dispose of when he cleared his desk. He wouldn't fetishise them – he'd learned from the le Creuset – but he couldn't disregard their significance. For a start, harvesting heaps of pamphlets from the shelves above his desk and the drawers beneath filled in time that delayed the gathering up of personal effects. If he'd had only to fill a box with his own property, he'd have been out the door in minutes, and he hadn't wanted to disappear so quickly.

Not that he'd been written out of the company history. Guy had provided a glowing reference, although the CV it was appended to was long out of date. Sarah had always been on at Jeff to keep it relevant, even when things were going well. 'Especially then,' she'd advised. 'Always make sure your CV and your resignation letter are current.' Sarah would be the ideal person to contact for career advice. It would be a professional enquiry. But it was too risky – he might swerve off piste and plunge into the personal. He might reveal just how little heed he'd taken of the guidance she'd offered when they were together, and drop a little lower in her esteem.

Trouble was, Jeff didn't want another job like the one he'd been released from. To be honest, Sarah had been right again; it wasn't such a great role. Maybe he'd given a signal to that effect, which had been noticed. But the reality of being unemployed at Christmas was bleak. If he contacted agencies, he might get his feet under the table in a new role before December. Or he could do some temping to tide him over.

One thing was for sure: Jeff never intended to start a business of his own, and so soon after leaving Go Aware. If asked, he'd admit to feeling daunted by investigating EU conventions and offering up years' worth of bank and mortgage statements. He had no plan, no model to follow. The fact is, however, we seek nourishment from the crumbs of continuity in life, like a chick gobbling whatever sustenance its mother presents to its desperate beak. Faced with vacant days, and going stir crazy, it's no wonder Jeff began to consider the merchandising opportunities that lay within the catalogues which glowered from various points around the living room.

He should have left them in the office, of course, but he didn't regret his actions. It had been a rescue mission. He'd never volunteered, let alone trained, to be custodian of the company archive. He'd asked if there was a successor in line? (His clients were swiftly handed over to other colleagues, apart from the sports charity, which was dropped.) His e-mails about it went unanswered. The team doesn't deserve the right to look after them, he thought. Well, they ditched three employees, why stop there?

Jeff contacted a specialist museum but they were waiting to be rehoused and couldn't store new acquisitions. He called some of the companies who had used Go Aware's services, not exactly spelling out the fact that he was no longer employed. He spoke with communications officers and marketing departments. 'Just checking if you have file copies?' He could offer to scan them, he supposed, it would be something to do. 'Are they worth keeping?' he was asked, and he realised he hadn't looked at them closely.

The second week of November was one of biblical rain and Jeff was glad to stay indoors. He decided to start sorting through his piles of publications, logging them in an Excel spreadsheet. It was a revelation: some of the brochures pre-dated Go Aware's inception by twenty years or more. In a paper envelope was a clutch of pristine brochures from the 1950s, advertising the latest household appliances. There were specs on cars and other cutting-edge technology. It seemed so quaint, and outdated, but had immediate appeal to Jeff who so often felt out of step with his present circumstances. He wondered if other people sought reassurance in this kind of material. Jeff got online and searched for websites and fan clubs and came up with limitless hits.

Jeff put one last e-mail into work – his old work – seeking direction for the archive, and waited a couple of days. There was no reply, but when he returned to the flat from the pool one afternoon he found three boxes on his doormat, full of additional print material.

Next day, Jeff began phoning the presidents and secretaries of societies he'd found on the web. Yes, they'd be interested in seeing his collection. (He made it sounded more extensive than it was.) Was he upset to break it up? 'No, I haven't got the space,' he improvised, and perhaps these older-sounding voices assumed he was parking a bachelor's obsession prior to getting married. There was no need to explain his actual misfortune.

In fact, Jeff felt far from pessimistic. Responding to approval, he began to sense a flicker of confidence that might just become a winning streak. There was an AGM in Watford he was invited to exhibit at. There were other meet-ups around greater London. If Jeff was willing to travel, he'd find homes for his collection. And so he did.

*   *   *

'You're doing a what?' demanded Steve, having been brought up to date. (At first he'd enquired: 'Are you harbouring stolen property?' which was ironic, since Steve had advised his brother to stock up on gel pens before he left.) The brothers were in a pub, of course; this one was just up the road from Blackfriars, near St Paul's, on a Monday evening.

Momentarily flattened, Jeff explained, 'It's a car boot sale. It's off the A3. Can I borrow the Audi?'

'Fucking hell! Has it really come to this?'

Jeff was certain Steve was teasing, but he wanted to be clear. 'To what?'

'My brother, like someone off *EastEnders*.'

'I never knew you were such a snob.'

Steve glowered. 'I never knew you'd sink so low.'

He and Steve hadn't argued since they'd physically fought as boys over second helpings or food or space allocated in shared rooms on holiday or penalties awarded in neighbourhood friendlies. Then, the physical release had been fun. Celia and Nigel had never had to worry that they'd come to any harm. Or perhaps they'd chosen not to worry. But that had been thirty years ago.

A beat passed, as if Steve were switching into a character. Suddenly, there seemed to be more than three years between them. Steve said, 'This year, Jeff, I've watched you give up, more and more, on everything and everybody. It breaks my heart.'

Jeff had a dreadful suspicion that he might cry, but fought against it. 'Well, you haven't done anything to stop it.'

Steve spread his hands. 'Who said it's up to me?'

'You mean I've got to drag myself out of the gutter. Thanks.'

'You could do with chucking out that shirt for a start. The collar's frayed.'

That was unnecessary, but he didn't want to retaliate. In his most reasonable tone, Jeff said, 'I'm going to do this, Steve. Whether I can borrow your car or not.'

His brother looked pained. 'But catalogues? Why can't you trade in something with a bit more wow factor. Vinyl. Old telephones. Anglepoise lamps. There's money to be made in the retro market, but you have to offer what people want.'

'I know that,' Jeff said, hoping he could still get Steve on board. 'I've had serious interest. I really think I'm on to something.'

He indicated their empty glasses, and stood, ready to fetch refills. Earlier, Steve had made a point of saying that Jeff ought to save money, but he did not object a second time. In fact, Steve seemed to have settled into a kind of sulk. Jeff felt suddenly buoyant – though at nobody's expense – and wanted to cheer his brother. 'I'll let you know how I get on,' he smiled. 'One of us just might be surprised.'

Jeff borrowed Celia's car, no questions asked. (He'd hoped for more of a conversation, to be honest; a spark of curiosity, at least.) He took to the A3 at dawn on Saturday, the back seat folded down to accommodate the cartons, and ended up in a field after a sharp turn off a sliproad. If Celia's silence was ominous and the empty dawn roads eerily apocalyptic, the day itself was enriching.

Apparently, anything print-related was a no-no for a boot-fair. 'As for books!' shrieked a fellow stallholder. 'Don't even go there. Unless they're children's books.' Other items which could not be disposed of for neither love nor money included picture frames, glasses, records and video tapes and kitchenware (Jeff did not enquire if this was brand specific). Hand tools were popular, and electrical goods. 'Just don't get them wet, obviously.' Jeff was also advised to bring a mate next time, or a partner. Well, chance would be a fine thing, wouldn't it?

Despite the fact he shifted nothing, the day was a happy one for Jeff. Fresh air. Mud (at least the rain had stopped). Camaraderie. Integrity: years of history carried in palm-pounded coins and sweaty, tattered bank notes. New faces, eager to be impressed, or persuaded or to have goals fulfilled or opportunities seized. It reminded Jeff – well, he hadn't quite forgotten – that he was, after all, a salesman. Maybe he *should* think about diversifying and using his contacts to source some really saleable end-of-line or second-hand stock. He could really see himself making it work.

If only they could see me now, he imagined thinking at the end of a future sunlit and successful day. People's faith in him would be restored. But the old question pulled rank. Who'd be looking?

Jeff had a tip-off about a church hall event in Egham the next Friday, and despite the location being way off home turf, decided to give it a go. He'd done very nicely with a stash of *Melody Maker*s he'd acquired by way of a first day cover specialist, on eBay, as it happened. A group of tourists with a taxi waiting had all but cleared him out.

Jeff had a missed call driving home and when he got to the flat, after a hellish journey through a sequence of school runs, another message from the same, unfamiliar number. He left both, ravenous for his dinner – these days, the fridge was always decently stocked. He'd just washed up and was getting ready for the ten o'clock news when the phone rang again. It was the same number.

Usually polite, Jeff couldn't disguise his irritation. He had PPI claims in mind. He said, 'Who is this?'

There was silence and a clearing of the throat. 'Hello, Jeff, I'm sorry to call you so late, but I wonder if I might take up a moment of your time?' The voice was precise but Jeff wondered if it were modified and suddenly thought of kidnaps and ransoms. He'd been warned about cranks and obsessives but could you spot them just by voice – or the slightly creepy tactic of a late-night call? He hurried to the window to see if Celia's car, which he'd kept all week, was still parked across the street. It was.

'I'm sorry,' said the caller. 'My name is Leonard D'Arblay and we met earlier today. I was interested in your Electrolux catalogues, circa 1980.'

Jeff checked the car again, for they were still in the boot. Nobody had touched them in three weeks. Lugging them in and out of the flat seemed a gesture that mocked his poor choice in acquiring them. (He'd need to watch his back – he'd felt a twinge the other day. He must find out if swimming helped or hindered, because he'd started going to the pool three times a week.)

'Not interested enough to buy them,' Jeff responded.

'I realise my mistake,' admitted Leonard. 'So I wonder if we could meet to discuss them further.'

'I don't make private appointments,' said Jeff. It came out sounding cocky, which wasn't his intention. Leonard sounded a polite sort of chap, and one-to-one appointments might be a warmer, drier route to lucrative business.

'I could make it worth your while,' said Leonard. 'Weekdays, I'm based in Hammersmith but at the weekends you'll generally find me just outside Reading.'

'Ah, I'm based in south-east London, and I tend not to ...' Jeff trailed off. He quite liked driving. It wasn't as if he had any other demands on his time.

'As I say, I'd make it worth your while.'

Did Jeff imagine the menace, or was it only in his mind? Instinctively, he tightened his grip on the conversation, trying to undermine Leonard, whose position as the customer was probably the stronger. 'What exactly is your interest in the catalogues? Are you connected to the firm?'

Leonard affected a dismissive laugh. 'No, no, it isn't that. I'm just an ... enthusiast. I'm sure you've met plenty of people like me!'

Clever, thought Jeff. I couldn't remember him, and now he's making it impossible to distinguish him from anyone else, and isolate a vulnerability or weakness.

'Oh yes.' Jeff maintained an agreeable tone. 'But enthusiasts hate to leave empty-handed. They usually buy at events, not phone up for chats.' Was it worth asking how Leonard had acquired his number? No, keep to the point. Targetted. 'I'm going to be in Farnham on Sunday, so you could come along then.' He added, cleverly, 'I'd recommend getting there early. So you don't miss out.'

Leonard said tersely, 'I'm afraid I can't do that. I'd prefer it if you came to me.'

'I don't do west London. Or Berkshire.'

Leonard was downright testy. 'But I want the catalogues.'

'Make me an offer, then, including postage and packing.'

Leonard was furious. 'What? Now? I need to see them again. To be sure they're in good enough condition.'

'They're in excellent condition.' I'm the only one who's touched them, he thought. 'You would have seen that today and it's why you're phoning me now. You obviously want them so, like I said, make me an offer.'

'May I ask about their provenance?'

'Their ... what?'

'How they came into your possession?'

'You want to go straight to my supplier?' Jeff blurted, clearly revealing his defensive position.

'I wouldn't dream of it,' said Leonard, perhaps hatching an idea. And why not? 'You asked about my connection so I thought I'd ask about yours.'

'I really don't have time for this right now. I've got to prepare for the weekend.'

Jeff had been warned about timewasters, the perils of passive-aggressive behaviour, the sheer exhaustion brought on by so-called experts who lecture you about your own stock. Did Leonard fit any of these categories? At least he wasn't a thief.

'Jeff, if you'd agreed to meet me we could have resolved this several moments ago.'

'And if you'd made me an offer . . .' Oh, god. Jeff was running out of patience, no – it was passion. The man could have the bloody catalogues for nothing, if he could be arsed to collect them. And if he played it straight with Jeff, who tried one last time: 'Look, come along on Sunday. I'll put them aside for you, all neatly wrapped up. How does that sound?'

A little desperate to Jeff's own ears, if he were honest. Leonard remained unmoved.

'I told you, I can't come on Sunday. You have to come to me.'

'I can't do that.'

'*Why* not, Jeff? Why are you making it so difficult? Don't you want me to buy them?'

'I don't mind whether you do or not,' said Jeff, but he knew that he should. He must. 'I mean, I'm not stopping you.'

'Yes, you are. You're being cruel.' That was surprisingly emotive. 'What do they matter to you? You don't know they're worth anything.'

'They are?' said Jeff, hoping it sounded like a rhetorical question. It had been ages since he'd negotiated prices – not that he'd ever enjoyed haggling or bargaining. It seemed so underhand.

'They are to me,' said Leonard.

'I still don't know who you are, or how you got my number.'

'Then meet me and let me buy them and I won't bother you again. I can guarantee it.'

'I don't accept cheques,' said Jeff, imposing the policy there and then. 'We are talking cash here, aren't we?'

'Oh, forget it!' Leonard snarled, 'just forget it!', and disconnected the call.

The suddenness struck Jeff like a blow. He'd seen a wide spectrum of behaviour in his fifteen years of paid employment, and had emerged from a negotiation the poorer party more often than not. He hadn't expected freelance life to abide by the same codes of conduct, but was there any reason why it shouldn't? He must ask Steve, if Steve didn't object to having his long-established business likened to Jeff's nascent enterprise.

Actually, Jeff already knew a big difference – if you're responsible for your own livelihood, you have to go above and beyond. Be extra courteous, as well as super resourceful. Lick arse when required. People talk to each other; your whole reputation can go down the pan if you cross the wrong person.

Jeff had been careless with Leonard, who for all he knew might be the chair of some international hobbyists' lobby group with a specialist chapter down the street. Even if Leonard was only Joe Public, Jeff's behaviour had been unprofessional. If Jeff had conducted a client meeting in the way he'd spoken to Leonard he'd have been out the door long ago. Perhaps he *had*?

Mollified, Jeff returned the call in the morning but Leonard didn't answer, and didn't respond to Jeff's grovelling message. Nor his second one. Not everyone has the hang of voicemail, but perhaps Leonard was furious. He had every right to be.

Then again, faced with Jeff's obstinacy he might have lost interest. Maybe Leonard hadn't really wanted the catalogues. Jeff supposed it's possible that the more you denied somebody something, the more they wanted it. You can create need by holding back something that wasn't ever desired. It sounded like a slippery tactic – not one in which Jeff wanted to engage.

He'd watch out for people like Leonard in future, but Jeff was more troubled by his own behaviour. He couldn't shake the fear that he had turned into an unlikeable person. Since when? Since the firm had let him go – had it made him bitter? Or had it been a gradual deterioration of character? He considered those unenviable qualities inherited from Celia – not that she was responsible for his behaviour. His mother wasn't a bad person by any means. But it hurt that she had offered no reciprocal support, apart from the loan of her car. He'd have trusted her guidance, because he envied her tenacity.

Just as Celia had persisted with her interest in Grace, Jeff longed – if the chance arose – to be equipped to say to Minna, 'I never stopped thinking about you.' He hoped Celia might shine a light on some quality of his that would unlock those words.

Jeff *did* think of Minna a lot of the time. After all, we value continuity more perhaps than innovation. The less attractive flipside was that because of this, he was still inactive when it came to making progress with Minna. Even though nothing was stopping him. It shamed him now – it *really* did. If only he'd achieved the rebrand he'd envisaged, because that was his dilemma: he couldn't see himself with Minna. No matter that no one was looking at him. Jeff just couldn't see *himself*.

Alone with his thoughts, Jeff was frustrated, embarrassed; as if his body was covered in scabs. If he couldn't bear his own company, how would that impact on his chances of seeking long-term, fulfilling work, and success, to say nothing of finding love? (When he wanted to say a great deal about that.) Nobody had warned him of this potential side effect of spending so much time on his own. They'd talked about loneliness, but not self-loathing.

That was something you had to discover in your own time and completely by yourself. But was 'by yourself' the only way to overcome it?

You can't hide for ever and Jeff's window of self-exile was short-lived, because it was his father's birthday the last week of November. Usually, it was quite an event in the Sullivan family, because Jeff, Steve and Celia's birthdays were all clustered around the May bank holidays. Celebrations were thin on the ground till Nigel's, for which they all paused, before girding their loins for Christmas. Jeff appreciated the pause more than he normally did, because he wasn't yet ready for the end of the year.

He phoned Celia, who didn't remark on his lack of communication, then asked what the plan was for Nigel.

'You'll all come round for lunch, I expect,' she replied, without much enthusiasm.

Jeff tried not to interpret this as a portent of doom for the day. So he wasn't over-compensating when he brought more effort than usual to his gift and card selection. He had more time to choose (was his excuse if needed) but the fact was 'the world's best dad' card really had been the only suitable one he could find in WH Smith. Quite a few others seemed to be missing envelopes. Everything else seemed geared to Christmas.

Perhaps any effort this year was overstepping the mark, pending more urgent but displaced resolutions. Alyx couldn't make it because she was in bed with a cold (lucky her) and Steve looked a bit sniffly himself (and threatened to leave early). Celia asked if they made 'world's best mum' cards, because she'd never seen one. In fact, both Celia and Steve regarded Jeff suspiciously at different points in the day. Steve took his brother to one side to ask, 'What are you trying to prove?' Jeff couldn't answer – not even to say 'Nothing' which was the truth. He just absorbed the blame like a sponge. He could have guessed the result of upstaging his brother would be nothing more than embarrassment.

Luckily, Nigel seemed oblivious to the tension. Until lunch, he sat in the living room listening to his new CD (from Steve and Alyx), wearing his birthday jumper (from Jeff – accompanied by a bottle of brandy it was the most prized gift), letting everyone else around him do the work. But he must have known that you can only trade on being the birthday boy for so long.

However limited his father's was, Jeff had no excuse himself. The minutes dragged slowly, painfully. Jeff longed to spirit himself away and as soon as the meal was over, he insisted that he'd wash up, so his parents could retire to the living room with coffee. He was relishing the solitude, the lack of imposition, when Celia sidled up to him and said: 'You've been quiet today, son. Anything the matter?'

Too tersely, he said, 'Apart from losing my job, you mean?'

Celia frowned. 'I know it's awful but you'll find something, won't you? And you'll be all right till you do.'

'Yes, I'm OK financially, Mum,' he said, feeling annoyed that he'd already squandered this opportunity to speak. 'Everything is fine.'

Celia nodded, though it might have been a shrug – Jeff didn't know because he couldn't look at her – and started putting plates in the cupboard. Jeff, rigid, immobile, wished she'd leave him alone.

She said, 'OK, OK. I can take a hint. I'll leave you in peace.' She closed the cupboard door. On parting, she said, 'Just don't tell me *you're* giving up on me too?'

He groaned. 'No, Mum, of course not!'

How strange it was to feel remorseful and wronged simultaneously. He flinched.

'So what's next?' he asked, fiercely scrubbing a pan with steel wool.

Celia took a step back, and her voice was sharp and guarded, as if suspecting Jeff had set a trap. 'What do you mean?'

Jeff wished he hadn't spoken. 'I just mean, have you got any other projects in mind?'

Celia sighed. 'Not currently.' She'd caught his drift. He hadn't foreseen she might be offended by it. She flicked a tea-towel so it nearly clipped Jeff across the cheek. 'But don't worry. I shan't darken your door with them if I do.'

What had Celia meant by people 'giving up' on her? How could she say that when she had Grace, her new discovery? Could she be referring to people at work? Jeff's heart quickened: Dad? No, not him. Surely now.

Jeff knew what it was like to be abandoned. He ought to be able to pick up on the fear in other people. But perhaps, in his absences, he had missed some major development. Oh, but wouldn't Steve have said something if there was a real problem?

'So what's next?' Jeff wouldn't have the courage to ask it of himself, so what had possessed him to demand it of his mother? And there was the risk he might learn something he didn't want to hear. With Celia's tart dismissal, he'd got off lightly. But it couldn't be the last word. It couldn't be the end.

On 1 December, Jeff set up spreadsheets to show his in- and outgoings. He had spaces booked at Christmas Fairs and into January, and no end of supply of possible stock. (His mind had turned to candlesticks and holders.) He contemplated buying a car – just a cheap runabout with a decent boot, which in turn put him in mind of insurance. The stock in his flat was of value, even if he wasn't always aware of its worth in advance. He needed to take this new business seriously.

One of the bright points in his new life was visits to the pool. It was ironic that having lost control of the sports account, possibly having let it deteriorate, Jeff now threw himself into swimming. Quickly, Jeff lost the weight he'd acquired and had toned up. He actually looked quite good, and was aware of the occasional glance of interest from both men and women.

By their very nature, routines bring recurrence – though they'd never yielded Minna (sigh) – and there was one woman he'd clocked who seemed to match Jeff's thrice weekly visits. Jeff wondered by what means their schedules coincided. On Thursday morning, Jeff came out of the men's changing room, fully dressed and ready to depart, when he saw her, hovering anxiously, in the doorway of the ladies'. It was a leg he noticed first.

Did she mean to catch his eye? Jeff said, 'Why are you hopping?'

'I've lost a shoe,' she replied, revealing a second leg, in a trainer, planted on the ground. The first, which Jeff had noticed and was bare was pressed against her other calf, as if in a yoga position. 'I'd say someone nicked it but why would they take one shoe?'

Jeff asked, 'Have you looked on top of the lockers?'

She looked anxious. 'Yes, *everywhere*. It's definitely gone. And I've a terrible fear of veruccas.'

Jeff nodded. He knew it was a hazard. 'Is there no one around to help?'

'As luck would have it, no. That's why I'm perched here, like a flamingo.' Her jumper was pink, he noticed. 'I was hoping someone I knew might pop along. Or one of the staff, but nobody, no . . . I don't suppose you—'

'Me?'

'Well, they sell flip-flops in the canteen. It's a bit of a walk . . . but I could give you the money. I'm a seven. Any colour would do.'

'What colours are there?'

'I'm not sure. There'll be red, I suppose, or blue. If I had a preference I'd go for red.'

'Even with that jumper?'

She seemed impressed. 'Are you in fashion?'

Jeff nearly laughed. 'No.' He almost blurted that he had no job at all. He said, 'Sorry. Of course I'll go to the shop. I'd be happy to. Wait there.'

To repay his kindness, she insisted on coffee. That is, she said she was gasping and would shout Jeff one, too. He accepted, feeling cold despite his dashing about; the last thing he wanted was illness.

Her name was Laurel, pronounced in a way so mellifluous she seemed exotic, as if from another world. Jeff couldn't imagine her equipped with a business card or noted as 'Absent with apologies' on minutes. He liked the fact that she worked part-time as a model, specialising in hands and feet (hence the need for protective footwear on the germ-ridden tiles of the changing area). It would have been rude to inspect too closely but Jeff gleaned enough to decide she could probably promote any part of her body that she chose. The rest of her time was spent child-minding, although she had no offspring of her own. Jeff ascertained that she was single.

How would he explain *himself* – or would there be no need? Laurel hadn't asked a single question, yet, but he didn't really mind. He just liked being in her company. She was sexy, for sure, although it didn't feel like a particularly sexy scenario. There was something slightly absurd about it – quite probably distasteful – like a scene from a 1970s sitcom in which a suited businessman chats up a woman in a bikini. After all, on each previous occasion, Laurel had been virtually naked. But then so had Jeff.

This wasn't a missed opportunity, that's for sure. Besides, any action – even in thought – would be a betrayal of Minna, the woman he wanted. Forewarned is forearmed, so Jeff felt he was on safe ground.

Luckily, there was no need to wrestle with his conscience because another set of thoughts had slid into view. They involved an idea which he'd been mulling over in quiet moments, most recently at the old Wimbledon dogs track. He'd jotted down a few notes and had named a file on his laptop for when he had a moment to write up details.

'Talking to you, Laurel,' he said with unpractised candour, 'has given me some really good ideas about the business I've been developing. You obviously have an entrepreneurial streak yourself.'

Laurel perked up at once. 'Sounds interesting, Jeff. Tell me about it.'

She wouldn't lose interest, he felt, but he knew he mustn't waste time. 'It's a sort of "Where are they now?" for people who aren't famous.'

'Oh really?' she said, warningly.

'I don't mean you—' said Jeff, flushing hotly, and gave a self-preserving laugh that sounded like a car with a flat tyre dragging itself across cobblestones. 'Of course not.'

Colour returned to Laurel's cheeks. 'Who *do* you mean, Jeff? All the world's a stage, as they say.'

No one I know would say that, thought Jeff. He said, 'It would be for people trying to connect with their pasts.' He buzzed with inspiration. 'The people they used to be.'

Laurel sniffed. 'That sounds a bit depressing, to be honest. I used to like Friends Reunited but with Facebook you can track anyone down for free. Only . . . well, where's the *glamour* in that? I like a bit of glamour, Jeff. I like excitement. Is there excitement in your idea?'

Jeff was excited now. His idea was full of possibilities. *Life* was. 'We'll see! So my basic idea would be to track down magazines where models appeared. I'm talking about the 8os and 9os, though earlier if possible. Complete copies, with all the ads and the fashions and the views of the days. I mean, the models would have photos.'

'Contact prints, in a pre-digital age.'

'But would they keep only clippings?' he asked. 'People move around, you have to throw things out. So you wouldn't keep complete publications which capture the mood and the details of the era. But context is so important.' He allowed himself a flash of pride at the smoothness of his delivery. Had he ever been so persuasive in an office presentation? And Laurel was nodding, as if completely sold on his idea.

'Would it be lucrative?' she wanted to know.

'Maybe not to start with,' said Jeff, 'but it would be fun.'

She clapped her hands. 'I love fun. But how would you keep afloat?' She lowered her gaze. 'Are you secretly rich, Jeff?'

'Not at all,' he admitted. With care, his redundancy would last till the spring. He wouldn't touch the equity from the flat sale, although he mustn't leave it too late to buy again.

Laurel finished her drink and smiled. She said, 'It's a *fun* idea, and it's been *fun* talking to you, Jeff.'

Dismay rippled through Jeff. They seemed to be at the end with no next steps agreed. 'We should talk some more about it.'

'Get carried away, you mean?' Her laugh was light and tinkly. 'It's *fun* to think of alternative jobs that won't ever happen, isn't it?'

His stomach flipped. 'Oh. I was being serious. You mean—'

'Of course it would never work!'

'You wouldn't be interested in giving it a try? As a hobby?'

'Jeff! We don't know each other. We're not about to go into business together.'

'Well, not immediately, no.'

'I thought you were going to ask me on a date.'

'Well, I was. I mean, I'd like to.' *A date?* They could meet. Go for a walk. Have a meal. Like with Alison, only not. So what, then? For fuck's sake. What did he want? What about Laurel? The mistake he'd made with Alison was neglecting her perspective. 'Would you?'

'Jeff, that's an afterthought if ever I heard one.'

He burned. 'No! I promise! It isn't.'

'You mean you wanted to get me into bed the moment you clapped eyes on me?'

'Well, yes ... no ... It's not ...' Just one more dig and he could jump in the hole, but Jeff stopped there.

'Sorry, Jeff, I haven't the time.' She pulled her phone from her bag. 'I certainly don't have time right now. In fact, I'm late already. I'm always late. Like I said, it's been lovely talking to you and thanks for your help. You're a lifesaver.'

Feebly, he offered, 'I enjoyed talking to you ...'

Laurel stood up. 'Tell you what, if in ten years' time I start wondering what I was doing today, I'll drop you a line and see if you can track me down.'

'I don't even know your full name.'

'Don't worry, it'll be on everyone's lips in a decade.' She blew a kiss from her own, and followed it with a peal of laughter. 'In my dreams!' She leaned across the table, and kissed him on the forehead. It was like being kissed by his gran.

When all he wanted was to be kissed by Minna. *Minna*. His whole body sighed with longing.

Shit. Even with eyes wide open, even with the benefit of lessons learned, he'd got it wrong *again*. Did that mean he would never get it right?

*　　*　　*

Jeff spent Friday gearing up for a table top sale in Farnham. It was a success – someone had actually come just to meet him, having read a snippet in a newsletter Jeff had forgotten he'd contributed to. It turned out that Jeff's catalogues covered the launch of a unique patent which had excited the motor industry in 1968. A local paper had wanted to interview him, but fortunately he was able to summon a real expert in time.

Sunday found him knackered. He returned his hired car first thing on Monday, after which he'd gone straight to a pool – a different pool, for the variety, not avoidance. To prove he truly wasn't inhibited by Laurel's rejection, Jeff devoted Tuesday to Googling actors who had been former models, tipped off by a piece in a freebie magazine tucked under the post downstairs. There *was* mileage in his idea, but it needed finessing. Jeff worked late on Tuesday night and designated Wednesday as a free day, before he began turning his mind to another weekend.

So it was just as well that Steve waited till the new week to summon his brother for a drink. 'I've finished for the day and I'm practically on your doorstep. Peckham Rye.' The invitation had been soured slightly by Steve's offhand postscript: 'You've got nothing else on, have you?' Jeff wondered if he ought to be offended at the presumption of idleness. He could have said he was about to go out. That he was out already (although the flat was silent and switching on the TV wouldn't create convincing noise). Or that he was waiting for an important phone call that might result in work. Anything to put paid to the notion that he was idle and could respond to any other person's beck and call.

But that seemed like such an *effort*. And, at the same time, needlessly defensive. When it's all said and done, we're *all* at other people's beck and call, aren't we? We need the push and pull to do things. Jeff knew he needed it, perhaps more than most people.

And Steve was being kind. It wasn't as if he were short of mates to invite to the pub. No doubt, there were people desperately angling for an invitation, who'd have clawed Jeff's eyes out in jealousy. Steve had Alyx, too, of course; a whole other life that would fill another category of person with envy.

Perhaps he should have invited Steve to his flat. Home was tidy-ish because lots of the catalogues had gone but there was new stock, in boxes, which he could shift into corners. Steve could see how busy his brother was. But the arrangement was made, and Steve liked pubs. So Jeff set off, glad he'd put on a waterproof jacket because the gunmetal sky started haemorrhaging rain before he got to the end of the road.

Unsurprisingly, when Jeff arrived cold and dripping, he found his brother toasty warm in a crisp white shirt, backlit by candles, reading the *Evening Standard*. Steve was full of beans, but when was he not? Jeff had the beginnings of a beard, because he'd not left the flat for three days.

When the brothers hugged, Jeff felt as if his ribs and chest would fracture, as if so starved he'd been of human touch that his bones had atrophied. Settled with drinks (Jeff bought them), he fired off questions about Steve's work (at lunchtime, Steve had heard he'd lost a tender to a rival, hence the early end to his day, but he was stoic), about Alyx (her cold had been nasty, but she was back on her feet), about many things like government lobbying and cycle lanes. Then Steve asked after him. It seemed a reasonable order of priority. Steve can't have been too worried or despairing of Jeff's situation or else he'd have cut to the chase. And presumably, their parents hadn't sent Steve to south-east London to check on his brother. Jeff was pleased about this, he supposed.

'What have I been up to?' Jeff said. Diminished already, he shrank a little more. 'I'm never in, these days.'

Steve was encouraging. 'Great. That's good. So what have you achieved?'

Was Jeff's upcoming schedule any more likely to impress Steve than his recent endeavours? It was scarcely the farewell tour of a legendary pop group. But the thought of falling stars reminded Jeff of Laurel at the pool. He shared the story. Perhaps it would sound comical instead of sordid.

Afterwards, Steve set his glass down on the table, and spoke above the din which had just encroached upon them. (Boney M, Jeff observed – no hiding from Christmas now.) 'Sorry if I heard – but you had a drink with a model?'

'Yes. That's where I got the idea.'

'The idea? The idea to sleep with her?'

'No, not that.' He didn't mean to sound prudish. 'My new idea – the one I just told you about. I think it's got more legs, in the long-term, than car boot sales. Don't you?'

'Sorry – whose legs are we talking about? The model?'

Jeff was over Laurel. But that didn't mean he had to write off their entire conversation. 'No, my idea.'

'Just remind me again – what *is* your idea?'

Jeff thought he'd made it plain. He made sure his explanation was even clearer, and more detailed (though it took some improvisation) the second time.

'And you're quite serious about this?' Steve said calmly. 'You've talked to other people?'

'Well, only Laurel. But she doesn't count. It's too early to share more widely. I need to run some figures. Make a few phone calls.'

Steve sat back, looking dubious. 'Is that so?'

Jeff looked away, suddenly coy. 'Yes.' His cheeks burned.

'What *about* Laurel?'

'She's not interested in my idea,' Jeff admitted.

'But you're interested in her. So what happened?'

'Nothing. She wasn't interested in me. Or my idea.'

'So you tried to impress her?'

'Well, sort of.' Jeff began squirming uncontrollably. Could this be guilt, at last?

'Did you fancy her?'

'Of course. She was stunning.'

'You made a move?'

'I didn't get the chance. She kind of nipped it in the bud.'

Steve frowned. 'What did you do wrong?'

Jeff's shaking had subsided. 'Why do you suppose I did anything wrong?'

'Stands to reason, doesn't it? You fancied her, she was obviously keen on you or else she wouldn't have joined you for coffee. So how did you fuck up?'

Jeff closed his eyes, shuttering himself from the external attack, which only brought his internal view into sharp relief. 'I didn't fuck up. Why do you think I fucked up?'

'You fucked up with . . . that girl. Whoever she was.'

It was a kick in the guts. No, lower. Jeff yelped. 'Minna!' He cursed Steve; no, himself. 'Fuck. Why did you mention her?'

What Jeff meant was, *Don't mention Minna in the same breath as Laurel.* But how dare he say that to Steve when he himself had done enough to wonder if he'd been betraying Minna by so much as thinking about Laurel? God, what if he had slept with Laurel? He so wanted to be true to Minna.

Steve glowered. 'I'm right, Jeff, aren't I? That's why you've done nothing to arrange for us to meet. You haven't been dating Minna. You never got that far.'

Jeff could only let out a desperate moan.

Steve softened. 'But you wanted to?'

Jeff imagined it, and an ache went through him again. 'Yes.' Oh yes.

'So what's actually going on?' Steve asked.

Jeff's shoulders slumped. 'Oh, well . . . Minna's still in the old building, presumably. I haven't been back.' If Steve queried this, Jeff could allude to stolen property.

'Is she locked in the turret, unable to escape? Surely you could pull up a ladder.' Steve slammed the table in frustration, unperturbed that other customers had noticed – even the guy behind the bar.

'You're making a scene,' Jeff said.

Steve fought back. 'And I'll bet you made a right show of yourself in front of Laurel.'

'OK, OK. So shoot me.'

'Don't be like that, Jeff. Do something constructive for once.'

'Like what?'

'Why don't you go and see Minna?'

'I can't just do that!'

'Why not? You'd have gone off with Laurel willingly enough.'

Ouch. But it was the truth, and truths were hard to come by. He'd have gone back for more of Alison, wouldn't he? And he'd have returned to Sarah like a shot. You might as well be hung for a sheep as a lamb, so Jeff took it all on the chin.

Steve checked his watch. 'It's just gone three. You could be waiting for her when she gets out of work.'

'I don't know what time she finishes.'

Steve's patience was endless. 'Surely you've got a rough idea.'

Of course he did. Jeff conjured an image of the ground floor foyer of the Eversholt Street building. You entered and left through doors at the side. Once inside, you had to pass a bank of sofas, set against the window, on the way to the front desk and the barriers that led to the lifts. Jeff could wait on the sofas, like any visitor; well, he no longer had his pass. There might be other people to make him less conspicuous. Ah, that could be a snag: staff didn't notice the sofas, unless they'd arranged to meet someone. If they were chatting to colleagues, they'd be preoccupied until they sailed out into the evening, into freedom. You had to be in an expectant frame of mind to notice …

Was Minna? Had it ever occurred to Minna these past few months to wait for Jeff? You had to have a reason to look, after all. Did she?

There was only one way to find out. 'I suppose I could …' He knew he must.

Steve beamed for the first time throughout the conversation. 'Why not? Have you got anything else on? Is there anything else you'd rather be doing?'

The third question clinched it. There was nothing in the world Jeff wanted to do more.

Jeff had omitted from his conjured image the annual transformation of the faceless foyer into Santa's Grotto. The building's managers went to town at Christmas, not only with the elaborately festooned floor-to-ceiling tree, but other decorations, such as tinsel on the security barriers (which rubbed off on to overcoats and suits), and artificial snow on the floor of the executive lift. It was always a shock the first day you encountered it, as it was today.

Jeff took a seat, his face averted from the tree so he wasn't blinded by the intermittent flashes of red and white light, and waited. He looked for changes to the set-up, but it was only six weeks since he'd left. He felt no anxiety about being here; that was all reserved for his encounter with Minna. Each time a new set of people was released from the barriers he looked up, anxiously. He knew he'd see old faces, and wondered if they would seem awkward. The first did a double-take, but smiled and made an excuse about having to hurry to meet friends. The second was on his phone but spotted Jeff at once, as if there was nothing unusual about his presence. Perhaps he didn't know that Jeff had left. No Guy. No Guy's PA, which was probably good.

No Minna, which troubled him. Taking a hint from his surroundings, Jeff wondered if it could be the evening of Macsamphire Strutt's Christmas party. The staff might have left early for the venue, or else be having warm-up drinks while people took turns to get changed. He vehemently hoped it wasn't – he could offer nothing to rival it.

When Minna appeared, at ten past six, she was one of half a dozen departees and luckily engaged with none of them. Jeff stood the moment he saw her, heart thumping, and moved to in front of the sofas so Minna could not fail to notice him. But it looked like she'd spotted him already.

'Jeff,' she said, quizzically. 'I haven't seen you for ages.'

He gestured at his jeans and sweatshirt. 'I don't work here any more.'

'Oh.' She nodded, perhaps reluctantly. 'That explains why, I guess. Are you here to see someone?'

I'm here to see you. It was the only thing to say, but nerves, suddenly, made speech an agony. That, and his astonishment that he was once again speaking to Minna. She was more beautiful than he'd remembered. Was he out of his depth? He said, 'I just came to drop off a parcel.'

'Christmas presents?' she said, not moving. 'That's nice. Chocolates for the old team, that kind of thing.'

No! 'Yes.' He suddenly felt the urge to move. 'But I'm done now. Are you off somewhere special, Minna?'

'Only home,' she said, and buttoned her coat. 'Are you heading to the tube?'

It'd be a start, wouldn't it? A slow stroll to Euston. A chance to re-establish the connection. To express what he felt. To listen to what Minna might have to say. Jeff nodded, and they emerged from the building into the chill evening. At least it wasn't raining.

'I was made redundant,' he said. He meant to say something witty, or more in tune with festive vibes, but once the words were out he was glad to have shed them.

Minna stopped and turned to him. 'Oh. I'm sorry to hear that. I didn't know.'

'It happened at the end of October.'

Was she making a mental calculation? *Our date was in February. You had eight months to get in touch again.* Or had she forgotten about the date? In the end she said, 'I'm not doing anything this evening. Do you want to go somewhere for a chat?'

'About my redundancy?'

'Well, not specifically. Just talk, I guess.'

Just say yes. Just say yes and avoid saying something else that's utterly stupid. 'Yes!' he said. 'That would be great. We could find somewhere on Tottenham Court Road.'

Minna agreed. Apparently, it was as easy as that.

'It was nice of you to bring the team chocolates,' she mused. They were in Starbucks because it looked empty but by the time they ordered, the only available table was at the very back. Still, it was cosy enough. Intimate. 'Or are you doing work for them as a consultant? You can't move for freelance panettone on our floor.'

'No, I made a clean break, more or less,' said Jeff, careful not to sound smug and create an inaccurate impression. He made a note: *Just don't go on about the catalogues.* 'I'll be looking for something permanent in the new year. Not sure what it'll be yet.' At least he wasn't holding anything back. This was as much as he knew.

'A change is as good as a holiday,' she said brightly.

Jeff admitted. 'I'm not very good at change.'

Minna nodded, slowly. Was she processing his words – wondering if he was referring to doors opening or closing? Wondering where she stood? Dare he wonder?

She inserted a diversion of sorts. 'I don't know who I'd keep in touch with if I left my job. I mean, I've no plans to, but if I were in your situation.'

Jeff liked the way Minna spoke without a hint of condemnation. He could continue to be truthful, which meant he might get around to saying what he truly felt. The chocolate box – which Minna had invented, but which he hadn't denied existed – was an obstacle to negotiate, but at least it meant he wouldn't blunder heedlessly on.

He said, 'I didn't make many friends, to be honest, even though I worked there for eight years.' The reasons no longer interested Jeff, so he doubted they'd enrapture Minna. He wouldn't elaborate, but he was curious: 'Do *you* think that's weird?'

He could imagine Steve's response, and that of everyone else in his small circle.

Minna shrugged. 'I wouldn't call it weird, Jeff.' She continued to sound as if anything was possible. 'I was just thinking, I wouldn't be surprised if the people I stayed friendly with might not be the ones I chatted to every day.'

Jeff took a sip of coffee. 'Really?'

Minna expanded: 'I've got my core group of friends – there's four of us, and we all used to work in the same pod until the summer; we've become really close – and there are some people who I thought were friendly, but aren't particularly. I still seem to see more of them than anyone else. So it's likely that there are others I've paid no attention to – haven't avoided them; we just haven't crossed paths – who I might get on with really well.'

Now Minna looked as if she'd said too much. She drank her coffee.

'And who you might get to know only once everyone else is out of the way?'

'Exactly, Jeff. What do you think about that?'

'You're probably right,' said Jeff. 'It's all a bit arbitrary, I guess. We're put into teams with people and we have nothing in common. Not even the same goals, sometimes.'

'Absoutely. And there's no reason to be friends just because we work together.'

'Assuming you need a reason, I suppose,' she said.

Jeff was going to volunteer the work/life balance, because it sounded more authoritative than anything he'd provide, but he snagged on the doubt that lingered in Minna's last observation. As if she, right now, was looking for a reason for this meeting. Wondering: *why* have we picked up where we left off? It's excruciating. (He hated to admit it, but it *was*.)

Jeff's only recourse against making it worse was to sock her with all the truth he had left. 'Minna. I haven't got *any* friends at Go Aware. I didn't come to the office to bring them chocolates. I came to see you.'

Minna placed her hands flat on the table, as if to anchor herself. If Jeff placed his upon them, which he longed to do, it would involve a lunge, which would do nothing to promote intimacy. He leaned forward slowly, subsiding a little in his seat. Overwhelmed.

She smiled. 'Oh, that's nice. I'm glad you did. I have thought of you, Jeff. I hoped I'd bump into you. And there was one day, actually, when I was determined to front up to your office to see you, to tell you how *I* felt. Because I feel the same way.'

'A day of days,' he said. 'When was that? I wish you had!'

Minna smiled. 'For a whole Sunday, I had just my own company and knew I wouldn't talk myself out of coming to find you. So on the Monday morning, I got to work early. I went up to my floor to drop off my bag, log on and then I intended to go straight up to the ninth to see you. Nothing would stop me. But then . . . one of my colleagues was in a flap about some survey that hadn't loaded properly. And I had to help. Then other people stuck their oar in. And the morning ran away with me, the way they do. And I did nothing about you. Not then, or the next day, or the next one.'

It was natural to beat yourself up, but Jeff hated seeing Minna do it. 'It just wasn't the right moment,' he soothed.

'Well, I think you'd gone by then. So it wouldn't have come to anything.' Still, she sounded regretful.

'I never stopped thinking about you,' Jeff said, at last.

Her face lit up. 'Then why didn't *you* . . . Oh, you don't have to answer.'

He should try. He didn't want to be withholding. 'Other people, I guess, like you said. I let myself be persuaded to stay away from you. I didn't mean to let it happen, but other things got on top of me – losing my job, but other stuff too – and somehow I got dragged down.'

'I'm the same!' Minna said, avidly. 'Crazy, isn't it, that we let it happen?'

Worse. 'But let's not talk about that,' he said. 'I wasn't going to mention—'

'Your ex.'

Jeff felt the blood drain from his face. 'Pardon?'

Minna blanched. 'Sorry! I don't know why—'

'I was going to say Niamh. My cousin. Your flatmate. I wasn't going to mention Sarah.'

'Yes,' said Minna. 'Of course. Niamh.'

'Why did you think I'd talk about my ex-wife?'

Minna was flustered. 'You did last time. People do talk about their exes.' She sighed, as if she regretted her own experience of the topic. She spread her hands. 'It's no big deal, Jeff. Like I said before, we can't always choose the people we stay close to.'

'I'm over Sarah, truly I am,' Jeff appealed. 'OK, probably, I wasn't before, not a hundred per cent, but now. I promise you, Minna. I am.'

'It's OK, Jeff,' she said. 'You don't need to say that.'

'But I do!'

'No, you don't. And to be honest, I wasn't really thinking about . . . Sarah. I suppose it was easier to mention her because I didn't know her. She doesn't mean anything to me. Sorry – that sounds harsh.'

'It's OK. It's fine.'

'Whereas Niamh,' said Minna, with feeling, 'I just hate the thought of her coming between us when she has no right to. I had this fear that she'd say all these horrid things to you about me.'

'We can't blame her entirely, Minna.'

'I guess not.' Minna looked at her cup, which was empty, as was Jeff's – it was cold to the touch. 'In fact, it was because of Niamh that I decided to come looking for you.'

'Oh. Let's not talk about her any more.' Jeff felt nothing towards his cousin and hoped he could make Minna forget about her – temporarily, at least. 'Hey, Minna, do you fancy going someplace else?'

Minna's eyes widened. 'Yes. Good idea.' Already she had grabbed her bag and started pulling her coat from the back of her chair.

'Only I don't really want anything more to drink here and it's not a very nice evening to be wandering the streets.'

'Well, Habitat is just down the road,' she said. 'We could look around there.'

Jeff beamed. 'Let's do that.' He had a flash of inspiration. 'In fact, I need to buy lampshades. I did some work on my flat a few months ago, but that's the one thing I keep forgetting to buy. But you could help me choose, Minna, and then have a drink afterwards. I always find shopping is thirsty work.'

'Sounds like a plan, Jeff. There's a bar in Heal's just next door to Habitat. We might need a pit-stop to compare and contrast. Colours, textures, shapes. There'll be so much choice. I wouldn't want to steer you towards something you ended up hating.'

'You wouldn't do that, Minna,' he said with conviction.

She smiled. 'After all, it's a bit early in the relationship to be buying home furnishings.' She laughed, then suddenly stopped, as if horrified at what she'd said.

By which point, Jeff had said, 'Well, all couples argue in Habitat. We might as well get used to it.'

At once, they froze and regarded each other. Why had they been joking? They'd made progress but it hadn't been easy. It wasn't funny. It was deadly serious.

Minna looked serious now. Was she thinking, Relationship? A couple? As if. Or could she be thinking, Why not?

It became a lot easier after that, although it still wasn't easy, but overall, Jeff believed his date with Minna had gone well. She seemed to have enjoyed herself too. They regained a lot of lost ground but there was plenty left to explore. (They never bought the lampshade.) That probably wouldn't happen until after Christmas, though. Minna's work do was this Thursday, and next week she had a few catch-ups. Jeff was working both weekend days – with early starts. At Christmas, Minna would be in Farnham with her parents, and Jeff was going to Alyx's dad's with his family. (It was a one-off scenario, which Jeff did not challenge. Steve would pick him up on Christmas Day and they'd end up somewhere in Kent.) They would keep in touch for sure until they could meet. He feared the consequences of moving too quickly and—

Well, going wrong.

But having agreed that no outside influences would corrupt them, that the only people at the wheel were each other – and both of them were committed to taking steps forward together – why did they entertain that fear?

And there were other flashes of reassurance, too, such as when he drove back from a fair the very next Saturday evening. Jeff was in a buoyant mood, albeit a little tired. It had rained on and off all day, but the car's windows were closed against the evening chill, there was music on, and his pockets were warmly lined with bank notes. He had chatted to other stall holders, joined in coffee runs, covered tables during loo breaks, helped pack up cars. People looked out for him now: 'Jeff's not here yet,' they'd say. 'Didn't he mention he was coming?' 'Hope he hasn't got lost – I'm sure he's got directions.' 'Let's give him half an hour, and we'll call.'

Next year, he'd be seeing Minna at weekends, he hoped. He doubted she'd want to tag along with him, and why should she? He'd need to earn money, to be occupied, at least, until he found his as-yet-unidentified new career. How would he balance the two? Well, one might have to go . . . Jeff felt guilt's familiar reproach, because he knew the boot fairs were just a temporary gig. So should he really be accepting friendship from these kind people? But was it really such a problem: Jeff realised – it seemed obvious really – that if you want people to look, you need to have something to show them. Surely these new friends could see as well as Jeff that this temporary life he had adopted wasn't it.

Nigel had never called his son at eleven-thirty on a Tuesday morning so Jeff could only assume there was an emergency. Nothing to do with Christmas, though it was days away, which remained Celia's domain – or had that altered this year?

It took a moment to find his voice. 'Dad, what's the matter. Is it you? Is it Mum?'

'Your mother's at work and fine as far as I know,' Nigel said mildly. 'Where else would she be this time of day?'

'Have you finished for Christmas already?'

'Not yet. I had a half day to take so thought I'd get in some shopping and collect a parcel from the sorting office.'

Jeff wondered, 'Is that what you've rung to tell me?'

'I knew you'd pick up the phone, with your new ... arrangements.'

'Just hanging round watching daytime TV, is that what you think?'

'Wouldn't suit me but fine if it's your bag. Anyway, I thought it was the five-roll toilet roll holder I'd ordered from the internet,' Nigel said. 'A little present to myself.'

'Five roll?' Jeff queried. 'Dad, there's only two of you in the house.'

'We still buy in bulk. It's too far to the pantry if anyone's caught short, so it makes sense to keep a decent supply in the bathroom. Anyway. It wasn't the loo roll holder. Or anything from Amazon, which your mother was hoping for. No, it was two boxes of photographs. I'd gone on the bus. Lugging them back nearly killed me.'

Photographs? Jeff couldn't recall the last time the camera had been in service at family functions. 'Photographs of what, Dad?'

'Come on, son, don't be awkward. Family photos, by the look of them. Question is, why didn't you just bring them round?'

'They're not mine, Dad.'

'They're not?'

'No. Why did you think they would be?'

'I thought you might have come across them by chance at one of your boot fairs.'

'Photos of *our* family? In a box on a trestle table? Dad, what are the chances of that happening?'

'I don't know what goes on in those muddy fields. You could be trading anything.'

Jeff sighed. 'It's all above board, Dad.' Had Steve said something about stolen goods? 'But I don't deal in photographs. Sorry. It's nothing to do with me. Was there a note?'

'If there is I haven't found it yet. I mean, I haven't really looked inside – so much dust. I didn't know where they'd been. As for storing them, we have trouble enough finding room for back issues of the Sainsbury's magazine.'

Back issues, Jeff considered. Was there a market in that these days?

Nigel continued, 'Well, if it wasn't you, then whose bright idea was it to—' The line went quiet. 'For pity's sake, I should have realised from the get-go. This is your mother's work.'

'*Mum?* What makes you say that?'

'Explains why the boxes had DO NOT LEAVE WITH NEIGHBOURS on them, which is why I had to traipse to the sorting office. Your mother has it in for Eve next door. Can't think why but *this* won't make life easy when it comes to replacing the fence next summer.'

'Dad,' Jeff interrupted, anxiously. 'What are you implying? What do you think Mum's done?' He could hear the unsaid *now* fall like a rotten apple.

'It's bloody Grace all over again, that's what it is. Cee'll have been haranguing my mother, and agitating my sisters. What *is* she playing at? What does she *want*?'

They were Jeff's questions, of course, but was it safer to let his father handle them? He ought to help if he could, without taking sides. 'So Mum's name was on the box?'

Nigel faltered. 'Well, no . . . it just said the Sullivan family.'

'Could Steve have been behind it?' He'd feel disloyal whatever he said.

'He's got better things to worry about,' Nigel said. 'That's why we thought it had something to do with you.'

Thanks for the vote of confidence, Jeff thought. But antagonism wasn't his game. 'Well, I'm sorry I can't help, Dad. Maybe Gran sent them herself. Was her writing on the boxes?'

'Doesn't look like it. Maybe she got someone to help. She's always losing her glasses.'

Was Nigel himself losing the will to fight? Maybe now that he'd had the chance to vent he wasn't so vexed, making Jeff the more exercised of the two. Not that Nigel (when Jeff thought about it) ever seemed ill-tempered for long. Or angry for the sake of it.

'There must be an obvious answer, Dad. Someone who might think we wanted two boxes of family photos. Can't be that many people. I'll give it some thought and get back to you if I come up with any names.'

'Well, all right then, son. I won't do anything with them just now.'

'I expect you're about to head off to work?'

'Yes.' Nigel sounded pleased as if offered a solution he hadn't thought available. 'I said I'd be in for one so I'd better get my arse into gear. Well, good to chat, son. Glad to hear you're keeping busy.'

'Thanks, Dad. Yes. I'd better crack on.' It was time to ring off because suddenly, blindingly, Jeff knew who was responsible for the delivery.

When he'd worked for Go Aware, Jeff had often been chided for resorting to e-mail instead of picking up the phone or, better still, walking across the floor to speak with someone. He wasn't lazy, he just preferred being one step removed. These days, he accepted any call because an enquiry could lead to work. People were looking beyond Christmas. He didn't resent his obligation to make two important calls today, but he did wonder if, since family were involved, he ought to have gone to speak to them in person. But phone calls are more economical, taking up less time and not requiring the expenditure of body language. Even if family deserved a greater effort.

At least he could phone in any order, but since Nigel had set the ball rolling, wasn't it only right to even the score and call Celia next? Assuming his call would be welcome. Would his mother want to follow eight hours of office politics with contentions of a domestic nature?

Maybe Jeff should allow his parents a few days to compare notes and reach a shared position. Perhaps they were doing it right now. His parents' lives had been of little interest when

Jeff had had a job and a marriage to occupy him. Was it too late to concern himself with it now? At any time, was it ever his *business*?

So perhaps it was safer to call Niamh. Her confirmation would exonerate Celia. But if he called Niamh before anything further happened with Minna – it was just a week since they'd met, though they'd exchanged messages – would that risk reprising Niamh's role of a kind of guardian? Oh, but you could argue that Niamh and her photographs were irrelevant. Celia had met Grace. Jeff had reconnected with Minna. So he almost didn't call. Then again, it seemed churlish to distance himself from anyone. He found her number in his calls log, and she answered straightaway.

Niamh sounded very different from the woman who had confronted him at the beginning of August. She was bright and breezy. 'Merry Christmas, Jeff! I thought you'd ring.'

He wasted no time. This needn't be a drawn-out exchange. 'To thank you for the photographs?'

'They arrived safely? Glad to hear it. It's nice to get surprise presents, isn't it? I'll bet your parents were pleased.' Already she was basking in the glory of her benevolence.

'They weren't expecting it,' Jeff said.

'But they wanted the albums,' Niamh reasoned.

'Yes,' Jeff replied, guardedly. How much did Niamh know about Grace?

'Oh, Jeff . . .' She sounded concerned. 'Have I got you into trouble?'

'Hopefully not in the long term,' said Jeff. He wondered

how deeply he should probe. Was Niamh a shit-stirrer at heart? 'Did you and Gran sort through the photographs before you sent them on?'

'Afraid not. There wasn't time. We just scooped them all up, and put them in boxes. It's a bit of a lucky dip.'

'Totally random?'

'Yes! Gran said your parents will have fun going through them. Needless to say, throw out any you don't want. Gran doesn't want them back.'

'Is that why you sent them?' Jeff remembered something Celia had said about a clear-out.

'Well, yes. Partly.'

'Only partly?'

'Well . . . to be strictly honest, Jeff, I sent them because of Minna.'

Suddenly, he bristled, feeling protective of Minna. 'What about her?'

It emerged in a breathless rush. 'Well, I was trying to make amends for keeping you apart for so long. Telling you to stay away from her.'

'You felt guilty?' Jeff asked, not quite believing it himself.

Niamh too seemed doubtful. 'I wouldn't go as far as that. I mean, I had a twinge of doubt that my advice might not have been overly helpful. But I just assumed you'd ignore me. I mean, nobody ever takes my advice. Ever. But then . . . well I realised you had.'

Did I? Both Jeff and Minna had rejected the idea. Plugging

in other names, other scenarios didn't move you on. Minna had wondered if you need reasons at all and Jeff felt that yes, you did: they were essential. You have to know what you think, or thought, because you were accountable. You'd never do anything if you weren't.

He said, 'What made you realise?'

'Minna said she's seen you, just last week.'

There was a lump in Jeff's throat. 'She told you that?' He pictured Minna coming home, into the flat, shrugging off her coat in a fizz of enthusiasm. Or—

'She did,' said Niamh. 'I was home when she got in. She had the time of her life, she said.'

'She did? Then why did you decide to get involved?'

'Jeff,' said Niamh. 'I've borne the brunt of Minna's temper so this was a welcome relief. In fact, it reminded me that it takes no more effort to help someone than to hinder them. So here we are.'

'So you do want to help me?' Jeff established, to be quite certain.

'If I can. And Minna, too, naturally. To be honest, things haven't been great in the flat for the last couple of months. We could all do with some cheering up.'

'Really? Why?'

Niamh tutted. 'You don't need to know about *that*. The upshot is, Minna is talking about moving out. I can't say I'm surprised.'

Minna hadn't mentioned that. Perhaps she was saving it for a later conversation. Unless she'd wanted to hurry the one they'd begun to a close. 'Why is Minna thinking of moving out?'

'Lisa, her sister, is getting married in the spring and Minna is talking about moving into Lisa's flat. Lisa's moving in with her fiancé. Well, he'll be her husband then.'

Minna had said nothing about her sister's marriage, either. Jeff longed to ask, 'Who is Minna taking to the wedding?' but said, instead, 'Why is that a problem? You've got a nice flat – you'd let a room easily there – and if things have been tense, surely it's a good solution.'

'It would be,' Niamh agreed, 'apart from the fact that I want to move out too. If Minna and I both go, Sharmila – she's our other flatmate and my best friend – would kill me.'

'But she's your best friend?'

'That wouldn't count in my favour if she had to move out too because she wouldn't want to live with strangers. I know her. And I don't think many people would want to live with Sharmila. I don't say that lightly. She is my best friend. But she can be . . . icy.'

Jeff resisted thoughts of pots and kettles. He asked, 'So what's this got to do with Minna and me?'

'I thought that if you'd got together she might want to move in *here*, with *you* and Sharmila – I've got the largest room – which would leave me free to go. Reading between the lines, Lisa's flat is less than ideal. It's further out, the heating isn't reliable and the windows need replacing. You wouldn't want Minna catching endless colds, would you, Jeff?'

'No, of course not.' But hang on – *what* was Niamh saying? 'Has Minna talked about moving in with me?'

'Not in so many words, Jeff, but I admit I wouldn't be her first choice of confidante given all we've been through. So that's why I made my direct approach to you.'

Niamh's vagueness was maddening. '*Do* you think Minna might want to live with me?' He was galloping ahead, he knew it, but there was no gainsaying it.

Fortunately, Niamh's quelling powers were in force. 'I'm not clairvoyant, Jeff. I just don't want her moving into Lisa's flat on her own. That wouldn't help me at all.'

'Why does it make a different *where* Minna lives if she isn't living with you?'

'Isn't it obvious? If Minna moves as a single person, she could live anywhere at all. She might *not* go to Lisa's – it isn't a foregone conclusion. The *best* thing would be for her to move with a boyfriend, and it *were* you, you could steer her towards my preferred situation which is the two of you and Sharmila here. Just think, there'd be a spare bedroom – Minna's is really just a box-room – for friends to stay over, or for storage. It would work well. If that's what Minna wants.'

'Do you think I'm what Minna wants?' Oh, don't ask Niamh – but too late . . .

'Well, you were back in the summer. I can't see that much has changed in that time. She hasn't seemed any happier, so I'm assuming she still fancies you. She just wishes it hadn't taken so long to get there.'

Jeff mused, 'Do you ever offer outright compliments, Niamh, or is everything you say a little bit twisted?'

'Truly, Jeff, I like to help where I can,' Niamh argued. 'Hence the photographs. Aren't you *grateful* for them?'

'We're back to that, are we?' Jeff said. It seemed like an adjacent concern. So much did these days, since Minna.

'Yes. That's another thing. I'm planning on moving into Gran's spare room, now that it's empty. I'll be able to get the tube to work, instead of a train and a bus, so it won't take much longer. Of course, it'll be rent-free. I've decided I'd like to go travelling in the first half of next year. It's all working out beautifully.'

'So it seems,' Jeff agreed.

'Only, don't tell my sisters, will you? Or any of the cousins. Especially Phoebe.'

What's wrong with Phoebe? But Jeff actually asked, 'About your travel plans?'

'No, about taking Gran's room. They'll be jealous and I don't want to deal with that. It's mine by rights, because I've done all the work in clearing it for her. Of course, it wasn't my intention to prep it for myself. I put family first. Mind you, I quite enjoyed doling out the family treasures, such as they are. The photos were a no-brainer, Jeff. They had to come to you.'

'Well, thanks,' said Jeff, mildly. 'I don't know if my parents have got any more storage space than Gran, to be honest.'

'You could sound a bit more grateful, after all I've done.'

'What *have* you done, exactly, Niamh?'

Niamh shrieked. 'Do I really have to spell it out, Jeff? I've urged you to come to your senses and make a go of it with Minna. Properly, this time. Not that you should need a helping hand if you're as into each other as you seem to be. Still, I suppose it's nice to be encouraged. I wish someone would do that for me . . .'

Jeff assumed it was an open invitation that didn't require his personal acceptance, so he closed that channel down, and focused on the photographs. 'I am grateful, Niamh. Honestly. Thanks so much. It was so thoughtful!' Could that be all Niamh wanted to hear? Jeff hoped so, because he had nothing more to offer her.

There was nothing Jeff wanted to offer *anyone*, in case it stole from what he wanted to give to Minna. It sounded mean-spirited, and instantly reminded Jeff of those unattractive qualities that lurked within him. (How would he hide them from Minna? How would he shield her from them?) His parsimony extended beyond Niamh to Celia, which was ironic, because hadn't he accused his mother of just that crime? But he was reluctant to speak to Celia, even to report in about the photos. She might be thrilled, she might be grateful (as Jeff was not). But he doubted she'd answer his question. She wouldn't tell him how you know when you're ready to love. But of course he called, out of duty.

Celia began with, 'Has your father upset you?'

'Mum, why d'you think—'

'Simmer down. I'm just asking. I know you chatted this morning.'

Jeff felt relieved, at least, that his parents had talked to each other.

'Dad was fine,' he said. 'He was just curious about the photos. I can explain where they came from.'

'Not from you?' She sounded disappointed.

'No, from cousin Niamh. She thought we'd like them. I guess she thought we'd want to give them to Grace.'

'Really? Is that what she thought?' Now she was surprised. Perhaps his mother believed that she alone spared thoughts for Grace, and was amazed that anyone else did too. 'How thoughtful.'

'Is it?'

'Well, yes, of course. It's company Grace is after, not possessions, but she might like to have a look next time she's in London. It might give her a reason to come down.'

'So you've no plans to see her?'

'Not imminently, no.'

'Is that because . . .'

'Because of what?'

Go on. Out with it. 'Because of Dad.'

Celia whooped with laughter, as if to say, Like *his* disapproval would stop me! She said, 'No, not because of him. Why do you say that, Jeff?'

'Oh . . . no reason.' He retreated. He always did. He must stop doing it.

'You're sounding troubled again, dear. What's this all about?'

Jeff stepped forward. He marshalled his thoughts so the words wouldn't leap out one step ahead. 'Before, I asked you "What's next?" and I admit, it sounded a bit bald, a bit rude, maybe. You were peeved, at any rate. All I meant, I think, was, will you see her again? Is she now a part of our family? And if she is, well – why, Mum? Why do we *need* her when we never did before?'

'Who said anything about *need*, Jeff? I thought it would be a nice thing to do. And it was. Grace was very happy that we'd helped her.'

'And you . . .?'

'I was happy that she was happy.'

'*Really?*' he said.

'Yes. I was. Why does that surprise you?'

'But I thought you wanted more from it. You put so much effort in.'

'Jeff, you've surprised me. I always thought you were more of the "ambition is its own reward" school of thought. As if you think it counts for more than achievement.'

'You did?' Jeff wondered. Is that what he thought? Ambition. It struck Jeff that you sometimes heard that word paired with 'naked', which was obviously inappropriate for a conversation with your mother. Anyway, it was more the case that he'd achieved so little that his ambition was bound to outrank it.

Although it was pleasing to think that any policy he might employ was worthy of quantifying. Supposing it *was* a bona fide policy. 'I guess I do,' he said.

'I've always admired it. It must mean you're not easily disappointed. More people should be like that.'

Jeff thought back over the past six months, when he'd really begun evaluating his life. He realised that, no, all things considered, in spite of his own array of failures, he wasn't disappointed. He wasn't dispirited, was perhaps more accurate. He said so.

Celia sighed. 'Oh darling.' She never called him that. 'How lovely to hear that. The optimism of youth. Well, not youth so much these days. Sarah always admired it in you.'

'Oh. Sarah,' he said, not quite wishing Celia hadn't said the name. Was Celia still upset about the break-up of the marriage? Had her disappointment leeched into all aspects of her life? Well, Jeff couldn't help her with that. He'd moved on. He *was* ready.

But he didn't want to leave her behind. Jeff still felt his sense of obligation. (*I owe you, Mum.*) Could there be common ground? 'What about you, Mum? Aren't you optimistic?'

'I'm OK, I'm pleased to say. I know your father thinks I'm not. I know he worries that I want more than I've got but I don't. I try and tell him that. He might believe me one day. I'll just have to wait. Hope he will too.'

It didn't sound like a plea. Perhaps she was just airing her requirements.

'Don't worry about *us*,' Celia cautioned. 'We're fine. Really we are. It's you and Steve who keep us awake at night, though fortunately not as much as you used to. You would let us know, Jeff, if there's anything we should be concerned about, would you?'

'Sure, Mum,' he said. What else was there to say? Maybe it was time to wrap up the call. Jeff was getting good at endings, but only because he was desperate to get on to his new beginning.

He asked, 'Will you tell Dad the photos came from Niamh? Gran's clearing out her spare room – that's all I know. I guess we can do what we like with them.'

Celia brightened. 'Well, I'll be casting about for something to tidy after the Christmas decs come down.' Then she added, 'I'm quite pleased about the new toilet roll holder, I don't know if he mentioned it. It should be with us any day. The little things make all the difference.'

Jeff had never been so relieved to return to work after the new year. (He'd stayed in, with a single bottle of Prosecco, and watched TV. He hadn't not enjoyed himself.) In the days that followed, he took care of as much admin as he could, and left the weekend clear, hoping he and Minna could meet. He was thrilled to receive a text from her on Thursday. It read: 'I'm meeting some friends this evening. Short notice, I know, but would you like to come along?'

It wasn't exactly what Jeff had had in mind for a next date, but at least it was another meeting. Jeff had become used to being a lone operator – but perhaps he always had been. You could say he and Sarah had led lives in parallel. Perhaps Minna was his total opposite in that she functioned better with back-up. Opposites attract, don't they? So that was good.

But maybe she wanted her colleagues to scrutinise Jeff, and score his suitability out of ten. That was daunting. But Jeff sought excitement from the fact that he was meeting Minna's friends early on – perhaps it was a sign that she was serious.

Oh, who knew? Jeff just accepted Minna's invitation and counted down the hours.

So Jeff wouldn't have to encounter any old colleagues, Minna suggested meeting at the pub. It happened to be the venue for Jeff's leaving do, which Minna couldn't have known, and was no better attended tonight. The staff seemed pleased to see the Macsamphire Strutt employees. Minna made introductions, and Jeff appreciated that everyone knew who he was and welcomed his attendance. The five of them secured a table in the corner that seemed to be a favourite, and shrugged off bags and coats. The evening began.

Kerry said, 'I'll go to the bar. Is everyone happy with the usual?'

As soon as Kerry turned her back to the group, Minna seemed to notice something odd, but was distracted by a comment from Adam. It was only as Kerry returned to the table, clutching a bottle and glasses, a bag of crisps between her teeth, that Minna started looking in earnest. Without wanting to pry, Jeff followed her interest closely.

'Kerry, what's that big white mark on the seat of your trousers?' Minna asked. She made a close inspection. 'It looks like a handprint.'

'As if someone's slapped you on the backside while finger-painting,' said Adam.

'Has it been there all *day*?' Steph gawped. 'Has no one *said* anything? Outrageous!'

'They didn't want to cause an upset,' said Adam.

'Whose handprint *is* it?' asked Minna.

Kerry twisted round to inspect the evidence, and promptly burst into tears – negating Adam's supposition. Her entire body was wracked with raw emotion, as never seen before within the group.

It was Stephanie who managed to stop staring and speak. 'What's *wrong*, Kerry? Can't you just sponge it off? Aren't all paints water-based these days?'

'NO!' wailed Kerry. 'You don't understand!'

Stephanie leapt. Her reaction reverberated around the room. 'What don't we understand?'

'It's the last straw! Really, this is the last straw. I can't take any more.'

'Any more of what?' Minna probed.

'*My life.* Do you know what it's like living in a permanent building site? Last night, we were both up ladders at midnight, doing the ceiling. The whole house stinks of paint, even with the windows open. We might as well pitch a billboard out the front saying "Come on in and slay us as we sleep" if it weren't for the fact that an intruder would be overcome with fumes before they got through the door. We have to do our own place in the week, because at the weekend, we're at one of the rental flats to sort some delinquent's fuck-up of the plumbing. We have no life!'

Adam moved a little closer. 'There, there,' he hazarded. 'It can't be as bad as that.'

'IT IS!'

'But I thought you *liked* DIY,' said Minna.

'I HATE IT!'

'Does Dave know how you feel?' ventured Steph.

'So it's his handprint,' said Adam. Then he coloured. 'No – no – I don't mean he *hit* Kerry. He didn't, did he?'

'Did you have a row?' asked Steph.

Kerry crumpled. 'No, of course he didn't hit me. We never argue – we're both too bloody tired. And there shouldn't be any *need* to argue because it's all so simple. I just want to live in an ordinary house that hasn't got anything wrong with it. I want to crash on my sofa after work and plump up the cushions and drink wine. Is that so unreasonable?'

All three of them warbled a chorus of endorsement: 'Nooo ...' 'Not at all.' 'No way.' Jeff looked on, spellbound at their cohesion.

Steph attempted to calm the waters by unleashing her own tale of woe. 'My place is a bit of a prison too,' she said. 'Because of this new friend I've got.'

Adam's gaze met Kerry's, both then met Minna's own, in what must have been a familiar way. But nobody spoke.

'She's moved into one of the flats downstairs,' Steph expanded.

'Oh, that sort of friend.' Kerry was dismissive. 'A neighbour.'

Steph frowned. 'What sort of friend did you think I meant?'

When Kerry looked to Adam, then to Minna who said, 'It's nice to have someone looking out for you when you live on your own.'

Steph shook her head. 'Do you think so? This kind of attention I could do without.'

They all leaned in. Drinks were forgotten, crisps left untouched. Adam said, 'So who's this neighbour?'

'Evelyn,' groaned Steph, as if she'd said 'Leprosy'. 'She seemed nice enough on moving day. I helped her bring a few bags up and made her a cup of tea. She hasn't left me alone since.'

'In what way?' asked Minna.

'She's always just "popping round" for a "natter", and I'm sure she watches my comings and goings from her window,' said Stephanie.

Because he hadn't had anything to say so far – much less the opportunity to get a word in – it occurred to Jeff to share the story of Leonard, who'd displayed stalkerish tendencies at first but who'd turned out to be the opposite. It might reassure Stephanie, but Kerry got in first.

'But you're never in!' she cried. 'You're always doing something.'

'Which makes it worse,' said Steph. 'When I get in all I want is peace and quiet. Some downtime. Then there's a knock at the door and my sanctuary is ruined. I'm beginning to dread going home.'

Minna said, 'Can't you have a word with her?'

Steph looked as if Minna had called for conscription to be reintroduced.

'I can't even cook my favourite meal any more,' Steph revealed. 'Vegetable curry – the smell wafts down to Evelyn's flat and summons her like a spirit from the underworld. It's *her* favourite too, apparently.'

'Couldn't you cook with the kitchen window closed?' suggested Jeff.

Minna nodded approvingly, but Steph just said, 'So at weekends I practically live on sliced tomato on Ryvita because *she* can't sniff it out.'

'You look really well on it,' said Adam. 'I think you've lost weight.'

'You look stressed,' corrected Kerry. 'Poor Steph. Minna is right – you'll have to shake her off. Or else move. I could help you there, of course . . .'

'That's good of you, Kerry,' said Steph. 'Especially given what you said about all the DIY. But I don't want to move. I shouldn't have to, should I?'

In unison, her friends offered agreement. It was a signal to resume drinking. Jeff wondered if any comment would be made on Minna's situation – he supposed her friends knew everything – but a deep sigh from Adam ensnared everyone's attention.

'What's up with you?' Steph wanted to know.

'Oh, nothing. Nothing, really. Well, Laura's pregnant. We found out today.'

'Baby number three!' intoned Kerry, as if speaking of excess when, after all, having eschewed parenthood, she had gone on to buy six properties. 'And there's poor Minna's friend desperately trying for just one. Funny what the hand of fate deals, isn't it?'

Minna said, 'Since Callie and Todd have never met Adam and Laura, I don't think it's going to upset them much.'

'No news, then, in that department?' asked Steph.

Minna shook her head. 'It could still happen. Anyway, it's *fantastic* news for Adam and Laura.' She raised her glass. 'Congratulations.'

'Thanks,' said Adam, gloomily. They all stared at him. 'No, it is fabulous,' he added. 'It's just that we only had our first unbroken night of sleep three weeks ago.'

'When is Laura due?' Minna asked.

'Not for ages. In fact, it's probably too early to talk about it. I shouldn't have said anything. Laura would kill me if she knew. I don't think she's told her mother yet.'

Steph said, 'Laura won't mind us knowing, surely.'

Kerry said, 'She does *know* about us, doesn't she, Adam?'

Adam looked cornered. 'Of course. She knows we go for drinks ... now and then. She knows I'm stopping briefly tonight. She's cool about it. But I shouldn't be too late back.' He drained his glass, eyed the others' jealously, but decided against topping up.

Jeff couldn't meet Adam's eye, unsure of the precise dynamics and frightened to offend. He didn't want it to seem he was automatically taking a fellow male's side, which wasn't his instinct, to be fair.

Perhaps it was the wrong move, because Adam faced Jeff, although he directed his question to Minna. 'So how did you two get together?'

'And when?' added Steph.

Minna consulted Jeff. What had she told them? Her fretful look gave no clues. To avoid duplication, or even contradiction, he had to let her speak, even though he felt sure she wanted him to explain their story.

So Minna began, 'Jeff used to work in our building.' She hesitated, probably nervous about mentioning his redundancy. They should have rehearsed their story in advance. He wanted to signal to Minna that it was OK to phrase it any way that came naturally. He really didn't mind. But she wasn't even looking at him when she said – practically blurted – 'Now, before you say it's Julian all over again, and I only go for guys who live or work nearby so I don't have to make much of an effort, or that I'm overly cautious and hate change, or worse, proves that I'm basically a big-time commitment-phobe—'

Everyone looked at Minna in astonishment, especially Jeff. His body sagged in an involuntary slump. Was Minna already reneging on their shared agreement not to speak of exes? For surely that's who Julian was. What other transgressions lay ahead? Should Jeff be looking for a way out – supposing these possessive friends would let him pass?

But he didn't want to go. So there he stayed.

Luckily, the others regained their voices quickly. Jeff wondered if they had been here before. It soon became clear that all were witnessing something entirely new.

'Minna,' whispered Kerry. 'None of us was going to say that.' She sharpened. 'Were we?'

With perfect synchronicity, Adam and Steph shook their heads. 'No.' 'Not me.'

Adam added, 'My dad has a saying about not shitting on

your own doorstep.' He pondered. 'But I don't think he'd apply it to this situation.'

Kerry glowered at Adam, but looked kindly on Minna. 'Why do you think we'd *mind?*' she said. 'We never had a problem with you dating Julian. We were sad when it ended, of course. Sad for *you*. Minna. Didn't you realise that?'

Suddenly, Minna had tears in her eyes. Jeff felt a surge of affection for her – no, it was love, already – and wanted to shield her, to protect her. But these people had a prior claim. Julian bothered him, though. Perhaps Minna *needed* to speak of her past because she lacked confidence about the future? But Jeff wasn't willing to make any accusations against Minna. He wished he could spirit her away, but luckily, shortly after, farewells were made, coats and bags were gathered, and the evening was at an end.

To Jeff's surprise, but delight, Minna stayed close to him as they walked to Euston Station. As soon as the others were out of earshot, she unleashed a tirade of apology. 'Oh god, Jeff, I'm so sorry, so, so sorry ...'

He tried to make light of it. 'About what?'

She said, 'I shouldn't have mentioned Julian. Or I should have explained about him. The thing is, Jeff, I had this terrible fear that everyone had *made* themselves forget about him, because of what happened – because of *me* – so it would be like he never existed. I'd have felt awful if that happened. I felt awful when it didn't, because it brought everything back.'

Jeff nodded. He would try to understand if he didn't already.

He realised, though, that he would be sad himself if he never heard Sarah's name again. He hoped people would speak of her to him. And that he would find things to say about her too.

Minna squeezed his hand, as if by way of endorsement. She kept hold of it as they approached the station forecourt. They stopped.

She said, 'You were brilliant, tonight. Honestly.'

'No, I wasn't. I just sat there. I should have—'

'What could you have done? They were all talking about themselves, it must have been so dull. The thing is, they're really nice people.'

'They're your friends. Of course they are.'

'I suppose it's been a while since they had a chance to really talk,' said Minna.

'It's obvious, Minna,' he said, delighted that it was. 'They were waiting for you. I could see that. They love you because you brought them together in the first place.'

She looked at him, as if giving the idea due consideration. Jeff wondered if it had occurred to her before, or was another new development of the evening, scoring its way through the familiar dynamics in which they found such comfort. Jeff liked the idea of bringing innovations to these gentle parties. Even more, he liked the idea of beautiful Minna's confidence blossoming, which he could see happening right now, before his eyes.

He wouldn't let her turn against herself. He wouldn't let anyone else keep them apart. He said, 'I really like that about you too.' And he pulled her close, and kissed her full on the lips.

It worried Jeff that he hadn't heard from Minna. She hadn't replied to his text, or the voicemail he'd left. It had been only three days since Monroe's, but it seemed an eternity. He was desperate to see her again. He tried to distract himself with work, sorting through the papers he'd acquired since leaving Go Aware. (The piles were teetering once more.)

He couldn't exactly remember who had given him the pair of tickets to a gig in London, but narrowed it down to a stallholder in Egham and one in Reading. The tickets were the spoils of a pub quiz and the recipient had no intention of going. But gigs might be your bag, Jeff (he was asked), is that true? Jeff accepted them gratefully, then promptly forgot about them. He now realised the gig was for next Saturday.

He wanted to ask Minna. Of course, what he really wanted was a date which comprised only the two of them, but wondered – and he'd given this a lot of thought – if Minna might not be ready for that yet.

'It's an indie group,' he told Steve when they caught up for a beer. 'From Carlisle. I hadn't heard of them but they've got a decent website.'

It was good to have resumed his regular meet-ups with Steve. At Christmas, the Sullivans had trodden on eggshells around their host, and perhaps also each other. Steve and Alyx seemed at ease, but for them it was a familiar environment. Jeff had longed to take his brother aside to ensure that relations between them had not been damaged. But Steve seemed oblivious to any need for a reality check. Jeff wondered if Steve had known with conviction that the brothers would not fall out for good – that it was somehow impossible – which is why he'd pushed Jeff the way he had, but not subsequently pulled him back. Steve can't have predicted how things would go with Minna, however, although he didn't ask. Jeff was miffed, at first, but decided the better course of action was to speed up and find something to report.

Steve took the tickets and turned them over, as if they might be counterfeit. 'It's good that you've done your research,' he offered. 'What's the music like?'

'They sound a bit generic,' Jeff explained, 'but it's pretty decent to listen to.'

'Generic is good,' Steve decided. 'It means you and Minna can chat between sets, even during them, maybe go up to the bar for a change of scene – keep things moving.'

Jeff nodded, vindicated by Steve's endorsement of all that he'd thought himself. But he wanted to check: 'I can't say I've listened to all their songs. Do you think I should? What if there's something that's a bit … well, culturally insensitive or anti-women?'

'Did you look in the comments log on the website?'

'I did. Couldn't see anything dodgy.'

'Then don't worry. Look, it's good that you're not proposing to take Minna to see your all-time favourite band, because what if she hated them? She'd be embarrassed. You'd be mortified. You don't need that at this stage.'

'No,' Jeff replied. 'We don't. If we find we both like it, it's something we can share. That's a good building block.'

'You're speaking my lingo,' said his brother, the architect. 'I couldn't agree more.'

He raised his glass and toasted Jeff's future success.

It didn't start disastrously, but Minna was very nearly late because she couldn't find her house keys – she laughed when she told him that Niamh had come to her rescue. Jeff made failure a true possibility by guiding them onto the wrong bus. Technically, this evened the score.

'This can't be it,' said Jeff, when Minna's phone (his had mysteriously lost power) guided them from the Caledonian Road up a sequence of back streets behind Kings Cross.

Minna presented her phone, but did not sound triumphant. 'I think it is.'

Jeff shook his head. 'But we're fifteen minutes late and nobody else is here.'

'And it looks as if the building's burnt down,' she added, trying to make it sound like an aside. And failing.

The venue, an old pub two streets from the canal, was heavily boarded up and showed signs of extensive damage by water and fire. Luckily, its true ugliness was obscured because the nearest streetlamp had been smashed into obsolescence, so darkness fell all around.

'They must have shifted the location,' Minna suggested, her tone especially bright in the surrounding gloom. 'You didn't get an e-mail, by any chance?'

'No,' said Jeff, wondering if his supplier had. 'There was nothing on the website about a cancellation, either.'

What was Minna thinking? Great. I'm on a date with someone even less certain about life than I am. But she said nothing.

Jeff said, 'Wouldn't you think they'd have people here to redirect us? Even if they had sent an e-mail with a new venue, how could they guarantee that everyone would have read it in time?'

Minna nodded, absently. 'Jeff, I don't think this is a recent fire.'

He turned to her. 'What do you mean?'

'Well, I can't smell any charred wood or smoke.' Then she pointed. 'And if you look at the newspaper stuck up in the windows — where someone's tried to pull the boards away — well, the date says July. It's January now.'

'I know it's January.' Jeff was annoyed at himself. Was Minna about to turn on him too? Before she turned on herself again? 'What are you saying, Minna? Do you think I must have known about this and that I've lured you here under false pretences?'

'Jeff! I'm not having a go at you.'

'You said you were happy to go on another date.'

'I know I was. I was happy to go along to a gig, too.'

'Well, if you didn't really *want* to go to a gig you should have said. I was only making a suggestion. There are plenty of other things we could have done.'

'I know that, Jeff. And I would be perfectly happy to go to the gig if the gig had been on.'

And on and on they went.

*　　*　　*

But a row so intense burns itself out, and its combatants with it. Eventually, Minna and Jeff took their cold bodies back to the high street, where buses swished past, showering them with muddy rain. They refined their list of options – a film in Islington, a meal at a curry house nearby. Minna was all for that idea until Jeff said,

'Why don't you come back to mine? I've got food and drink and DVDs. We can sit on the sofa and pretend we bought a lampshade.' He paused, and looked at her, earnestly. '*Will* you come back, Minna?'

Thankfully, Minna said yes, she was ready to go.

They caught the tube and a taxi the last part of the way, Jeff being too impatient to wait in the cold and wet – it had begun to rain – for a connection. Nervously, he stabbed his key in the lock until it almost snapped. But at last, they were indoors, in the safe and warm.

Jeff had never felt happier. He hadn't dared think this would happen. Not yet. But no other resolution would do.

Jeff led the way into the bedroom, and at once they began to undress in a tangle of leg-holes and sleeves and elbows, so that by the time they achieved the bed naked it was all they could do to burrow into it. Then they explored; they offered, took and shared. Hungrily, eagerly, but not insatiably. At the end of it there seemed to be a great deal left.

Minna stretched luxuriously, as if she had at last allowed herself to relax. Perhaps she was scrolling backwards through the events of the evening, just to check she was comfortable with its progress. Only, she seemed to go back much further than that.

'I like this,' she said, running her hand down his chest. 'It feels like . . . well, being in love. That's what I want, you see. I'm not desperate. But for ages I assumed everyone else was in love, but they're not, are they?'

'They aren't,' Jeff agreed, excluding himself defiantly.

'But that wasn't the difference between me and everyone else,' Minna explained. 'I guess I thought that love was my thing, but actually it was pleasing other people while trying not to embarrass myself.'

'Minna . . .' he urged.

'No, it's OK, Jeff. I don't think that any more.' She turned to him, really looked at him. 'I'm just thinking about us. The two of us. Maybe we – us – well . . . maybe. Sorry – that sounds vague, but actually it isn't vague at all. I know what vague is, you see. It's not this.' She traced a line down his body again.

Then she told him about the weather forecast she'd seen in the pub. She told him about her misty start to thirty. Jeff wondered why it was important to share it now, but he listened, willingly, more than happy to accept any burden offered if it meant Minna could shrug it off.

He smiled. 'Maybe that could become one of those everyday weather expressions. You know like, "it never rains but it pours."'

'A storm in a teacup,' said Minna.

'A bolt from the blue.'

'To steal someone's thunder.'

'Or just to make heavy weather of something.'

'Maybe,' said Minna. Then she leaned in close. 'Jeff, please, *no*. That's not it. That's not what this is.'

Jeff knew what she meant. He held her tightly, absorbed her, but still managed to free one arm from the bedclothes. He said, 'Let's shut out the weather,' and then he switched off the light.

About the author

Jon Appleton was born in Sydney in 1974 and has lived and worked in London since 1996. *Ready to Love* is his first novel. For updates, more stories, and more about writing, visit jonappletonsbooks.com and follow him on Twitter at @appletonsbooks